GHOSTMAN

Barbara Arent

Cord Books
3Cord Publishing

3Cord Books are published by

3Cord Publishing
5963 CR 1114 W Suite A
Kilgore, TX 75662

All scripture from the King James Version unless otherwise noted.

ISBN: 978-0-9835324-0-8

First printing: September 2012

Printed in the United States of America

Acknowledgments

I would like to thank Brenda Smith and Carole Arent for their valuable input and work in helping me bring this story to life. Also, Paula Bowker for walking through scenes with me and helping me get them from my mind to word picture format. And, Jason Smith for his work on the awesome cover.

A special thanks to Vickie Phelps for helping me with the final editing process.

PROLOGUE

He took a deep breath and slowly squeezed the trigger. As the bullet left the chamber, a boy jumped from behind the car and into the man's arms. The bullet struck, slicing through both of them and burying itself in the wall of the house. A look of surprise crossed the man's face, then man and boy dropped to the ground.

Pandemonium immediately erupted in the compound. A screaming woman ran out of the house and threw herself on the bodies. Men, yelling 'Get in the house', tried to pull her off the bodies. Others fired off a few shots in his general direction. Some scattered out of sheer panic.

He watched as a man knelt over the bodies and felt for a pulse: first the boy, then the man. A waste of time. It was a clean kill. They were dead before they hit the ground. It wouldn't take long for the men to come to their senses and begin a methodical search of the area. He should have already been on the move.

His hands, moving of their own volition, removed the rifle from the stand and broke it down. The zip of the draw string on his backpack sounded deafening in the silence that lay around him. He looked down surprised to see the gun and stand secured and the area clean. All he had left to do was scatter some debris to cover his presence.

Without raising his eyes, he covered his tracks as he slowly moved away from the compound. By the time they organized a search and found where he had been, he would be at the extraction point waiting for his ride. With great will power, he cleared his mind of any thought and settled into a gentle ground eating lope.

When he heard the whirl of blades over his head, he blinked. He was standing at the edge of the clearing with no idea how or when he had gotten there. He glanced at his watch. It had been six hours since the successful completion of his mission.

As the helicopter started its descent, he leaned over and threw up. Once started, he couldn't stop. Like waves rolling over him, his stomach heaved until there was nothing left but a dry racking sound that seemed to come up from his toes. He stayed there until his body calmed. With slow deliberation he straightened, wiped his mouth and jogged to his ride. Without a word, he climbed inside and nodded at the pilot. The pilot nodded back and the bird lifted off the ground as easily as it had sat down.

Leaning back, he turned his face toward the door. It would take two hours to get to base and then he would have several hours of paperwork before he could move out again. They would already have an assignment waiting for him. He had been doing this for eight years. He knew the drill.

When the bird landed at base, he stepped off and went directly home. He filled out his report, put it in the pick-up box outside his door, and called for someone to come get it.

In the bathroom, he turned on the hot water and stepped into the shower. He stood there with his head bowed and let the water wash over his back. When he realized no amount of hot water was going to ease the tension in his muscles, he opened his eyes. Blood, oozing from deep fingernail cuts in his palms, mingled with the water at his feet. At the sight of the blood, something inside him burst. He dropped to his knees, covered his face with his hands and let the sobs rack his body.

CHAPTER 1

Linda heard a scream. When another scream rent the air, she tried to sit up but couldn't. She twisted and turned but the more she moved, the tighter her bands got.

"Lin! Lin!"

Penny! Penny was calling her. Linda tried to answer but no words came.

"Lin, wake up!"

She had to help Penny. She threw out her hand.

"Ouch!"

That one word penetrated the fear clouding her mind and she stopped struggling.

"You're having another nightmare."

She forced her eyes open. Penny was leaning over the bed. Linda sighed. She had done it again.

"You can't keep going this way." Penny sat down beside her. "These nightmares are getting worse. You are working too hard, not getting enough sleep and with the weight you've lost, it's obvious you aren't eating."

"Okay, *Mother Hen*."

"Don't sass me, young lady."

Linda smiled. She untangled her legs from the sheet and sat up. "I'm too close to finishing the polymer to back off now. I promise I'll..."

Penny rolled her eyes. "Like I haven't heard that before."

Linda started to speak but Penny stopped her. "This obsession is killing you."

"Seriously? Pen, I'm not even close to dying."

"Right," Penny said.

"And," Linda interrupted her, "I promise I will take time off when this is over. Maybe the three of us can plan a trip together."

"I'd like that." Penny smiled.

Linda looked at the clock: 4:40 am. "Go back to bed. You need to be bright eyed and bushy-tailed so you can ace that exam. Then you can get a job and quit bumming off of me."

Penny raised an eyebrow.

Linda laughed and waved her hand. "Go. I'll be alright."

Penny stood and headed for the door. "I *could* use a little more sleep."

Guilt clinched Linda's stomach. She was the cause of Penny's sleepless nights. That's why she had been sleeping at Cy-Rac lately. At least there, no one could hear her scream.

With a shaking hand, she pushed the hair out of her face. The nightmares *were* getting worse. If she could only remember what they were about, maybe she could deal with them—get some peace. But they were elusive. She always woke up wrapped in a thick blanket of fear with no memory of why she felt so afraid.

Linda picked up the well-worn Bible sitting on her nightstand. She had always found comfort in its pages. But since her father's death, it seemed like God was nowhere to be found in the mess that had become her life.

At the thought of her dad, a familiar ache spread through her and she dropped the Bible. She had to get up; had to get moving. She would not waste time on grief. She needed to finish her dad's research. She owed him that.

Gathering her things, she headed to the bathroom. If she was extremely quiet, she could shower and get ready for work without bothering Penny again.

As she passed the mirror, Linda glanced at herself. The image stopped her. Penny was right. She had lost a lot of weight. Her clothes looked like they belonged to someone else. She shrugged. These days eating ranked last on her list of priorities. She preferred being awake a while before she ate breakfast and by the time she got to work... And, of course, she worked through lunch. By the time she got home, eating took too much energy. Linda sighed. She would have to do better. She couldn't afford to get sick now.

She padded down the stairs and into the kitchen. It was still too early to leave for work so she turned on the coffee pot then sat down. Opening her briefcase, she took out the top folder.

Recent tests had been promising and according to the numbers, the polymer should work. It didn't. There was always a breakdown in the last phase of bonding and it wouldn't hold under extreme pressure. Yesterday, she had printed a hard copy of the files in hopes that looking at paper instead of a screen would help her locate the problem. It hadn't. Everything looked...right.

She sat back in the chair. As much as she hated to admit it, someone else needed to look at the numbers. In the past it would have been her dad. Now she was her dad. At least as far as Cy-Rac was concerned. Everyone turned to her for help. Who, she wondered, did the Head of Research turn to? In all the years she had been working for her dad at Cy-Rac, she had never wondered who he asked for help. Truthfully, it had never crossed her mind that he would need help. He had been...her dad.

In the last six months, she had often questioned whether taking her father's place as Head of Research for Cy-Rac Industries had been the right thing to do. Maybe she was too young, too inexperienced or just too stupid to handle the job. Was she in over her head? She needed to answer that question. Not knowing wasn't fair to Cy-Rac or the people in her department. She needed to be one hundred percent certain of herself so she could be one hundred percent for them.

Linda looked at the clock, then looked again. She had been staring at the file for over an hour. She put the folder back in her briefcase. Getting up, she poured coffee in her travel cup. By the time she got to Cy-Rac, the building would be open.

She stepped into the garage and started to open the garage door. Her finger hovered over the button but she couldn't make herself push it. It always felt like someone was watching, waiting for her to open the door. In her head, she knew it was nonsense. There was no one out there. This was her neighborhood. She had grown up here.

But, what she knew and felt were two entirely different things. Sometimes she could almost feel them right beside her; hear them breathing. She never opened the garage door anymore until after she was in the car. She always scanned the area as she pulled out; always watched her rearview mirror. She was even worse at work.

She got in the car and punched the button for the door. She had just cleared the garage when she hit the brakes. Was something moving in the walkway? She let her eyes adjust to the dim light and watched the bushes beneath the kitchen window. The shadows in that area seemed bigger than just a few bushes would make. The familiar blanket of fear wrapped around her and began squeezing the breath from her body.

Linda closed her eyes and opened them again. Everything looked the same but it didn't. She shook herself. Penny was right. She couldn't go on this way.

She was driving herself crazy. The best solution would be to finish the polymer. That alone would be enough to make most of her problems disappear.

She eased down the driveway and onto the street. She would immerse herself in work and put everything else out of her mind. Right now, it was all she was capable of.

The silent streets moved by in a quick succession of twists and turns. It took about forty-five minutes to get to work at this time of the morning. Leaving the house thirty minutes later could extend the time to one or one and a-half-hours, depending on traffic. She pulled in the parking garage and glanced at the guard shack. There had been men working on it for several days now and it appeared to be finished.

There had been other changes going on within Cy-Rac since Cyrus Randal had died; most of them having to do with security. Linda wondered if Peter Burk, Cyrus' foster son, had insisted on the upgrades since Mrs. Randal had almost been killed within the walls of the building itself. He had been Head of Security for Cy-Rac until he had started his own business.

Someone outside of Cy-Rac had to be overseeing the upgrades because their new Chief of Security, Darrel Foss, didn't look like he would be inclined to do much of anything. And, he certainly didn't *act* capable of initiating all the upgrades himself. How he had gotten the job, she would never know. Yes, he had worked for the Cy-Rac security division for several years but he had never been particularly noticeable in anything he did. It had been surprising when he had been named Chief of Security.

Linda parked the car and leaned her head back. "Please, please, please, let me finish the polymer today. Help me see what the problem is so I can fix it and move on."

She sat up and opened her eyes. That was the closest she had come to praying for several months now. Silent tears slipped down her cheeks. "Father, I know I haven't been talking to You lately and I'm sorry. It's just that everything seems so...hard and I can't...

Linda swiped at the tears dripping from her chin. Suck it up. The Head of Research can't be seen bawling her eyes out in the parking garage. She flipped down the visor and opened the mirror. Her eyes were red, her mascara was running and her hair looked like it hadn't seen a brush in days. She had brushed it, right?

She opened her briefcase and pulled out her emergency kit. She pulled the brush through her hair, twisted it into a loose French knot and fastened it. She removed the runny mascara and touched up her makeup. She couldn't do anything about her red eyes. Hopefully, anyone seeing her would assume she wasn't getting enough sleep. Satisfied, she nodded. When she put her lab coat on, it would complete the Head of Research look.

She opened the door and stepped out of the car. Suddenly, that feeling of being watched settled over her. She slid a key up between her fingers and closed her hand around it. She tried to casually scan the parking garage but fear made her movements jerky. Her thumb hit the panic button and her car horn blared. She turned it off and closed her eyes. So much for trying to act calm.

She grabbed her briefcase, hurried toward the elevator and punched the button. That feeling flitted across her neck again and sent a chill racing down her spine. Without looking around, she opened the door to the stairs and started running up them. She pushed through the first floor door and slammed into a solid wall. Strong arms held her for a split second and then hands steadied her as she stepped back.

"Are you alright, Ms. Brown?"

Linda looked up into the brownest eyes she had ever seen.

CHAPTER 2

Darrel Foss looked in the mirror and wondered if he was in over his head. He had known Cy-Rac had holdings all over the world. Known he would be over security not only at the corporate facilities but also worldwide. What he hadn't realized was corporate espionage was a very big, very dangerous business. He didn't know who had recommended him but he took it as a sign he should step up and take more control of his life. He sat on the side of the bathtub and put his head in his hands. How stupid could he get?

He usually stayed at a job about six months then moved on. Temp agencies were a wonderful thing for a man on the move. He'd been working in security at Cy-Rac for four years. The big question was why. What had made him stay?

The money was good but it had never been about the money. Living like he did, didn't take much money. Most of what he made went straight into investments. Always had. Now that he was officially Chief of Security, his salary had jumped substantially.

He looked around the tiny bathroom. The tub was the only place he could sit without banging his knees. The rest of the apartment was on the same scale. Even though he'd been living here two years it had never felt like home. He'd lived in a flea-bitten motel on the outskirts of town before he'd moved here. He could move into an upscale apartment or a house in the suburbs. He shuddered. The 'burbs' wasn't his thing. That whole 'knowing your neighbors' was not for him. Living on the edges of society suited him just fine.

He sighed. Since he'd become Chief of Security, he was moving into areas outside his comfort zone. Cy-Rac had always run like clockwork and with a few exceptions, this job should have been a piece of cake. Even someone like him should have been able to handle it. Now he wasn't so sure.

The recent upheavals caused by Cyrus Randal's death, the disappearance of his sons, the take-over bid that had been launched against the company, and the attempted murder of Mrs. Randal and Mr. Burk had taken him places he didn't want to go.

He rubbed the back of his neck. He had that feeling again and he hated that feeling.

Darrel moved into the combination living room and kitchen. His furnishings, a small TV on a cart, a coffee table and an old couch, didn't look like much. The couch was so comfortable, though, that he slept on it. He had one plate, one bowl, one glass, one pan, and one set of silverware. More times than not he ate straight out of whatever the food came in.

Everything he needed could be packed in a duffle bag within minutes and he kept the duffle bag ready to receive his worldly possessions at a moment's notice. Even now his fingers itched to pack it. His feet itched to take it and go. His mind was already searching for a good place to stop for the night. He hadn't felt this way in...well, four years. He walked over and picked up the bag. It felt good in his hand: real good.

For the last ten years he had refused to let himself be personally responsible for anyone in any way. He had gone to work by himself, come home by himself and been happy about it. It was much easier to move on if you didn't care about anyone around you. When the need to move on hit, all he did was walk into whatever agency he was working for and give notice.

He could do the same at Cy-Rac. No one would miss him. Oh, they would wonder about him. His sudden departure would probably be big news for the next day or two. Then things would return to normal and move on. He had three months of vacation saved up so he could give two weeks notice taken as vacation and leave today. The vacation pay would be a hefty deposit into his account. Enough that he wouldn't have to find another job for a month or so.

Darrel fingered the bag and grunted. Who was he kidding? He wasn't going anywhere. He had given his word. It was the only thing left of the boy he had once been. He dropped the bag and glanced at his watch. The security staff was meeting this morning to review procedural changes for the new security system.

Even though the person responsible for the recent trouble at Cy-Rac had been caught, he wasn't satisfied that the threat was over. It was that stupid feeling. It danced around the edges of his subconscious and had him peering into shadows. He wasn't going to be caught off guard again.

The new security measures at Randal Towers, Cy-Rac's home office, had gone live yesterday. Because of the upgrades, he had to add twelve people to his department. That meant screening a hundred or more applicants. Conducting at least thirty or more initial interviews. Thank goodness, Karen Eckels, his secretary, could weed out the majority of the applications. He just had to make sure she understood what he was looking for.

He made a fist and rolled his wrist. It had been four months since he had been shot during the SP affair. His arm wasn't one hundred percent but it was better. He opened the kitchen drawer and lifted out the case inside. He punched in the numbers and the lid popped up. He picked up the gun. Licensed to carry it, he went to the range once a month to keep himself sharp. A small shudder ran through him and he gently placed it back in the case. He picked up the knife, strapped it to his leg and put the case away.

He glanced at his watch again. If he left right now he could stop at Momma Dona's for breakfast. A hot breakfast, even if it was just a burrito, would be good. Plus, he could use a large latte.

Darrel closed the door and locked it. With his body shielding his actions, he placed a small piece of clear tape across the door frame and the door. He stepped back and looked. Of course, the tape jumped out at him but he knew it was there. He doubted anyone else would notice it. Satisfied, he headed to the front of the building.

The early morning sunshine struggled to break through the clouds as he climbed into his car. The four door late '90s sedan matched his apartment and the neighborhood he lived in. It wasn't old enough to be considered vintage or new enough to be worth stealing. Still, it got him where he wanted to go.

When he walked inside Mama Dona's Deli, there was a burrito and a large latte sitting on the counter. He smiled at the girl and handed her his money. He walked outside and paused. He didn't want to stop coming here. But when your food was waiting on you before you walked in the door, eating here had become a habit. Habits came back to haunt you.

He grunted. Being offered the Chief of Security position *had* been a sign. Only, instead of it meaning he should stay, it had meant he should go. After the department was back on an even keel, he would recommend someone to replace him and leave.

Darrel pulled into the parking garage and parked close to the guard shack. He unlocked the door and went inside. It now had re-enforced walls, bullet-proof glass and a new computer that allowed the guard to raise the tire guards at the entrance and lower the steel bar gate to block the exit.

As he stepped out the door, an uneasy feeling swept over him. He slowly turned towards his car so he could do a three-sixty of the parking garage. The lights were off and the two left corners were deep in shadows. It was impossible to tell if someone was there. Moving closer would defeat the purpose. If someone *was* there, they would be gone the moment he started in that direction.

He rubbed the back of his neck. That nagging feeling was still there. He turned around and headed for the stairs. When he reached the door, he did a quick perusal of the area and made a mental note to have the timer for the lights reset so they wouldn't go off until the sun shone into every corner.

Darrel took the stairs two at a time. There were a few things he needed to do before the staff meeting. They wouldn't take long but he wanted everything in order before his people arrived. He walked into his office and a large latte sat on his desk.

Karen grinned at him. "I know how you are about that first latte of the morning. I wanted to make sure things went as smoothly today as I could get them."

Darrel raised his eyebrow.

Karen pointed at the latte. "The first step was making sure *you* were in a good mood."

Darrel grunted. "Is everything set for the meeting?"

"I have the schedule here for you to sign off on and I took the liberty of doing an initial screening of the security applicants. Not knowing the exact criteria, I put them in order based on what I thought you would be looking for."

"How many so far?"

"Thirty. I grouped them by experience and work history." Karen tapped the stack of folders on his desk. "The blue folders on top are retired or ex police, military, or private sector security. The green folders contain all public sector security. The yellow folders contain those new to the security field and those looking for part-time work. The pink folders, I rejected out of hand. Let me know if you agree with my assessment."

Darrel silently sighed. It was going to be a long day. "Thanks. I appreciate you taking the initiative on this."

Karen grinned. "Sure thing, Boss."

Darrel shook his head as she sash-shayed out of the office. Young and a little sassy, she was a bulldog when it came to him and his office. And, a good right hand.

He walked over to the window. The need to move on was strong. But he had tried staying on the move and that hadn't worked. Evidently, staying in one place wasn't working either. Maybe it wasn't possible to get away from his past. Maybe...he was going to have to live with it. That thought chilled him to the heart. He shook it off and walked into the control room

Darrel glanced at each monitor. With a building as big as Randal Towers, total coverage was impossible but he had been given more or less carte blanche to spend whatever it took to update the system and he had taken full advantage of it.

Movement on one of the screens caught his eye. He turned toward the bank of cameras covering the parking garage. A compact car was pulling in. He watched with satisfaction as the cameras showed its progress from the street to parking space. A young woman stepped out of the car. She looked...uneasy.

He tapped the monitor. "Zoom in." The camera zoomed in on the woman. "Isn't that Ms. Brown?"

"Yes, Sir."

"Zoom in a little closer." Darrel watched as she slid a key between her fingers. She tried to appear casual but her movements were jerky and anyone watching wouldn't be fooled. Suddenly, her car horn went off. She silenced it, grabbed her briefcase and hurried towards the elevators.

He remembered his uneasy feeling. "Keep an eye on her and call me if anything happens."

"Yes, Sir"

Darrel headed for the elevators. He was probably overreacting but he would rather be safe than sorry.

When he reached the elevators, the stair door opened and Linda Brown slammed into his chest. He automatically wrapped his arms around her and she fit within the circle of his arms like she was made for them. Surprised, he stepped back but kept his hands on her shoulders. Her breathing was shallow and she quivered from head to toe.

Her honey-gold hair looked soft to the touch and was trying to free itself from the bun she had it in. He had the oddest desire to see what it would look like down. When she looked at him with big hazel eyes surrounded by thick lashes, he was lost.

"Ms. Brown, are you alright?"

CHAPTER 3

Linda had never seen eyes that looked so luminous they seemed liquid. They were surrounded by long black eyelashes that had *the* perfect curl. Something she would have to put time and effort into to achieve. Why, she wondered, did men always have beautiful eyes and perfect hair while women had to work so hard at it?

She blinked and realized she was staring into Darrel Foss' eyes. The oddest sensation ran through her. She had just been thinking about him and here he was. Several impressions lodged themselves in her brain at once. She had never been this close to him before and he was bigger than she thought he would be. He had a solid chest and remembering the feel of his arms around her, he was strong. Even now, she could feel the power in his hands as they steadied her. The fear was still pressing against her chest and she had the strangest urge to step back within the circle of his arms and stay there.

She saw his mouth moving but the words weren't registering. Surprisingly, she was having trouble concentrating with him so close. She took a deep breath and stepped back. Raising a shaking hand, she tucked her hair back into its knot.

"Is everything alright, Ms. Brown?"

Not ready to look in his eyes, she looked down and groaned. So much for trying to look like the Head of anything. Rumpled. That was the only way to describe herself. She straightened her coat, smoothed her hair again and focused on the top button of Darrel's shirt. In her best head scientist's voice she said, "Yes. Why do you ask?"

"Well...," he held up a finger, "...you hit your panic button."

"Accidently."

He continued like she had not spoken. "...scurried through the parking garage..."

"I—do—not—scurry."

"...ran up the stairs instead of waiting for the elevator, slammed into me with enough force to knock the breath out of me...."

How in the world had *he* noticed so much in such a short amount of time? The events he was describing only took minutes. This was the man who never bothered himself about anything, right? Her eyes narrowed. Besides, what was he doing spying on her?

"...and, if I'm not mistaken, you have been crying."

That was going too far. She straightened to her full height. It didn't help that she was still looking at his top button. "If you will excuse me, *Mr.* Foss, I have work to do."

"Are you sure there is nothing I can help you with?" Darrel asked

Linda finally looked him straight in the eye. "Perfectly sure."

When he stepped back, she walked past him with her head held high.

*****

Darrel slowly smiled. Feisty. Not at all like he thought she would be. *And* try as she might to look the Head of Research part—with that hairdo, the lab coat, and those granny shoes—her eyes told a different story. A beautiful woman lived in those eyes; one, that at the moment, was running from something.

What spooked her like that? Everything he had heard about her said she was calm and level headed. He rubbed the back of his neck. First he had felt like someone was in the parking garage. Now, Ms. Brown had acted like she thought someone was there. It was too much of a coincidence.

He stood still while she stepped into the elevator and the doors closed. Then he went down the stairs, gently opened the garage door and stepped out. He huffed. Daylight was beginning to creep into the shadows and employees would start filling the parking garage in just a few minutes. If someone had been here, he was gone now.

Darrel walked over to Linda's car and did a slow three-sixty. In his mind's eye, he saw her enter the parking garage and get out of the car. Had she looked or moved in a certain direction? No. She had been looking all around when she hit the panic button. He glanced at his watch. Policing the area would have to wait.

He walked to the elevator and punched the button. The doors quietly opened and he stepped inside. That feeling ran across his neck again and he quickly stepped out. He did one more three-sixty and...nothing. He stepped into the elevator. That feeling had never been wrong before. Something was going on and after the meeting, he needed to find out what it was.

Darrel walked into the glass conference room and nodded at his people. "Thank you for coming in this early. I realize that this is a quick turn around for some of you so we'll make this brief."

"As you know, we have updated the entire building security system. To properly man the system, we will be hiring twelve new people. So if any of you know of someone looking for a job in security, have them fill out an application." He paused. "What this means for us right now is overtime and lots of it."

Groans filled the room.

Darrel smiled. "Ms. Eckels is handing out the new schedules. Some of the new computer software for the building will require training. Your schedules will include time for that."

He waited until Karen had the schedules handed out. "Please keep in mind that time off will be at a minimum. If any of you have a firm conflict with the hours you have been assigned, make an appointment with Ms. Eckels and she will work with you."

"Now, let's look at the new procedures for the monitor room. If you have not done so, walk through there before you leave. We have more than doubled the security cameras in the building; so, the number of monitors has more than doubled. We will start with two people working the room for the morning and evening shift; one at night. If we find two people can't adequately monitor the new system during the day, we will hire additional personnel. Remember, there are always minor glitches with a new system. Please be patient while we work through them."

"Each guard manning the monitor room will fill out an on-line shift log. When you arrive, log in with your ID number and log off when you leave. Even if the log is empty, we want a record of who manned the monitors during every shift. This log is for comments, notation of anything irregular: things like that. It is fairly simple and easily mastered."

"The front desk will be manned at all times. I don't want to come in and see it empty. The two guards manning the desk will be on rotation: four hours at the desk; four hours roving patrol. Until we get the extra manpower, it will be six and six.

As it stands, the roving guard will man the guard shack during peak employee arrival and departure times. The gate can be opened from the monitor room but I prefer to have a live person manning the shack during peak times."

"I know the next few weeks will be trying." He smiled. "So be patient with one another and the new system. Hopefully, you will be able to return to your normal schedule within the next three months. Are there any questions?"

He looked around the room. No one spoke up.

"This meeting is adjourned then." Darrel started to leave and a picture of Linda standing by her car, scared and alone, came to his mind. "Wait."

Everyone stopped.

"When you are on monitor duty and there is only one person in the parking garage, I want them watched from the time they leave their car until they are in the elevator or inside the building."

Several people started to ask questions but Darrel held up his hand. "Nothing is going on. This is only a precaution. Starting tomorrow, the parking garage lights will be on from 5:30 to 7:00 am and when required, from 4:30 to 7:00 pm so that no one has to come or leave in the dark." Darrel waved. "That's all."

He watched his people walk out. They were good people but Bailey and Jarvis were both nearing retirement and three months of twelve hour days might be rough on them. He needed to hire four people—quickly. Maybe Cole or Mr. Burk could give him some leads. It wouldn't hurt to ask. Karen had already saved him a lot of work by sorting the applications.

Darrel stepped into the monitor room. Instead of black and white images flickering on the screens, there was digital color. Sharp and clear with the ability to zoom in close enough to count someone's eyelashes. The thought of eyelashes brought to mind a pair of big hazel eyes. Darrel shook his head. The owner of those eyes had made it very plain she didn't care for his company.

He sat down and pulled the stack of six blue folders towards him. He flipped open the first folder, glanced at the picture attached, and closed it. The man had been fired from his last job for excessive cruelty and was in the middle of a drug investigation.

He opened the next folder and read through the application, references and cover letter. The young man had been an MP in the Army and still wore his hair high and tight. He had been honorably discharged two months ago. He was fresh enough Army to have that yes, Sir; no, Sir mentality. Darrel put a note on the folder: Contact CO and ask for phone conference.

He read through the next three folders and noted those accordingly. He opened the last folder, glanced at the attached picture and dropped it like it was on fire. Erik Vaughn. With his talents, this guy had to be pulling down six to seven figures a year.

What were the odds that Erik would apply for a job in security at Cy-Rac shortly after he had taken the Chief of Security position? Slim to none. That Erik didn't recognize his name was possible. But his face was an entirely different matter. If they had a face to face, his past would come back to haunt him with a vengeance and he didn't need that. He was haunted enough already. He sighed. He should have taken the duffle bag option.

CHAPTER 4

From the moment she had awakened to now, nothing had gone right. Linda leaned back in her chair and closed her eyes. The tired burning sensation that had been nagging at her was now a full-blown, class-A headache. The intense pain even made her teeth hurt.

She rubbed her temples. It was lack of rest and she knew it. If she went home, she could play some praise music, stretch out on the couch and relax. Going home in the middle of the day seemed like admitting defeat. She hated to admit defeat.

A chill ran across her neck. She didn't even have to look to know who was behind her.

"Ms. Brown?"

Linda sat up. "Mr. Waters?" She had a hard time keeping a straight face. His parents must have been originals because they named him Wade Waters. It sounded like a spy's name and Wade looked more like a spy than your stereotypical scientist. Everything about him was manicured. From the top of his perfectly styled hair to the tips of his Italian shoes.

He had been her father's 'right hand' from the day he started less than a year ago. She had expected him to be offered the Head of Research position. He knew the research department inside and out. Everyone in the department seemed to like him or at least respect him.

"Would you like me to do the polymer testing today so you could take a break?" He raised one perfectly formed eyebrow. "Maybe get something to eat. It is after one." He leaned over her shoulder and looked at the screen. "Since I worked with your father, I *am* familiar with the project."

Something about the way he studied the screen made Linda turn off the monitor. "I appreciate the offer but I think we need to take a break from this particular project. Since we don't seem to be making progress, I don't think one more day is going to make a difference."

Linda pushed her chair back and stood. "I had, just this moment, decided to go home." She picked up her briefcase, sat it on the desk, and opened it. "Is there anything that requires my immediate attention?"

"No. All the other projects are on track."

"Good." She picked up the folder containing the hard copy of the polymer formula and tossed it into her briefcase. "You know how to reach me if anything comes up."

He nodded and walked away.

She waited until Wade was at his desk before she turned the monitor on. He *had* worked on the polymer with her father so he did know everything about the formula. He might not look like a lab-coated, wild-haired scientist but he certainly had the credentials. He was the logical person to ask for help.

A shudder ran through her. She wouldn't...couldn't. It didn't make sense but he was too—perfect. Always willing to do what was asked of him. Always ready to take the backseat and let someone else get the glory. The outside image he maintained didn't fit the persona he projected. He embodied the perfect arrogant male in the way he dressed and carried himself but he acted mild-mannered and self-effacing. The difference was too extreme to be believable.

Linda saved her work and shut down the file. She ejected the flash drive and put it in her briefcase. Then she deleted her temporary files and shut down her computer. Anyone who really wanted to could find a copy of the files on her computer but she wasn't going to make it easy.

She paused. Her father had never gone to such lengths to hide his research. Why was she? Had she become that selfish and glory-seeking? Did she want to be the person who perfected the polymer and got the write-ups in the scientific journals, the lecture tours, and all the attendant fame possible in the scientific community?

She stepped to her office door and looked out across the lab. These were her people. She had been one of them until her father died. She'd had a job and a family she loved; it had been enough. Had she changed that much?

She caught movement out of the corner of her eye. Wade had seen her and was getting up from his desk. She smiled and waved him back down. If she didn't get out of here, he would be back asking questions.

Linda picked up her briefcase, stepped out of her office and locked the door. It felt odd to be leaving early. She never left early, not even on the Friday before she started vacation. She stepped on the elevator and breathed a quick prayer. "Please let me get to my car and out of the garage without doing something embarrassing."

She stepped into the garage and looked around. The sun was shining into every corner. No one was lurking in the shadows. Still, she couldn't shake that feeling of being watched.

She was halfway to her car when she heard footsteps. She started walking a little faster. Why hadn't she parked in her designated space close to the elevators? Habit, that's why. She had been parking in the same spot since she had started work here.

By the time she reached the car, the footsteps were right behind her. She punched the button to unlock the doors and the horn started honking. The sudden noise startled her and she dropped her briefcase. She took a deep calming breath and turned the horn off. When she bent over to get the briefcase, she felt light headed. She leaned over too far and hit her head on the side mirror which caused her to drop her keys. Standing up abruptly, she hit her head on the mirror again. Pain shot in all directions. She opened her eyes and the garage tilted. The floor buckled beneath her. She quickly closed her eyes and willed the garage to stop moving. It wasn't working. She started falling forward. Two hands settled on her shoulders and stopped her forward motion.

"Are you alright, Ms. Brown?"

Linda kept her eyes closed. She refused to confirm what she already knew. This was the second time today she had made a fool of herself in front of Darrel Foss. Embarrassed was too mild a word for what she was feeling right now. She settled for nodding her head and he let her go. She turned and opened her eyes at the same time. It was the wrong thing to do. She could feel herself falling forward. Once again, strong arms wrapped around her and held her steady. She gave up and relaxed into them.

*****

When Darrel felt Linda relax, He sighed deep within himself. He didn't need this complication in his life but having her head on his shoulder, seemed...right. He rested his chin on her head and pulled her in a little closer. They stood there like that until she finally shifted within his arms. "Better?"

Linda nodded against his chest then started shaking her head.

"I think I'm going to be sick."

He quickly turned her around and kept a steadying hand at her waist as she leaned over. She heaved; a dry hacking sound that ended in a coughing fit. When she recovered, he helped her upright and handed her his handkerchief.

*****

Linda looked at the square white cloth in her hand and smiled. Most men didn't carry handkerchiefs anymore. At least, not the men she knew. It was such an old-fashioned gesture; like something out of a Regency romance novel. The hero rescues the damsel in distress and invariably hands her his handkerchief.

The fact that that was her favorite genre, made this feel a little surreal. If this was one of those stories, she would look up into Darrel's eyes and they would fall instantly in love. This was real life, though, and she was *not* going to look in Darrel's eyes. She was embarrassed enough.

"Better?"

"Yes."

"Do you think you can stand by yourself?"

"Yes"

"Here, lean against the car until I get the door open."

Linda leaned against the car while Darrel retrieved her keys. He unlocked the door, helped her sit down and then squatted in front of her. She would have had to turn completely away to avoid his gaze so she looked up. He looked neutral but gentle at the same time. It was the only way she knew to describe it and it set her at ease.

"Ms. Brown, what would you like me to do for you?"

Linda sighed. No one had ever asked her that question before and it brought all kinds of images to mind. He could fix the problem with the polymer. He could put her on a plane to New Zealand for a lifetime vacation. He could ride in on a white charger and slay whatever dragon haunted her nightmares. He could wrap her in his arms and kiss her senseless.

Linda popped her hands over her mouth. She hadn't said that out loud, had she?

"Are you going to be sick again?"

Linda gently shook her head. The headache was intensifying. She closed her eyes and rubbed her temples.

"Would you like to go back inside and lie down?"

"No, thank you. I'm going home. It will be peaceful there and no one will disturb me."

"I don't think you should be driving in this condition. You can lie down in my office. I'll make sure no one disturbs you."

"No! I don't want to stay here. I want to go home." Linda knew her voice was becoming shrill but she couldn't seem to help it.

"When was the last time you ate?"

"What?" The sudden change in topic caught her off guard. "What kind of stupid question is that?"

"Breakfast?"

Linda barely shook her head.

"Supper last night?"

Linda shook her head.

"Lunch or breakfast yesterday?"

"I don't remember but what has that got to do with anything?"

"Ms. Brown, your sugar level has probably bottomed out."

"I do seem to have the mother of all headaches." She looked at Darrel. Big fat tears began to slide down her cheeks. "I just want to go home." She used the handkerchief to try and stem the flow but for some reason they just fell faster. "I'm sorry. I'm not usually such a cry baby."

He smiled. "Cry. It relieves stress and will reduce the pain in your head. Let me make a phone call and we'll get you home."

CHAPTER 5

Darrel stood and walked a few steps away. The smart thing would be to take her back inside and hand her off to Karen. But he didn't always do the smart thing. He took out his phone and dialed Karen.

"Hey, Boss."

"Get me Ms. Brown's address."

"What's up?"

"She is feeling ill and I am taking her home."

"Okay, but why are *you* taking her? I could call a cab."

"Just get the address and knock off the third degree. Even though you are the Chief of Security's secretary, there are some things you don't need to know."

"O-o-o-h, attitude."

"Karen!"

"1617 Elmwood. That's out in the Briarwood Addition."

"Emergency contact?"

"Sister, Penny Brown."

"Call her. Let her know I'm taking Ms. Brown home. Tell her it isn't an emergency but Ms. Brown really doesn't need to be by herself."

"Will do."

"Give her my cellphone number and have her call me if she can't be there by the time we are, which should be in about an hour."

"You got it."

Darrel shut the phone and looked at Linda. His head kept saying 'you need to walk away'. It was right; he knew it. Not walking away went against all the rules he had set down for himself. Instead of listening, he walked back to the car and held out his hand, "Let's get you home." She took his hand and he slowly pulled her up. She swayed slightly, so he put his arm around her waist to steady her.

"What are we going to do?"

"First, we are going to get you in the passenger seat. Then, we are going to drive you home."

"But you don't know where I live."

"Yes, I do." Darrel opened the passenger door.

"But..."

"Get in. We'll work the details out as we drive."

"But..."

Darrel held up a finger. "Don't. This is the way it's going down. Besides, arguing will only make your headache worse."

*****

Linda got in the car, shut her eyes and leaned back against the seat. She shouldn't let him take her home. She should have him call a cab or insist she drive herself. But it felt nice to let someone else be in charge, if only for a little while. Tomorrow she would deal with the fallout.

When they pulled out of the garage and turned left, she sat up. "Where are we going?"

"A small detour. I want to pick up a few things before we get you home."

"What things?"

"Good things. Trust me on this."

Linda settled deeper into the seat. At this moment, she would just go with the flow.

The car stopped. Linda opened her eyes. They were in front of a small store that had several different kinds of fruit outside on display. A small bubble of panic started forming around her heart. Nothing looked familiar. The buildings were old and semi rundown. Trash lay in the gutters and a couple of homeless people sat in the doorway of an abandoned building. Alarm bells rang in her brain.

She knew nothing about Darrel Foss except that he worked at Cy-Rac. Yet, she had let him take complete control of her person. He could be a pervert or a homicidal maniac for all she knew. Just because he *seemed* nice didn't mean he was. You heard about that kind of thing on the news all the time. The guy next door turns out to be serial killer or a child molester and none of the neighbors suspected a thing. Stupid. Stupid. Stupid.

The panic continued rising until her heart sounded like a bass drum pounding in her head. She began rubbing her temples. What had she done?"

"You allergic to any fruit?"

Linda jumped. "What?"

"Fruit. Are you allergic to any fruit? I make a mean fruit slush. Drinking one will do wonders for your blood sugar."

The panic oozed out of her body until she felt like a deflated balloon. Her heart slowed its rhythm. "Uh, not that I know of."

"Anything fruit you don't like?"

"No", she paused, "at least not that I know of."

Darrel grunted, got out and walked up to the fruit stand.

Linda watched as he picked up an orange, turned it over in his hand and then smelled it. After checking several he put some in a basket. Then he picked up a couple of bananas, some strawberries and a pineapple. He took them inside and came out with a bag in his hand.

Linda blinked. Was this the action of a serial killer? It could be, but she doubted it. When he was back at the car, a peace enveloped her. It was the oddest thing. It's probably the headache, she thought. Nothing seemed normal with the pain coloring everything.

"What kind of bread do you like?"

"Bread?"

"Rye, wheat, sour dough, pumpernickel?"

"I prefer flaky croissants drenched in butter."

"Really? That's two blocks down. It will be easier if I walk. Are you okay here by yourself for a few minutes?"

Linda looked around again. This place didn't seem so bad, especially since Darrel was so comfortable being here. "Sure."

"It might not look like much but it is a good neighborhood full of good people. You won't be bothered but lock the doors if it will make you feel better."

Linda nodded. Darrel stepped back and she rolled up the windows, and then locked the doors. She watched as he walked over to one of the men sitting in the building doorway. Darrel said something to him. The man nodded, looked her in direction and saluted. Then he walked back to the doorway and sat down. How odd, Linda thought.

*****

Darrel walked away satisfied. Gino would watch over Linda like she was his sister. He grew up in this neighborhood and could smell trouble a mile away. He might look like a homeless man sitting in front of that building but he actually owned it and was renovating it.

Well, they owned it. It hadn't taken long to realize that everything Gino touched made money. Financing him was a sound investment.

Walking into Mama Dona's, the smell of fresh baked bread made his stomach rumble. He glanced at his watch. It was almost three and he hadn't eaten since this morning.

"What are you doing here this time of day? Nothing is the matter?"

"No, Mama. I am just a hungry man in search of the best sandwich in town."

"You have come to the right place. But, of course, you already know that."

Darrel smiled as Mama Dona walked through the swinging doors. She was as wide as she was tall and swayed back and forth when she walked. She made the best sandwiches in the city *and* she had a heart of gold.

In a couple of minutes, she came out with a bag and set it on the counter. "Do you want chips or a drink today?"

Darrel snagged a root beer out of the cooler and set it on the counter. "I also want six honey butter croissants."

"You, a croissant?" She came around the counter. "Bend down."

Darrel did as he was told.

Mama felt of his forehead. "No fever. You are not ailing in the stomach?"

"No, Ma'am. The croissants are for someone else."

"Ah-h-h." Mama went back through the swinging doors and came back with a box in her hand. She set it on the counter. "I put in extra butter so you can impress."

Darrel smiled. "Now, Mama, I'm not buying croissants to impress anyone."

She wagged a finger. "You can say what you want, Darrel Foss, but Mama knows it is a lady. This is a first for you and I will help anyway I can."

Darrel felt the heat rise in his face. "Thank you, Mama."

Mama reached up and patted his face. "It is time the sadness left your eyes."

Darrel leaned down kissed her cheek. Then he laid twenty dollars on the counter and walked out.

His cellphone rang. "Yes?"

"Penny Brown is in the middle of final exams. Her brother is at the beach with some friends. She said if Mrs. Kennedy is home, she will stay with Ms. Brown. Mrs. Kennedy lives two houses down to the right. She also said if you need her to come home now, she would."

Darrel looked at his watch again. By the time he got Linda home and settled, it would be time to knock off work anyway. "What's her number?"

"555-661-1919."

"I'm gone for the day. Shut down my office and lock up."

"Will do."

"Thanks." By the time he put his phone away, he was at the car. He looked at Gino and nodded. Gino stood and disappeared into the building. Darrel pulled the keys out of his pocket and hesitated. Linda was asleep. He hated to wake her. He could sit close by and eat his sandwich while she slept. As he started to turn away, she stirred. Home it was, then. When he unlocked the door and got in, she briefly opened her eyes and smiled.

"Home?"

The tone of Linda's voice vibrated across his skin. A vivid image of his mother standing at the kitchen sink with his father's arm around her floated into his mind. He closed his eyes against the pain. It had been years since he had been home.

Darrel pulled into the driveway of the two story brick home with the minute manicured front lawn and shut off the car. It was everything he expected of suburbia. The houses on either side were only separated by three or four feet. It sounded weird coming from a guy who lived in an apartment but the closely built houses made him feel claustrophobic.

Linda didn't stir when he opened the car door so he retrieved the packages, went to the front door, unlocked it and eased it open. It opened onto a neat little foyer with several old pieces lining the walls. He walked into the living room and on through to the kitchen. It was small and obviously not the center of this family. Everything was too neat.

His family had lived in the kitchen. Everything important that had happened to them had been around the kitchen table. He sat the packages down, looked around and grunted. There was a blender sitting on the counter so he would be able to make the slush the easy way.

He went back to the car. "Alright, Ms. Brown, you're home. Let's get you inside."

*****

Linda opened her eyes. The light sent shafts of pain shooting through her head and her stomach jumped into her throat. She quickly shut her eyes again. It helped. She put her hand out and when Darrel took it, pulled herself out of the car. She didn't let go of his hand. He was going to have to lead her because she wasn't opening her eyes until they got in the house.

They stood in the driveway for what seemed like forever.

"Why aren't we moving?"

"It would be easier to navigate the driveway with your eyes open, Ms. Brown."

"The light hurts too much."

Linda heard a sigh. Suddenly her feet left the ground and she was resting in Darrel's arms. "What do you think you're doing?"

"Carrying you."

"Well, obviously. Put me down this instant. What will the neighbors think?"

"Ms. Brown, we can either spend the next five minutes with you staggering around like a drunk or I can have you in the house and away from prying eyes in two minutes."

Neither way was acceptable but appearing sickly was infinitely better than appearing drunk; especially in the middle of the afternoon. "Carry on."

"Your wish is my command."

CHAPTER 6

Darrel eased Linda onto the couch and put a pillow behind her head. He took the afghan lying nearby and covered her with it. "Comfy?"

Linda nodded and rolled to face the back of the couch.

"I'm going to make that slush. Stay awake long enough to drink it." Darrel turned toward the kitchen. A hand stopped him.

"My briefcase?"

"In the car."

"Would you mind bringing it in first?"

"The car is locked."

"Ridiculous, I know but lately I want it where I can put my hand on it. Please bring it in first."

Darrel looked at the hand resting on his arm. Life from here on out could become complicated; very complicated if he didn't guard against it. "It can wait ten minutes."

She rolled over and looked at him. "No, it can't." She rubbed her forehead. "Don't ask me to explain why because I don't know. I just know I need it in the house with me."

Darrel looked at her. He was here because of what happened in the parking garage this morning. Something had definitely spooked her. Besides, getting the briefcase would be faster than arguing about it. "Okay."

Darrel walked out to the car and unlocked it. He shrugged. Might as well put it in the garage. He activated the door opener and that feeling ran across his neck. He swung his arm and 'accidently' dropped the keys behind him. As he turned around to pick them up, he did a slow three-sixty of the neighborhood. Nothing seemed out of place. Not a curtain twitched. The cookie cutter houses were...well, cookie cutter. Every lawn was cut to the required one and a half inch height. Neatly trimmed shrubs, designed to deter intruders, circled each house.

Darrel smiled. If someone wanted in, a shrub wasn't going to stop him.

He glanced around again. Nothing. Maybe being in the burbs was making him uneasy. People, like Ms. Brown, reveled in suburban life. He shuddered.

Darrel pulled the car into the garage, went back outside and closed the door. He started to the front of the house and stopped. Might as well check out the back yard.

He walked around the side of the house glancing back and forth between shrubs. He stopped at the kitchen window and turned around. This part of the yard was visible from the driveway. He looked in the big window and shook his head. The kitchen was an open book for anyone who wanted to read it. It plainly said 'here, this is a good place to break in'. He started to walk on when his eye caught a glimpse of white. He squatted. A cigarette butt.

He didn't think Linda smoked. He didn't know about her siblings but it seemed odd that a cigarette butt would be in this particular spot if it came from someone in the house. He stood and finished circling the house. None of the other windows had such an open view into the house.

After trying several keys, he found the one that opened the kitchen door. Stepping inside he said, "It's me, Ms. Brown." Silence greeted him. He went through to the living room. Linda was asleep with one arm across the back of the couch.

You *know* nothing can ever come of this, his mind said. She is leagues above you. You need to walk away—fast and never look back'.

"I know."

Linda stirred at the sound of his voice. She sighed and rolled over.

Darrel backed up until he was in the kitchen doorway. "*You* know we are not going anywhere."

'I know', his heart answered.

Darrel searched through the kitchen cabinets until he found a plastic sandwich bag and some tongs. He went back to the cigarette butt. It had been laying there for a while and getting evidence from it would take a miracle but he picked it up anyway. He noted the brand, dropped it into the bag and slipped it into his pocket. He would label and hold on to it until something else surfaced that made it evidence.

He went back into the house and checked on Linda again. Still asleep. He glanced at his watch and was surprised. He had only been here for thirty minutes.

In the kitchen, he searched the drawers and couldn't find a sharp knife so he got his out. Balancing it on the tip of his finger, he flipped it in the air and caught it by the hilt. He rarely had to use it anymore but he still kept it razor sharp.

He set the fruit out. With the palm of his hand, he rolled the oranges to soften them then stemmed the strawberries and washed them. He sliced the pineapple and cut the heart out. Putting it in a bowl to catch the juice, he sliced the pulp into chunks then poured them into the blender. Breaking up a banana, he dropped it into the blender. He cut the oranges in half, squeezed the juice into the bowl, removed the seeds and added that to the blender. Next, he added some honey and pulsed the mixture to mix the honey in. Then, he put some ice into the blender and pulsed it until it was a creamy texture.

He had just finished dicing the strawberries when a blood-curdling scream erupted from the living room. A solid thud quickly followed. Darrel flipped his knife into fighting position and sprinted into the living room. Linda was lying between the coffee table and the couch fighting the afghan like it was a living, breathing thing.

"Ms. Brown?" Darrel moved closer to the couch and raised his voice. "Ms. Brown!"

She stopped fighting.

He watched shudder after shudder run through her body. He wanted to stay. Hold her. Comfort her. Dispatch the monster that haunted her dreams. But, he didn't remember locking the kitchen door and he hadn't checked the rest of the house either. It might be a nightmare but there could have been someone in the house. He needed to do a sweep to make sure.

"Ms. Brown, I'm going to sweep the house. I'll be right back."

When Darrel came down the stairs, he found Linda curled into a ball whimpering. The sound tore at his heart. He sheathed his knife. Bending down, he touched her shoulder. She jerked and her fist connected with his eye. The surprise set him back on his heels.

*****

After the shrieking sound of metal being twisted and torn apart, the stillness was deafening. Linda waited for the blackness to envelope her but this time it didn't come. She heard her father groan. She didn't want to look. Didn't want to see. Didn't want to remember.

Another moan drew her gaze to her father's face. Blood oozed out of a deep gash on his forehead. His eyes fluttered open and he reached for her. She tried to take his hand but she couldn't move.

When he started pulling away, she tried to follow him but her legs were lost in the darkness. She couldn't budge them. She called out to him but he kept moving farther and farther away until he was just a small dot in the distance that flickered and then vanished. She was alone in the darkness.

"Ms. Brown?"

Linda came fully awake at the sound of her name. She looked straight up into liquid brown eyes. "Mr. Foss."

"You were having a nightmare and fell off the couch."

Linda looked around and saw the overturned coffee. Not again. Why, she wondered, do I keep embarrassing myself in front of this man? This is the third time today. "So I see."

He smiled. "The slush is ready and I'll heat up one of the croissants. You will feel better with some food in you."

She nodded. He scooped her up and before she could protest, sat her on the couch. She began fussing with the afghan and the pillow; anything to keep from looking at him.

"I'll be right back with that food."

Linda watched Darrel's retreating back. Had she heard amusement in his tone? She looked down at herself and groaned. Yes, she had. Her clothes were rumpled beyond repair. The afghan was wadded up in knots around her legs. Her waist length hair curtained around her. She must look ridiculous. Holding her hair off her neck, she looked on the couch and floor but didn't see her band anywhere. Finally, she shrugged and let go. It was too late anyway. Darrel Foss had already seen enough to make him run for the hills.

Linda stilled. Did what Darrel Foss thought of her matter? She shook her head. No, she just didn't want anyone from work seeing her out of 'work' mode. Simple solution; she would avoid speaking to him after tonight.

She looked toward the window and realized the light wasn't hurting her eyes. The screaming pain had become a dull ache. Maybe crying had helped. She slowly stood. The room dipped and then quickly righted itself. She stood there until she felt oriented, then she pulled the afghan off of her legs and dropped it on the couch. The smell of warm bread drifted into the living room and her insides rumbled in protest. Surprised, she patted her stomach. It had been a long time since she had been hungry. Walking around the overturned coffee table, she headed for the kitchen.

Darrel set the timer on the microwave and turned it on. The smell of warm bread filled the air and his insides started rumbling. He glanced at his untouched sandwich. Now it would be an early supper instead of a late lunch. When he turned to finish the strawberries, he saw Linda standing in the doorway. "Better?"

"I think so."

"The headache?"

"Down to a dull throb." She walked into the kitchen and sat down at the island.

"Good." The microwave dinged. Darrel set the bread in front of her.

Linda picked it up and started to take a bite.

"Wait."

She jumped and dropped the bread.

"Sorry, I didn't mean to startle you but Mama Dona sent extra butter. She would have my hide if I didn't use it." Darrel spread some of the butter over the croissant. It immediately melted and ran down the sides.

She caught some of the butter on her finger and put it in her mouth. "Mmm. Honey butter, my favorite. Tell Mama Dona, thank you very much."

"Will do."

Darrel watched as she broke the croissant in half and swirled one piece in the butter that had pooled on the plate. She started to bite it and stopped. She closed her eyes and mumbled, then opened her eyes and took a big bite. She closed her eyes again as a look of pure pleasure crossed her face.

Darrel smiled. "I did buy six of them so you don't have to make this one last forever."

Linda covered her mouth with her hand and laughed. "Good." She put the rest of the piece in her mouth, picked up the other half and handed him the plate.

Darrel put another croissant on it. He showed it to her and she looked at him like he had lost his mind. He set another one on it and raised an eyebrow. She gave him a thumbs-up, so he put those in the microwave to warm. When he turned around, Linda pointed at the blender and covered her mouth again.

"Is that the slush you were talking about?"

"Yes, Ma'am."

"You said something about it being ready."

"I just need to add the strawberries."

She watched as he gathered the pieces of strawberry and put them into the blender. With a long spoon, he gently stirred them into the mixture. Then he poured some in a glass and handed it to her. Next, he got the warmed croissants and put them in front of her.

Linda picked up the glass and took a sip. "This...is good!"

"You sound surprised. I told you I make a mean fruit slush."

"Bragging and being able to back it up are two different things." Linda waved her hand in the air. "But this is good."

Darrel laughed. He put the pitcher in the refrigerator. Next, he cleaned the cutting board and propped it up in the sink to dry. Then, he wiped down the counter.

"You seem to know your way around a kitchen."

"Cooking can be very relaxing."

"You've got to be kidding. I never willingly cook. Every time I try, nothing ever comes out right and I end up frustrated. Take out or delivery is much less stressful."

"I can tell."

"Oh? How?"

Darrel tapped one of the copper-bottomed pots hanging over the island. "These pots, in a well loved; well used kitchen, would not be this shiny. They have rarely, if ever, been used." Darrel spread his arms. "It's a shame, too. This is a nice little kitchen."

"My father bought those pots for my mother right before she was diagnosed with cancer." Linda sighed. "She loved to cook."

"Accept my condolences for your mother..." Darrel hesitated,"...and your father."

"Thank you."

CHAPTER 7

Darrel realized he was staring at Linda and mentally shook himself. "Okay, finish eating while I get your briefcase."

Linda eye's narrowed. "Is this the same briefcase I asked you to bring in before you did anything else?"

"Yep."

"The same briefcase that you agreed to get."

Darrel chuckled. "Yes."

"So what's it still doing in the car?" Linda's voice sounded shrill.

Darrel raised his eyebrows. "I'm glad you're feeling so much better, Ms. Brown. The car is safely locked in the garage and the briefcase is locked in the car. I don't think it's going anywhere."

Linda raised her hand. "Sorry, I didn't mean to sound like a shrew. For some reason I'm paranoid about my briefcase."

Darrel remembered the piece of tape he put across his door. "Everyone has some habit, if examined closely, would be pushing the edges of paranoia. I'll get the briefcase."

*****

Linda watched as Darrel opened the garage door and walked through without hesitating. He seemed very familiar with the layout of her house, especially since he had never been here before. He was definitely at home in the kitchen. That thought should have worried her and she waited for that uneasy feeling to creep up the back of her neck but...nothing. It was the oddest thing but having Darrel in the house felt right.

He came back in with the briefcase and she immediately stuck her hand out for it.

"Tell you what; you grab the food. I'll carry this and we'll get you settled on the couch."

Linda picked up the food and walked into the living room. She waited while he sat the briefcase down. When he righted the coffee table, she set the food on it and started to reach for the briefcase.

Darrel snatched it up, walked over to the desk and set the briefcase down. "I'm going to put this right here. Do not touch it tonight. It will be here in the morning and you can work then. Right now, you're going to finish eating and then either go back to sleep or watch some TV but you are not going to work while I'm here."

Linda put her hands on her hips. Did he honestly think he could tell her what she was and wasn't going to do in her own home? "Uh...who do you think you are that you can tell me what to do?"

Darrel picked up the croissant. "I am the man that controls the bread drenched in honey butter. Which, I happen to know, is your favorite."

Linda snorted and reached for the plate Darrel held above his head. To get it, she would have to stand on the couch. Considering her day, she would probably fall off and land on him. She remembered the strength of his arms when he'd caught her as she slammed into his chest. Remembered how mesmerizing his liquid brown eyes could be and knew she did not need to get that close. Instead, she sat back in her corner, crossed her arms, and raised an eyebrow at him.

"Seriously, you came home to take a break from work. Don't undo the good you have done just because you feel better."

Linda stopped and did an inventory; actually she did feel better. The tension in her neck and shoulders had eased and it hadn't taken all she had to drag her body from the couch to the kitchen and back. He was right, though; the first thing she had thought about was work. She sighed. She could at least finish the croissant. Maybe by then, her headache would be a memory and Mr. Mother Hen would leave her alone.

Immediately, Linda felt guilty. Darrel had gone out of his way to help her and she was irritated because he was telling her not to work. Which was stupid since that is exactly why she left work in the first place.

*****

Darrel watched the emotions race across Linda's face. Did she know how easy it was to read her thoughts? He tried to recall if she was that way at Cy-Rac but he couldn't honestly say. Until this morning, they had been two people who happened to work in the same building.

"Okay."

Darrel kept a straight face but could not keep the smile out of his voice. "Okay?"

Linda threw up her hands. "Okay, we'll do it your way but only because I *did* come home to rest."

Darrel set the plate on the coffee table, picked up the remote and held it out to her. "Do you want to choose or should I?"

"I never watch TV anymore. You choose." Linda picked up the croissant and stopped with it halfway to her mouth. "As long as it's not some macho man thing with lots of fighting, car crashes and killing."

Darrel grunted. "Take all the fun out of it." He didn't watch much TV either. "Let me know if you see anything you want to watch." He began flipping through the channels. He paused long enough to get an idea of what was on and then changed channels.

Linda finished the croissant and settled back against the couch.

When he came across a channel showing an old Three Stooges movie, she touched his hand. He looked at her. "Really?"

"Really. I've probably watched this a hundred times with my father. I laugh every time."

Darrel shrugged. "Works for me."

They laughed as Larry, Moe and Curly slipped and tripped and fumbled their way through the movie. During one of the commercials, Darrel took Linda's glass to the kitchen and came back with more fruit slush. She nodded her thanks.

Suddenly Linda sniffed. "Dad and I watched a Three Stooges movie the night before we left for Philadelphia."

Darrel reached over and took her hand. A sad smile spread across her face and she burrowed deeper into the couch.

Her hand gradually relaxed in his. He looked at her. She was asleep. He turned the volume down on the TV and eased his hand out of hers. When he did, she rolled over and put her feet up on the couch. He stood to get out of her way; then he spread the afghan over her. She pulled it under her chin and snuggled into it.

Darrel shook his head. This woman had captured him with that first look. He'd like to think it was just the damsel in distress factor but he knew it wasn't. It was those eyes and spending this time with her hadn't helped. He was beginning to appreciate the different parts that made up Linda Brown. She was a contradiction to everything he thought she would be. He shook his head again. Imagine, a woman that liked the Three Stooges as much as he did.

His insides rumbled. Darrel picked up the dishes and headed for the kitchen. Maybe he could get to that sandwich now.

A little girl voice said "don't go". When he turned around, Linda had her hand out toward him. Her eyes were closed and her breathing regular. She was sound asleep and he doubted she even knew she had called to him.

He sat the dishes down and pushed the coffee table away from the couch. He pulled the wing backed chair over and sat down. He took her hand in his and gently rubbed it. "I'm not going anywhere."

She sighed and seemed to sink deeper into sleep.

He tried to find a comfortable position in the chair but it was impossible. It was a woman's chair and had not been made for someone built like him. He finally gave up and eased the coffee table closer to him. He put his legs on the table and leaned back in the chair. At this rate, it was going to be a long evening.

The sound of the key turning in the lock brought Darrel fully awake. He stayed perfectly still as a younger version of Linda walked in the door. This must be Penny. When she moved closer, he could tell there were subtle differences. Linda's beauty was classical; all clean lines and mature features. Penny was Hollywood gorgeous.

*****

Penny opened the front door and stopped. Her sister was asleep on the couch and there was a large man sprawled across her grandmother's winged-back chair and the coffee table. He was holding Linda's hand and appeared to be asleep, too. She walked to the desk and hesitated. She shook her head and set her things down.

When she turned around, the man was staring at her. She walked to the chair and knelt down beside it. She liked what she saw. Besides, anyone who would stuff themselves into the most uncomfortable chair in the house just so he could hold her sister's hand had to be alright.

When she smiled, he smiled. That did it for her. She whispered, "Penny".

"Darrel."

"Mr. Darrel," Penny nodded towards Linda, "how long has she been asleep?"

Darrel turned his hand slightly so he could see his watch. "Roughly four hours."

Penny's eyebrows went up. "That's the longest she's slept at one time since the accident. Maybe you should come hold her hand more often."

Penny's frank gaze and voice made Darrel a bit uncomfortable. For the second time that day, he felt the heat rising in his face. It was almost like she could tell how he... Darrel shook his head and broke eye contact. He was *not* ready to go there.

He shifted his weight and an involuntary grunt escaped as pain shot from his hip up through his back. Linda stirred. He stilled instantly.

Penny smiled. "Not very comfortable, is it?"

Darrel rolled his eyes.

She went around the coffee table and took Linda's hand out of his. Linda stirred again. "Hey, Sis, I'm home."

Linda's eyes flickered open and she smiled. "Good. Don't let them get the briefcase."

"I won't."

Linda sighed and turned to face the back of the couch.

Penny leaned closer to Darrel. "Need help?"

Darrel shook his head. He wasn't so old that a few hours in an uncomfortable position would require him to need aid. He set his feet on the floor and another pain shot through his back. He grimaced.

"You sure?"

He looked up and Penny was silently laughing. "Yes, I'm sure."

"Okay, I'll take the dishes and meet you in the kitchen."

Darrel nodded. He waited until Penny had her back turned before he attempted to get up again. It took three tries but he managed to get up without waking Linda. He stood and stretched. A bone popped in his shoulder and his left calf started cramping. He rolled his neck and it cracked. He put the chair back where it belonged and moved the coffee table further away from the couch in case Linda decided to take a nosedive to the floor again.

He walked into the kitchen. Penny was standing at the counter spreading mustard on the top piece of bread from his sandwich. "You know that's a sacrilege, don't you? Rye can only be truly appreciated with mayonnaise."

Penny looked up and popped her hand over her mouth. She began to laugh. "I see you have met my sister's left jab."

"What?"

Penny pointed at her eye. "The shiner. It's lovely."

Darrel touched his eye and winced. He had a shiner. From the look on Penny's face, it must be a beaut. His knife had a mirror surface so without thinking, he pulled it out to look.

He heard a gasp. When he looked up, Penny's eyes were as big as saucers and she had backed up as far as she could. He quickly flipped the blade down and away from her. To him it was a thing of beauty; perfectly balanced and just made to fit his hand. But to her, the serrated edge and curved blade probably looked like death calling.

"Sorry. I carry this instead of a gun."

Penny just nodded.

"Here," he set the knife on the counter with the blade facing him and then took several steps back, "check it out. It's standard gov..." Darrel stopped. She didn't need to know where it came from; she just needed to know that in his hands, it wouldn't harm her.

Penny slowly picked the knife up and turned it over.

He saw her swallow hard and her face paled. In a slightly shaky voice she asked, "So, what's this red stuff?"

CHAPTER 8

"What red stuff?"

"This," Penny pointed at the blade, "red stuff."

Darrel walked around the counter and took the knife. There was a dull red stain on the blade and it had bits of leather stuck to it. He shook his head and started laughing. No wonder Penny had reacted the way she did.

"That would be strawberry juice. I was dicing them when your sister screamed."

Penny visibly relaxed. "So, that's how you got the shiner. You tried to wake her."

"Yes."

"My brother and I have learned to duck."

"Does she do that often?"

Penny pointed towards the end of the counter. "Is that your sandwich?"

Darrel blinked at the sudden change in subjects. "Yes."

"I should have known. Linda would never bring home rye bread. No one in this house eats rye because it's too dry."

"That's what the mayonnaise is for."

Penny made a face. "I'm not a mayo person. Give me a spicy mustard any time." She got a knife out of the drawer and cut the rest of the sandwich in half. Then she cut the bread with mustard on it in half. She took another plate down, put the bread on it and then took a small portion of the meat, cheese and vegetables. "I hope you don't mind. I thought since I had already put mustard on one side, I might as well eat it."

Darrel folded his arms across his chest and stood there.

"Uh, you don't like mustard, do you?"

He raised an eyebrow.

She tilted her head and gave him a sad puppy dog face. "I'm very hungry." Then she made a cross on her chest. "I promise I don't have cooties."

Darrel tried to keep a straight face but his stomach rumbled and made it impossible. He grinned. "I guess that settles it. No, I don't like mustard and since you have touched everything on the sandwich, it's a good thing you don't have cooties."

She waved her hand in the air. "Alright then, sit. I'm going to check on Linda, and then I'll be back."

He squeezed mayonnaise onto the bread then cut his half of the sandwich in half again. He took a bite and savored the flavors.

"She is still out. What did you give her? ...and will she wake up in the morning?"

Darrel sighed and sat his sandwich down. He was beginning to wonder if he would ever get to eat. "Sit and I'll get you a small glass."

Penny sat.

Darrel took the pitcher out of the refrigerator and poured some in a glass then set it in front of her. "What is it?"

"My famous fruit slush. Of course, most of the ice is melted so it won't have the same texture but it still tastes good."

Penny picked up the glass. "This is a *fruit* slush? Not one of those carrot and beet things disguised as fruit?"

"It's fruit."

She lifted the glass to her nose, smelled and shrugged. She took a small sip then she took a big drink and smacked her lips. "No wonder it's famous."

Darrel watched as she took a bite and then stopped, bowed her head and mumbled the way Linda had. So, blessing the food was a normal thing in this household.

"Where did this sandwich come from? I know it wasn't from our grocery store. This bread doesn't taste like it came straight out of the Sahara.

Darrel chuckled. "It's a little place called Mama Dona's. They bake their own bread."

She took another bite and then covered her mouth. "This is good."

Darrel smiled. "In my short acquaintance with the Brown women, I would say that you know how to enjoy your food."

"Most definitely. We may not eat a lot but what we do eat, we enjoy." Penny sat down her food. "Okay, tell me what happened."

"I missed lunch today. Do you mind if I eat while we talk?"

"By all means, I'm going to."

Darrel got his root beer out of the refrigerator. "I was in the parking garage and saw your sister swoon. She had a migraine headache. I think her sugar level bottomed out because she hadn't eaten since some time yesterday. Long story short, I decided it would be easier to bring her home because she didn't need to be driving."

*****

Penny blinked. A very short version. "And?"

"She fell asleep before we got here so I carried her into the house and laid her on the couch."

Penny smiled. She could just see him sweeping Linda off her feet, carrying her in the house and depositing her on the couch. He made it sound like something he did every day.

"And?"

Darrel shrugged. "She screamed. She woke up, ate some honey butter croissants, drank a fruit slush, watched some TV and went back to sleep."

While they munched on their sandwiches, Penny digested what he had said. She took a sip of the fruit slush and smiled. There was no real food in the house, period. They usually brought home take-out. There might be some chips or nuts to snack on but there certainly wasn't anything here capable of making the slush, the sandwich or the croissants. So instead of sending Linda home in a cab, he had driven her home after stopping to get fruit, this sandwich, and some croissants. Point one, two and three; his favor. Then he had stayed, fixed the slush, watched TV and held Linda's hand while she slept. Point four and five; his favor. Point six for doing his best to put her at ease about the knife.

She looked at him. Oddly enough, he seemed to fit here. He had certainly taken good care of Linda and Linda definitely needed help. Penny sighed. *They* needed help. She was getting as bad as Linda. When Linda wasn't home screaming and keeping them awake, she still woke up at every little sound. She had been praying for help. Maybe this was it.

"Every night."

"Every night what?"

Penny pointed at his eye. "She does that every night. I think that's why she started sleeping at the office. When she's home, none of us gets much sleep."

"And how long has she been doing this?"

Penny hesitated. She desperately wanted help but she wasn't sure how much to tell him, finally she settled for the basics. "Ever since the accident. She wakes up screaming in terror. As you found out, sometimes she is fighting something in her sleep." She smiled. "I was on the receiving end of a few of those punches until I learned to duck."

"Is she seeing someone about it?"

"No. I have tried to get her to. She keeps saying she will as soon as the polymer is finished. She insists she is so close she can smell it but I don't think she is any closer to finishing it than Dad was. She is totally obsessed. She doesn't sleep because of the nightmares, she works twelve hour days and she has all but quit eating because she is so focused on the polymer."

"That explains the briefcase obsession."

"If only that was all."

Darrel sat down his sandwich. "What do you mean?"

"It's the little things."

"Such as?"

"Linda is neat but I am fastidious. Everything has a place and should be in its place and lately...they aren't. I know it sounds crazy but small things, especially around the desk, are moved by a fraction of an inch. Most people wouldn't notice but I do."

Penny rolled her eyes and stood. "It does sound crazy when I say it out loud."

"No one knows this house like you two do. Have you talked to the police?"

"And tell them what?" Penny slouched and started twirling a strand of hair. "Uh, Officer? I left that notepad one centimeter further to the left this morning and uh, I know this paper was closer to the end of the couch than in the middle, like it is right now." She pushed the hair out of her face. "They would call for the men to bring the little white jacket and rightly so."

"I noticed you hesitated before you set your things on the desk."

"You were awake?"

"From the moment the key turned in the lock."

"I would have sworn you were sound asleep." She frowned. "Did you or Linda use the desk?"

"No. I just put her briefcase down beside it. Why?"

"It was the notepad thing. That and one drawer was slightly open. Linda and Teddy both have a desk in their room. I am the only one that uses the desk downstairs."

*****

Darrel felt the hair on the back of his neck stand up. Maybe the house hadn't been as empty as he thought. "Would you be able to tell if anything had been disturbed on your sister's desk?"

"Maybe."

"Let's go check."

When they got to the stairs, Penny hesitated.

"Want me to go first?"

Penny shook her head. "Not really. Someone could come up from behind just as easily as they could be waiting upstairs."

"I think you have been watching too many cop shows." Darrel put his arm around Penny. "If it makes you feel any better, I went through the whole house right after Linda screamed."

"Actually, it doesn't."

Darrel chuckled. "Come on. I'll be right here."

Penny walked into Linda's room and stopped so abruptly Darrel bumped into her. He stepped back. "What?"

Instead of answering, she walked to the desk and looked it over. "I don't think anything has been moved on the desk but", she walked over and picked up a stuffed bunny that was sitting on the foot of Linda's bed, "this has."

"You sure?"

"Yes. Mom gave this to Linda right before she died and it always sits right here." Penny set the bunny between the pillows at the headboard. "If Teddy was home, I might accuse him of moving it but he isn't here. It's almost like someone is deliberately trying to make us think we are crazy or...scare us."

"What is Linda's take on this?"

"We haven't talked about it. We haven't really talked about anything since the accident. She is under enough stress as it is and I don't want to add to it by freaking out over minor stuff like this."

Darrel studied Penny for a moment. She didn't seem to be the drama queen type. Her voice had been calm and steady the whole time she had been talking to him. She had told him her concerns in a practical, straightforward manner.

"Actually, I'm glad Linda's home. Without Teddy in the house, I don't think I could have stayed here by myself."

Darrel felt anger build in his chest. These women should feel safe in their own home. This should be a haven for them, not a torture chamber.

He threw his arm around her shoulder. "Tell you what, I'll bring Linda upstairs and then we'll look through the house together. I won't leave until you are ready for me to. Sound like a plan?" He felt Penny relax.

"Sounds like a plan."

Downstairs, Darrel picked Linda up in his arms and headed back up the stairs.

Linda opened her eyes. "What are you doing, Mr. Foss?"

"Carrying you upstairs, Ms. Brown."

"Thank you, Mr. Foss."

When she snuggled into his shoulder, Darrel brushed the top of her head with his lips. "You are most welcome, Ms. Brown."

Darrel laid Linda on the bed and turned to Penny. "I'll wait downstairs while you get ready for bed. Don't be in any hurry; I'm not. Come down and we'll go through the house together, okay?"

CHAPTER 9

Darrel sat down at the kitchen counter and rubbed the back of his neck. This day had definitely not gone according to plan. Just this morning, he'd been thinking he might be in over his head. He wasn't in over his head; he was drowning. He picked up his sandwich and mechanically took a bite.

This morning his biggest problem had been interviewing enough people to hire twelve new associates. This evening, he was in the middle of ...he shook his head. He didn't know what he was in the middle of. He only knew that now there were two women who needed someone to depend on. He kept shaking his head but he couldn't shake the image of two big trusting hazel eyes looking into his.

The sandwich suddenly tasted like cardboard so he threw it in the trash. He turned out the lights and walked over to the kitchen window. The view looking out was just as good as the view looking in. If someone had been standing at this window, surely one of the ladies would have noticed. One thing was certain, this window needed to be covered.

"Darrel?"

Penny's voice sounded small and unsure. He walked over and flipped on the light. "In the kitchen."

When she walked in, he had to smile. She had on a kimono type housecoat covered with huge red, blue, and yellow flowers with green parrots thrown into the mix. She had a towel wrapped around her head and frog slippers on her feet. For the first time, Darrel wondered what he had missed by not having a sister.

"It was so dark; I thought you had changed your mind."

"No way. You ready to make that sweep?"

Penny barely nodded.

Darrel pulled out his knife and flipped it into fighting position. He held his hands up in front of him and bobbed back and forth on his feet. "With or without the knife?"

Penny laughed. "Without, please."

He tossed the knife up, caught it and put it away.

"You seem pretty handy with that thing."

Darrel shrugged. "Practice and lots of it.

"Do you always carry it?"

"Always."

"Why?"

"I am in security."

"Wouldn't a gun be better?"

Darrel shook his head. "I don't do guns." He smiled. "Now, enough with the third degree. Since we're in the kitchen, I say we start our sweep in the garage.
"

"Okay by me."

*****

Penny followed Darrel through the door and watched as he checked behind and under things. He even looked in the small spaces. He took the keys down and went through each car. Then he dropped to the ground and looked under the cars, from front to back.

Darrel stood. "Did you see anything?"

Penny shook her head.

"To the kitchen then."

"But we just came from there."

"True; but we are sweeping the whole house, remember?"

Penny trailed behind Darrel as they went from room to room. She was amazed at how thorough he was. Before they left a room, he checked all the windows and doors. She would have just stuck her head in the room and glanced around. There would be no doubt in her mind that no one else was in the house by the time he got through. They searched her room last.

Darrel stood in the hall. "I'm satisfied. You?"

Penny nodded and covered a yawn with her hand.

"Need me to stick around?"

Penny yawned again. "I think I'm okay."

"I'll be leaving then. Follow me downstairs and lock up after me."

Penny started down the stairs and paused. "Wait a minute. Didn't you bring Linda home in her car?"

"Yes."

"How are you going to get home?"

"I'll call a cab."

"No. Take Linda's car. This was my last day of school. I can take her to work in the morning." He started to say something but she interrupted him. "I won't take no for an answer. Not after what you've done for us. If I have to, I'll get dressed and drive you home myself."

"That would make the sweep we just did pointless."

Penny smiled at him. "Exactly."

Darrel chuckled. "Okay. I'll leave Linda's keys at the security desk." Darrel started out the door and stopped. "Can I have a sandwich bag?"

Penny gave him an odd look. "Sure."

He went to the cabinet and pulled out one of the bags and slid it into his pocket. "Thanks."

Penny followed him out to the garage. She waited while he got in the car and backed out. When he was clear of the door, he stopped the car, got out and hit the button to close the garage door. When it was closed, Penny went back in the house, closed the door to the garage and locked it. She leaned her head against it. "Point seven; his favor".

*****

Darrel waited until the garage door closed then he slid into the car and backed onto the street. He punched in a number into his cellphone.

"How can I help you, Mr. Foss?"

"I'm coming in with a car. When I get there, I'll flash my lights twice for you to open the parking garage gate."

"Yes, Sir."

"Turn all the lights on. I want it bright as day."

"Will do."

Darrel hung up. He had just started sweeping the parking garage when Linda had come in. Since it was only a whim, he had planned to leave it until the morning. But after what Penny had said plus finding the cigarette butt, it needed to be done tonight.

He pulled into the garage, stopped and flashed his lights. The gate opened and he drove to the Head of Research's designated parking spot next to the elevators. If Linda parked here, she would step out of the elevator and be right at her car. He would strongly suggest she do so.

Darrel smiled. Keats had taken his request seriously because the parking garage was as bright as the noonday sun. He went to the middle of the garage and studied each corner. If someone had been here this morning, they would have stayed where the shadows were deeper.

He did a slow three-sixty. Only one spot allowed someone to see the entire floor. He walked over and began a slow sweep of the area. Little piles of debris lined the edges. He made a mental note to have these areas routinely swept on every level.

Darrel turned his back to the wall and positioned himself where he could see the whole garage. He took his sunglasses and laid them on the floor at his feet. Then, he took four steps to his right, looked around and took one more to the right. Taking his pen out of his pocket, he gently sifted through the debris piles, spreading each pile out until he could see everything.

He found what he was looking for when he was one step to the left of his sunglasses. He rolled it over until he could see the brand name. Same brand. Taking the sandwich bag out of his pocket, he rolled the cigarette butt into it and closed it.

Darrel sat back on his hunches. Now, what to do with it? Penny was right. The police would dismiss the notepad being moved as hysterics due to women being alone. They would also need more evidence than a cigarette butt of the same brand being in the Cy-Rac parking garage. Several Cy-Rac employees lived in that general area and both butts could have come from one of them. Trash blew around even in suburbia.

He stood and put the bag in the pocket with the other one. That feeling of unease settled in his neck again. He pulled out his cellphone and pushed redial. "Keats, kill the lights—now." He closed his eyes to help them adjust. When he heard the lights click off, he opened his eyes and looked across the street. He caught the flicker of a cigarette as it went out.

Crouching down, he moved four feet to his left and vaulted over the wall to the ground below. He oriented himself to the position of the glow and headed across the street. When he reached the general area, no one was there. It was irritating but expected. He would police the area in the morning but if he didn't find anything it wouldn't matter. They—whoever they were—had tipped their hand because now he *knew* someone was watching.

*****

The man scowled as he hurried away. The boss wasn't going to like this. He wasn't too happy about it, either. He had taken particular pleasure in harassing those pretty little ladies. He would have to find out who this gent was and take care of him. This was his first solo job and he didn't plan on blowing it. He thought about the Brown women and laughed. Plus, he really liked the perks.

CHAPTER 10

Linda rolled over and looked at the clock. 6:45 AM. She was late. She stood and waited for the dizziness to come but it didn't. She gingerly stretched and then touched her toes. She straightened and the sudden movement made her light-headed but not enough to make her pass out. The bed was fairly neat and the clock said 6:47.

She blinked her eyes. She had slept all night. When had she fallen asleep? The last thing she remembered, she and Darrel were laughing at the antics of the Three Stooges.

More images filled her mind. Darrel steadying her while she had the dry heaves. Handing her his handkerchief. Putting her in the car. Carrying her into the house. Holding her after the nightmare. Fixing the slush and croissants then watching TV with her until she went to sleep. Had he carried her upstairs and put her on the bed? She groaned and sat on the bed. Had she really snuggled into him while he was carrying her?

She would never be able to look him in the face again. What was worse, he would never be able to see her as a colleague again, only as a sniveling female watering pot. That last thought made her want to crawl back under the covers and not come out for about six years. Maybe by then she would have the courage to face him.

Linda heard a soft knock and looked up. A sleepy-eyed Penny stood in the door. "Hey, Sis."

Penny rubbed her eyes. "Hey to you." She yawned. "Let me know when you are ready to leave. I promised Darrel I would drop you off at work today."

"You promised Darrel?"

"Yeah, it was the only way I could get him to take your car." She rolled her eyes. "He planned to call a cab and wait outside. I had to threaten to get dressed and drive him home." She turned to walk away.

"Wait!"

Penny turned back around and slumped. "Wha-a-a-t?"

Linda laughed and then looked at the clock. She didn't actually have to be at work until nine o'clock. She patted the bed. "Come sit and tell me what happened last night. Some of it is a little fuzzy."

"I can only start from when I came home."

"That will be good enough."

"Actually, I can start a little before that. Karen, Darrel's secretary, called me and said you were taken ill... She used those exact words, which seems odd because she sounded young and 'she was taken ill' sounds like something a matronly woman would say."

"Penny?"

"Sorry. ...and that Darrel was going to take you home. That it wasn't an emergency; you just didn't need to be alone. I told him Mrs. Kennedy would stay with you." Penny moved back on the bed and crossed her legs. "I guess she wasn't home because he was still here when I got here."

"What time did you get here?"

"Around nine. Since he didn't call, I thought Mrs. Kennedy was here so I went to work." Penny laughed. "Imagine my surprise when I walked through the door and saw this large man stuffed into grandmother's chair with his legs hanging off the coffee table, holding your hand."

"Holding my hand?"

Yeah, and it was so..." Penny got a dreamy look on her face and heaved a big sigh.

Linda covered her face with her hands. "It's worse than I thought."

Penny laughed. "You better believe it. Sometime during the course of the evening, you gave him a shiner."

"What!"

"Evidently, you fell asleep and had a nightmare. When he tried to wake you, you must have landed a solid hit because it is a beaut; all purple, black and blue."

Linda groaned. Six years with her head under the covers wouldn't be long enough. How in the world would she ever face him? "Okay, so what else did I do?"

"Nothing after I got home."

"So, what time did Mr. Foss leave?"

Penny looked puzzled. "Why so formal?"

Linda sighed. "Mr. Foss is a colleague of mine. As such, he deserves my respect."

"I don't know, Sis. It's a little late to be formal. The man stayed in *that* chair for fours hours so he could hold your hand while you slept."

"Four hours?"

"That's how long he said you had been asleep. Let's look at this objectively."

Linda rolled her eyes. That was usually what she said when one of her siblings was arguing with her.

Penny held up her fingers and counted as she talked. "You gave him a shiner, he fed you, you watched TV together and he carried you upstairs when I was ready to go to bed." She crossed her arms. "I would say it is a little late to be concerned about being formal, wouldn't you?"

Linda groaned and fell back across the bed.

"He told *me* his name was Darrel, so that's what I'll call him. Beside, I ate part of his sandwich—which was very good—and he saw me in my frog slippers. I am way past calling him Mr. Foss." She stood. "I'm going to get dressed. Let me know when you're ready."

When Penny left, Linda rolled over and buried her face in the pillow. Penny was right; it was too late to worry about being formal. There was only one thing she could do, avoid Darrel Foss like the plague. How hard could it be? She rarely left the lab and she could get in the building without going near his office. Maybe, at some future date, she would be able to see him without feeling mortified but she doubted it. She glanced at the clock. Right now, she needed a shower.

She went to the closet and grabbed the first suit that came to hand. When she walked in front of the full length mirror, she stopped dead still. She had a bad case of bed hair and still had on the suit she worked in yesterday. At least she didn't see any food stains. That was one thing to be thankful for. She sighed as she got ready to shower. It really shouldn't matter so much but it did.

Linda put down the towel she was drying her hair with. She really did feel better. Amazing what food and a good night's sleep could do. She stepped in front of the mirror and looked at herself; really looked at herself. Her suit hung on her like a sack.

She walked over to the closet, rummaged through the clothes hanging there and huffed in disgust. All her suits were basically alike; different colors with maybe a different cut around the collar. They were all the same size, so they would all hang on her like sacks. She needed some new clothes. She made a good salary so surely she could afford to get some new clothes. It wouldn't hurt to check.

She went downstairs and got her briefcase. When she walked into the kitchen, Penny was sitting at the counter. She set the briefcase on the counter, went to the refrigerator and opened the door but the pitcher wasn't there.

"What are you looking for?"

She turned around and saw it was sitting in the sink. She looked but didn't see the box for the croissants either. Disappointed, she walked back to the counter.

"Earth to Sis, what are you looking for?"

"I had the best fruit slush and honey butter croissants last night. I saw Darrel put the pitcher of fruit slush in the fridge and there were three croissants left. "

The smell of warm bread filled the air. When the microwave dinged, Penny took the plate out. "You mean these croissants?"

Linda's eyes narrowed and she grabbed the plate out of Penny's hand. "He bought those for me."

Penny acted shocked. "You're not going to share." She put on her sad puppy dog face. "I'm your little sister. You're supposed to share."

Linda laughed. "I suppose you can have one. But if you want anymore than that, you're going to have to get your own." Linda sat the croissants on the counter. "Did you see any extra butter? I distinctly remember extra butter."

"You mean that yellow-brownish stuff?"

Linda nodded.

"I threw that away. It sat out all night and I wasn't willing to take a chance on it."

"Oh man, that was the best butter." Linda got another plate, put one of the croissants on it and handed it to Penny. "What about the slush?"

"Well, by the time I got home it wasn't very slushy but it did taste good."

"Don't tell me you drank the rest of it. There was at least half a pitcher left."

"No, there was one glass left but I'm not going to let you anywhere near it until you promise to share that, too."

Linda started tapping the counter and looking around the room.

"You're not going to find it. Share or no deal."

Linda put out her hand. "As long as I get the bigger share."

Penny grabbed her hand and shook it. "I can live with that, especially since I've already had some this morning."

"Not fair."

"Love you dearly", Penny got the glass, "but when it comes to this stuff; you snooze, you loose."

Linda grabbed another glass and Penny poured some into it. They sat down and Linda reached across the counter and took Penny's hand. Penny looked up, surprised.

"I know," Linda said. She bowed her head. "Father, thank You for the food we are about to eat. You have been good to us. You have kept us sane and together. Thank You. I ask that You bless Darrel Foss for helping us and providing this wonderful food. Amen."

Penny jumped up, ran around the counter and threw her arms around Linda. "It's good to have you back."

Linda hugged Penny. "It's nice to be back." She laughed as Penny danced back around the counter and sat down. "So, do you have any big plans for your first free day?"

"Not really. I'll probably spend the day around the house, catch up on my reading or re-arrange the pantry. You know me."

"Think you can handle an afternoon shopping with your sister?"

Penny grinned. "Could I ever. Especially if you let me pick one complete outfit for you and promise to wear it at least twice before you consign it to the back of your closet."

"I don't know; that's a pretty big order."

"I promise I will pick something you can live with. When do you want to go?"

"Let me see." Linda opened her briefcase and looked at her schedule. All it said was work on polymer. "This is a light day. Why don't we meet for lunch and take the whole afternoon."

"Lunch and the whole afternoon?"

Linda nodded again.

Penny punched the air with her fist. "Alright! Where do you want to meet?"

CHAPTER 11

Darrel examined his eye. He'd already encountered several smirks, pithy comments and pointed questions as he walked through the department. He couldn't blame them. It *was* a beauty and it wasn't everyday your boss came in with a black-eye. He smiled. It gave him an air of mystery.

He rolled his shoulders and then rolled his neck. He flexed his fingers and stretched his arms. The couch in the lounge was not as big or as comfortable as his and he felt cramped all over. He could use a good workout.

He pulled off his shirt, wiped down with paper towels and put on deodorant. He ran water over his head and face and toweled dry. Then he got a fresh shirt out of his briefcase and put it on. He folded yesterday's shirt and put it in the briefcase. He had three suits made exactly alike. No one but the night guards would know he had been here all night. He tied his tie and shrugged into his coat.

Darrel walked into his office and grunted. A large latte and a breakfast burrito sat on his desk. He punched the button, "Thanks."

"You're welcome."

He picked up the latte, took a sip and sighed in pleasure. The burrito was still warm and when he opened it, the smell made his stomach rumble in protest. He was going to have to push for Karen a raise. She was fast becoming worth her weight in gold. He ate slowly, savoring every bite. He had another long day ahead and now he had two more things to add to the list. He punched the button.

"Yes?"

"Brief me on the day."

Karen walked in. When she looked at him, she started laughing.

Darrel crossed his arms and kept a stern look on his face. "Want to let me in on the joke?"

"That is some shiner. Care to elaborate on where you got it?"

"It was an accident and no, I did not run into a door or fall down and hit something. Now, brief me on the day."

Karen saluted. "Yes, Sir." She sat down and laid some folders on the desk. "There are three more applications. The color codes still apply."

Darrel nodded.

"You have a conference call with Darin Whitfield's CO at 10:30. Interviews with Steve Crowder at 1:00, Adam Davies at 2:00 and Benjamin Hart at 3:00. And a meeting with Mrs. Randal and Mr. Burk at 9:30."

He had forgotten about that meeting. Now, he could kill two birds with one stone. He shoved a sheet of paper across the desk. "Type this up and make a copy for each interview. Do you have anything scheduled at 11:00?"

"No."

"Put me down."

"Yes, Sir. Is that all?"

Darrel nodded. He drummed his fingers on the desk. He wanted to call the security desk and see if Linda had picked up her keys. He wanted to go to her department and make sure she was alright. He wanted to stand guard over her twenty-four/seven. All of those options were out but there were a few things he could do.

He walked into the monitor room. He tapped the monitor for the ground floor of the parking garage. "Email me a copy of yesterday's video feed from 5:30 to 7:00am."

"Yes, Sir."

They probably wouldn't get a face off of the video but it could confirm someone with a cigarette was in the parking garage at that time. Darrel went back to his office and straightened his desk for the CEO's visit.

The intercom beeped. "Mrs. Randal and Mr. Burk are here."

Darrel walked into Karen's office. He bowed slightly. "Mrs. Randal, Mr. Burk."

Peter Burk pointed at his eye. "Nothing we need to be concerned about, is there?"

"No, Sir."

Peter smiled and held out his hand. "How's the arm?"

Darrel shook his hand. "Good. How's your leg?"

"Better but I would appreciate it if we didn't have to see every new camera."

Darrel laughed. "That won't be necessary, Sir. We'll stay in the monitor room unless you want to see something specific."

"Good." Peter looked at his watch. "I hate to rush you but we have to be in court at 11:00."

"Then let's get started." Darrel opened the door to the monitor room. "If you will just step through here."

Peter Burk whistled. "Impressive. How did you manage it in such a short time?"

"Organization and Mrs. Randal's generous budget."

"Okay," Katie Randal said, "show us what that generous budget bought."

Darrel glanced at her. He *had* spent a lot of money but she had signed off on all expenses. She was smiling, so he relaxed.

He waved at the array of monitors. "We now have cameras in every corridor, elevator, and office in the building. Some of the other businesses weren't thrilled with the updates so..." he looked at them, "I sort of twisted their arms."

Peter nodded. "They will be happy enough if they ever have a problem with security."

Darrel sighed to himself. That had been the one thing he had worried about them approving.

"Plus, we have a camera on each corner of the building." He pointed to the parking garage gate camera. "We installed a gate, a spike strip and a card swipe panel on the entrance and exit. Plus, the shack will be manned during peak arrival and departure times. We have also installed automatic locks on all exterior doors."

"Step over here." He stopped in front of a console. "Each area has the ability to control the new features installed in that area but that can be overridden and controlled from this central panel."

"Eli, show them the gate and the spike strip." They watched in silence as the spike strips shot up and the gate quickly closed. "I had them set on a short timer. If these had been here, Samantha couldn't have left the parking garage."

Darrel saw Mrs. Randal shudder. "I'm sorry, Ma'am. I didn't mean to bring up painful memories."

"That's okay, Mr. Foss." She took Peter's hand. "We're working through it."

Seeing Mrs. Randal and Mr. Burk together, it was obvious how right they were for each other. The sudden image of Linda snuggling in his arms sent a shaft of jealousy shooting through him. He mentally shook himself. Because of his past, he would never have that kind of relationship with anyone. Especially someone like Linda. He smiled at Mrs. Randal. "I'm glad."

"This room can be barricaded and there is a backup generator to keep it running if the power is cut to it. We can also zoom in close enough to count a person's eyelashes." He walked over to the bank of cameras and pointed at one. "Watch this. Eli, slowly zoom in on camera three."

They watched as Karen's face grew closer and closer until they were looking at the lashes on one of her eyes. He punched a button. "Smile, Ms. Eckels, you are on camera."

She batted her lashes and Darrel chuckled. "Can you tell we used this camera to work out the bugs in that particular system?"

Both his guests smiled.

"Is there anything else you would like to see or any questions?"

"Aren't the cameras in the offices a bit intrusive? What if someone becomes obsessed with another person in the building? Couldn't these be used to stalk them?"

"That is a possibility, Mrs. Randal. We have policies in place for that issue. The senior VPs and the Head of Departments can turn off the cameras when they're in a meeting that requires privacy. Of course if we have reason to believe there is some sort of threat, that can be overridden also."

"I would like a copy of those policies."

"Yes, Ma'am. Hard or electronic?"

"Electronic is fine."

"We'll get that right to you."

"I see that you have tried to prepare for any emergency," Peter said

"Yes, Sir. It is my firm hope that we never have to use any of it."

"Amen," Peter said.

"I, for one, think the money has been well spent." Katie stuck her hand out. "Thank you, Mr. Foss, for the overview."

"You're welcome, Ma'am. This door is open anytime you have questions or need assistance."

Katie and Peter turned to walk off and Darrel touched Peter's arm.

"Sir, if I might have a moment of your time?"

Peter looked at Katie.

She looked at her watch. "Go ahead. Conan has something he wants to review with me. Buzz me when you're ready to go."

Peter waited until Katie had walked off. "What can I help you with?"

"Let's go to my office." Inside, he motioned Peter to the chair. "First, we are hiring twelve new people. I would appreciate anyone you could send our direction."

"Jason might be able to help." Peter took a card out of his pocket, flipped it over and wrote 'Jason' and then a phone number. "This is his number. Call him and let him know what you're looking for."

Darrel took the card. "Thank you. I will do that." He sighed and sat down. "This may sound a little odd but please hear me out."

"Sure."

"Yesterday morning, I was checking the monitors when I saw Ms. Brown—Head of the Research Department—arriving. Upon exiting her vehicle, she seemed highly agitated and hit her panic button. She almost sprinted to the elevator. I went to the elevators to meet her and she burst out of the stairwell door straight into me. She was shaking from head to toe and seemed a little dazed. I asked her if anything was wrong. She said no and went on to work."

Darrel rubbed his neck. "I wouldn't have thought much about it except that I had a..." Darrel looked a little uncomfortable. "I got here about ten minutes before Ms. Brown and had the feeling someone was in the parking garage watching me."

"People with our training—who do the kind of work we do—depend on that feeling. What else?"

"The short of it is, Ms. Brown felt ill and I drove her home. I decided to sweep the perimeter of her house..." Darrel opened his briefcase and took out a sandwich bag "...and found this."

Peter picked up the bag labeled 'kitchen window' and examined it. "And?"

"After talking with Ms. Brown's sister, I decided to sweep the first floor of the parking garage where Ms. Brown parks." He pulled out another bag. "And found this."

Peter picked up the second bag labeled 'parking garage'. "What did the sister say?"

"That things were being moved in the house: things only they would notice and some only by a fraction of an inch. I asked Penny, that's Ms. Brown's sister, if she had talked to the police but she believes they would think it was probably hysterics brought on by their father's death." Darrel sighed. "I had to agree with her. But...then I saw the flicker of a cigarette across the street last night while I was in the parking garage. I investigated but they ran. I went back and looked this morning." Darrel pulled toilet paper out of his briefcase and set it on the desk.

Peter carefully unrolled it. With a pen, he examined it. Same brand. "That's a little more than coincidence."

"That's what I think."

"You're right, though. The police might note this but wouldn't take it seriously without more proof. A stalker, maybe?"

"Maybe. No. It's that stupid feeling. Penny didn't say anything about weird phone calls or emails. My question is, where do I go from here? I can't, in good conscious, walk away from it. Especially since it's probably work related."

"What makes you believe it's work related?"

"Ms. Brown guards her briefcase with her life. She believes someone is trying to get her research."

"What is she working on?"

"All I can tell you is that it is a new polymer. I don't know its applications or who would be interested in it."

"Anything to do with big business has big money potential. The polymer could mean millions in revenue and there are people who will do anything to get their hands on that kind of money." Peter leaned back in his chair. "I only have a vague knowledge of polymers but with everything that has happened lately, let's err on the side of caution."

Peter pointed to the cigarette butts. "I have a friend that can analyze these for DNA. If they match, it would lend weight to our case. I'll also ask Katie the specifics of the polymer. That might give us a clue who might be behind this." Peter picked up the cigarette butts and put them in his pocket. "You'll know as soon as I know. Let me see the card I gave you."

Peter took the card and circled a number on it. "This is my beeper number and I can usually be reached anywhere at anytime. If anything comes up on your end, call this number. Give me your number." Peter pulled out his cellphone and put Darrel's number in his phone. "If an emergency arises, type in 'darrel911' and I'll get back to you as quickly as I can. If you have more information you want to pass on, type 'darrel211'. That will let me know to check my email for information."

Peter headed for the door and stopped. "Oh...if you need help protecting the ladies, call Jason."

"I'll do that and thank you, Sir."

CHAPTER 12

Linda started at the beginning and ran the numbers again. It had been four months since she had reconciled her checking account. She had received a substantial pay raise when she became Head of Research but she had taken over all the household bills at the same time. She had been adding the bills up and if they didn't exceed her monthly income, she hadn't worried about it. She compared the total to the piece of paper in her hand. They were the same.

She started laughing. Her checking account was healthy: very healthy. An afternoon shopping with Penny was not going to endanger their finances. She had been hoarding every penny she could since her father had died. When she started working at Cy-Rac, she began paying half the household bills. After her father's death, she had feared that without both of their incomes there wouldn't be enough money.

Her parents had dealt wisely with their money and taught them to do the same. They had opened a savings account for each child when they were born. Over the years, they added money to each account. Hers had almost completely paid for college. Penny's had completely paid for college. Teddy had enough, that if he lived simply, he would not have to work while he was in college.

The estate had paid off all outstanding bills, including the house and left a little money for each of them. They hadn't formally discussed it, but she was planning on buying the house from Penny and Teddy. Her part of the money was set aside as a down payment.

She looked at the numbers again. Maybe they could get a facial and have their hair and nails done. Penny would be ecstatic. For some reason, she was getting excited about it herself. She had never cared much about her appearance. Being neat and clean had been enough. Suddenly, it wasn't anymore.

The image of shimmering liquid brown eyes filled her mind followed swiftly by images of her with her hair sticking out and her rumpled clothes. No, neat and clean wasn't enough anymore. She was willing to admit *that* but not ready to admit *why*. It was sufficient enough that she was ready to change her image.

Linda dialed Penny's number. "Hey!"

"Hey, yourself. You're not calling to cancel, are you?"

"No. I was wondering, since we are going to get some new clothes, if you wanted to really go all out and get a facial, maybe hair and nails?"

Penny squealed and Linda held the phone away from her ear. "Calm down."

"You have no idea how long I have wanted to get you in Tabatha's chair. She will love your hair."

"Do you think you can get us in on such short notice?"

"I'll see what I can do."

"Did you manage reservations for lunch?"

"Of course." Penny changed to a deep southern drawl. "Manny is a particular friend of mine and he was more than happy to accommodate us."

Linda laughed. "I'll see you at noon, then."

She put down the phone and looked at her desk. Having decided to take the rest of the week off from working on the polymer, she felt a little lost. Maybe she should start with her emails. It had been a while since she checked them. She brought up her email and blinked. They went on and on. She arranged them by sender and started with the As.

After reading three, she went back to the first one that had been sent directly to her. This particular one had been three months ago. She went through the emails from each person in her department and they were all the same. Each one had sent their first queries to her and copied Wade. When she had ignored them, Wade had replied accordingly. For the last two months, the whole department had been sending their queries to Wade first and copying her.

Linda sat back. She really had no idea what was going on in her own department. Wade was essentially doing her job. That had to change and today was a good a day to start. She was responsible for work currently being done in the department. If there was fallout on any project, it would stop at her desk and rightly so.

She bowed her head. "Father, forgive me. I've left You out of my life lately and have been trying to do this myself. I haven't done a good job. I have no idea what is going on in my life, with the polymer or with my department. And, I'm feeling overwhelmed by it. Your Word says to 'cast all our care on You for You care for us 1'. Today, right this moment, I give the worry of all of this to You. You are much bigger, much smarter, and definitely more competent than I am. Please tap me on the shoulder and let me know if I try to wrestle this away from You and do it on my own again. I love You. You're a great Father."

Linda dialed Wade's extension.

"Wade."

"Are you busy?"

"I'm looking over Toby's numbers. He's at a standstill and wanted me to check his findings. If his numbers are correct, it will be back to square one. Do you need something?"

"Could you work me in this morning?"

"Sure. What about now? This can wait. Give me a few minutes and I'll be there."

"No. Let me come to your office. I want to ask about the current projects and we'll have instant access to the information at your desk."

"Okay."

She hung up the phone. Grabbing a pad and pen, she headed for the door. It was time she found out whether she was capable of being the Head of Research for Cy-Rac Industries or if she needed to step down so someone more qualified could take the position. The first test would be to see if she could put aside her feelings about Wade and work with him.

Wade stood as she approached. He motioned to his desk chair. "Why don't you sit here, Ms. Brown?"

"No, you sit there." Linda pulled up a chair and sat down. "First, let me apologize for dumping the responsibility for running the entire department in your lap."

Wade started to speak but Linda held up her hand. "Wait. Let me finish. I have been focused on the polymer and acting like an employee instead of the supervisor. I really appreciate you stepping up and taking the initiative where the department is concerned. It made *me* look good. So...thank you, very much."

"You're welcome."

Linda smiled. If it wasn't absurd, she would say the polished Wade Waters was squirming. "I would like for you to bring me up to speed on who is working on what and how they are doing."

Wade looked surprised.

Linda didn't blame him. She had always studiously avoided him. "I know we can't do it all in one day but I thought we could start with Toby's project since you're working on that."

He smiled. "I'd like that. You have a good group of people working here. I have enjoyed helping them."

Linda looked at Wade. What an odd choice of words. He made it sound like he wasn't part of the team.

"If I might make a suggestion?"

"Sure."

"Call a meeting and tell your people what you just told me. Every one of them worked with your father and have been dealing with his loss. It would do them a world of good to hear you say you appreciate their efforts to keep the department going during this hard time."

Linda closed her eyes as a wave of guilt washed over her. More evidence that she wasn't capable of running the department. She had been so focused on her own grief, her own driving need to see her father validated that she had ignored everything and everyone around her.

"You're right. You know everyone's schedule. Is it possible to have that meeting now?" Linda thought about Penny. She was so excited about their shopping expedition. Linda didn't want to disappoint her again. "I have a meeting at noon and will not be back until tomorrow morning."

"No one is doing any testing today. I can call an impromptu meeting. Five minutes? Ten?"

"Make it fifteen. That should give everyone enough time to close what they are doing and get here, shouldn't it?"

Wade nodded and then shook his head. "Everyone but Casey. He might not check his email until this afternoon. And he has effectively learned to ignore all the bells and whistles set to let him know he has new email. I'll send this out and go get him."

"You send the message. I'll go." Linda started to stand. "Just have them come here. You don't mind if I use your desk to hide behind, do you?"

Wade smiled. "Not at all. I have been waiting for this day for six months. You can stand anywhere you want to."

"I'll get Casey."

Wade nodded and started typing.

Linda walked half way across the room and looked back. Wade seemed excessively happy about the meeting and...his choice of words had been so odd. She shook her head and walked on.

She stopped behind Casey. He had headphones on and was bobbing his head in time to the music. No wonder he didn't hear the bells and whistles for his email. She tapped him on the shoulder.

He squawked and jumped at least a foot off the ground. Then he spun around and yelled. "What do you think you're doing? Trying to scare me to death?"

Linda shook her head.

He jerked the headphones off and started stammering. "I'm sor-ry. I d-d-didn't k-k-know it was you, Ms... Ms...Brown."

"Casey?"

"I d-d-didn't mean to ye-ye-yell at you."

"Casey."

"Please d-d-don't..."

"Casey!"

Casey looked startled and then turned red. "Ma'am?"

"We are having a quick meeting at Mr. Waters' desk in...," Linda looked at her watch , "...ten minutes. Are you at a stopping point?"

Casey nodded.

"Alright, I'll see you there."

"Yes, Ma-Ma'am."

Linda turned her back to him and started grinning. Casey had to be somewhere in his mid-twenties and he reminded her of Teddy. Evidently he was good at his job because she had never heard one complaint against him.

By the time she got back to her office, most of the department was gathered at Wade's desk and they were all trying to talk at once. Wade raised his hands and said something. It must have satisfied them because they began quietly talking among themselves.

She looked at her watch: five minutes left. She stepped inside her office and watched them. She *really* didn't want to walk out there and talk to them. Which was silly. These were her people. She knew them and they knew her.

Linda leaned her head against the door. Who was she trying to kid? That was the problem. She had been friends with them, occasionally gone out with them for supper or to see a movie. They knew all her quirks and foibles. To step past that and be their boss seemed impossible. How was she supposed to act towards them? How did she find the balance between boss and friend? Her father had done it for years and made it seem effortless.

Suddenly, the image of two wrestlers locked in combat flashed into her mind. She chuckled. "Okay, Father." Taking a deep breath, she walked out her door.

CHAPTER 13

Darrel looked up as Karen walked in.

She hesitated. "We're still on for 11:00, aren't we?"

Darrel blinked then looked at the clock. "Yes. Come in and take a seat." He leaned back in his chair and waited until she sat down. "I really appreciate the way you have taken the initiative in sorting through the applicants. It has saved me a lot of time."

"Happy I could help."

"Would you conduct the initial interviews?"

"Me? Shouldn't someone higher up the food chain do that?"

Darrel chuckled. "You have proven that you are a good judge of character. The way you sorted the applicants only reinforces that. I'm sorry to suddenly spring this on you but I ..."

Darrel stopped. What could he say? I have this weird feeling on the back of my neck and I need to check it out. I found some cigarette butts connected to...he didn't know what. The woman I lov...whoa! Where had that come from?

"That's okay. I know how busy you've been. If you're confident I can handle the interviews, I'll do them."

"You can handle it. Do you have those copies I asked for?"

"Yes."

"Good." He opened a file and then turned the monitor where Karen could see it. "That paper has the questions I want you to ask. Most of them are straight forward. Put down their answer and your perception of the answer."

"Will do, Boss. Is there anything else?"

Darrel paused. "I didn't ask but do you have time to do these interviews?"

Karen smiled. "I'll make time. If you're pleased with the job I do, it will be a feather in my cap." She cocked her head. "I don't plan on being your secretary forever, you know."

Darrel frowned. "I might have to rethink this then unless you promise to stay until I move on."

Karen shook her head. "Can't do that. This job fits you like a glove and you will probably retire right here. I'm not willing to wait until my fifties to start moving up the corporate ladder."

Darrel stared at her. Fit him like a glove? He did like his people; liked this place but stay here till he retired? No-o-o. He wasn't the staying kind. Couldn't be the staying kind.

"Will there be anything else?"

Darrel continued to stare at her.

"Sir? Is there anything else? I need to take lunch now to be ready for the 1:00 appointment."

"Oh," Darrel shook his head. "Sorry. Darin is a definite go. See if you can work him in this afternoon. From what his CO said, he will probably make the time to get here if you call him right away."

Karen nodded.

"Also, make sure each applicant knows they are being video taped by security cameras. We don't want anyone having privacy issues because of an interview." Darrel thought about the 'SP' affair. "On that note, if there is anything odd—like a tick or an obsessively nervous habit; even an odd feeling on your part—note that. I might want to review the taped interview before going any further in the application process." Darrel smiled. "And that really will be all."

"Okay."

Darrel drummed his fingers on the desk. He wanted—no, needed to be up and moving. There was a threat and he hadn't identified it yet. DNA testing could take several days or even weeks according to the priority placed on the cigarette butts. But there were things that needed immediate attention. Like what to do about Linda and Penny? And how to do it without making them more afraid than they already were? He *wanted* to move in with them until this whole mess was over. It would make things much easier.

He sighed. That was unrealistic, though. For one thing, the ladies didn't know him and would freak if he showed up and announced he was moving in for the duration. Plus, their suburban reputations would be in tatters after the first night he was there.

Darrel glanced at the clock. He would do a walk through. If he focused on something besides the lovely Ms. Brown, his subconscious might come up with an answer. He went to the monitor room. "You guys doing okay?"

Both men looked up and nodded.

"Any questions or concerns?"

Both shook their heads.

Darrel grunted and went out the door. If the rest of the round went that quickly, he would be back in his office in twenty minutes. He went to the front desk. "All quiet here?"

Bailey saluted him. "Yes, Sir."

Darrel smiled. "Good." He took the elevator down to the parking garage. He stepped out the door and stood jingling the change in his pocket. He should be in his office tending to paperwork. That wasn't going to happen because he couldn't seem to sit still. He shook his head. In the past, this kind of behavior would have gotten him killed.

He should have done the interviews himself. Now the afternoon stretched before him and he was at loose ends. He flexed his hand and rubbed his bicep. He could use a workout. If he left now, he could hit the gym and then grab lunch. It would get the kinks out and help him focus on the problem at hand. He dialed Karen's number. It went straight to voicemail.

"Karen, I will be out of the office this afternoon. Beep me if you need me." Darrel paused. "If I'm not back by five, lock up. Thanks."

Darrel looked at the phone in his hand. Now why had he said that? He was just going to the gym and grabbing a bite to eat. He unlocked the door and started to get in when that feeling moved across the back of his neck. Instead of sitting down, he reached across the seat and got his book. He locked the door and walked toward the elevators. He didn't see anything but the feeling was still there so he took the elevator up. He would just make sure Linda was in the building and planned on staying a while.

He went back to the security desk. "Bailey, has Ms. Brown picked up her keys?"

"Yes, Sir. Just did. That little sister of hers was here. Said they were going out for lunch."

Darrel turned back toward the garage and stopped. He had just come from there and hadn't seen them. "Were they headed to the parking garage?"

"No, Sir. Went out the front. I think they were taking the younger Ms. Brown's car."

"Thanks." Darrel took the stairs two at a time. He jumped in his car, pulled out of the garage and turned toward the front of the building. When he reached the stop sign irritation crawled through him. Lunch time traffic was bumper to bumper. Hopefully the Browns would have to wait for a break in the traffic also.

He turned on his blinker so the other drivers knew he wanted to go with the flow. Maybe one of them would be kind enough to let him in. He drummed his fingers on the steering wheel. Should he put the car back in the garage and try to catch them on foot?

Suddenly a horn honked. When Darrel looked up, a man was waving him in. He waved back and slowly pulled into traffic. It would take a miracle to find them in this mess; still, he kept looking. Penny drove a late model, bright red Ford. He should have memorized the license number last night.

Darrel huffed. Why in the world had that woman left the building in the first place? He caught himself up short. She didn't have all the facts. Neither did Penny. But he knew and he couldn't ignore them. That feeling crawled across his neck again. Had someone been watching for her? Waiting for her to leave?

The ladies could be walking. He searched the cars and the sidewalk as he inched forward. Or they could have taken a cab. Maybe meeting boyfriends. Darrel felt his heart squeeze. He didn't know that much about Linda or Penny. But he did know that two such lovely ladies wouldn't stay unattached for long.

He kept scanning the cars ahead. Suddenly a semi moved over and he saw a red Ford, with its right blinker on, four cars ahead of him. He eased into the opening left by the semi and prepared to turn. A silver compact two cars ahead turned on its blinker. All three cars turned and the silver compact stayed two car lengths behind the Ford. Darrel looked for a way to pass but there was no opening. He put a car's length between himself and the compact. He would have to hope the Ford was Penny's.

They drove three blocks and the Ford turned into Manny's restaurant. The silver compact pulled into the parking lot and so did he. He parked two cars away from the compact and waited. Linda and Penny got out and went into the restaurant. Darrel breathed a sigh of relief. He was trying to think of a good excuse for being here when he realized the man driving the compact had never gotten out.

He looked that direction and watched as the man opened a paper and laid it across the steering wheel. Then the man picked up a sandwich and took a bite. Darrel's eyes narrowed. The sedan had kept two cars behind the ladies from the time he had found them. Then the guy pulled into the parking lot of one the best restaurants in town and ate a sandwich? Ten-to-one he had found the watcher.

He leaned back. Might as well get comfortable. This could take awhile. As he rolled down the windows, his stomach rumbled. He looked toward the restaurant and laughed. Knowing the Brown women was definitely interfering with meals.

CHAPTER 14

Wade wanted to reach through the phone and choke the man on the other end. He would have settled for raking his fingers through his hair but with all the mousse and spray he used to achieve this look, it was impossible. Instead, he tapped the pencil on the desk. "It's not working."

"You don't know that."

"Yes, I do. There has been no activity since Dr. Brown died." Wade threw the pencil he had been tapping onto the desk. "There wasn't much activity for the year before that. I'm telling you the best thing to do would be to let her succeed. If it was known that the polymer worked..."

"Not yet."

"She's working herself to death: not eating, not sleeping."

"That's not your concern."

"Look, she would not take the result upstairs until we had run the test several times as proof positive it worked. Especially since there have been *so—many—FAILURES*." He couldn't help his rising voice. He wanted to slam the phone on the desk to emphasize his point but he knew the man on the other end would not take kindly to that.

Silence met his tirade. He took several deep breaths to calm himself. "With the polymer finished, we could step up the timetable."

"You do the job you are being paid to do and let me worry about the rest."

A click sounded in Wade's ear. He looked at the receiver in his hand and very gently hung it up. Sighing, he put his head in his hands. He had done the one thing someone in his position could not afford to do; he had let himself get to know and like the Browns.

First, the father and now, the daughter. He picked up the formula for the polymer and ripped it in half, then half again. He looked at the pieces in his hand and chuckled. Now he would have to print it out again. Someone coughed. He turned around and saw Casey standing there.

"Anything wrong, Sir?"

"No." Wade threw the paper in the trash, "Just another almost but not quite. Do you need something?"

"I f-f-finished those c-c-calibrations you asked f-f-for. I...I was wondering if," Casey hooked his thumbs in his back pockets and rocked back on his feet, "if I c-could help you test t-t-today."

Wade smiled. Casey seemed like a good kid and he never complained about doing the menial work. "Sorry, no testing today."

"Not even the p-polymer?"

"Ms. Brown has halted all work on the polymer."

"But, I th-thought the p-p-polymer was the h-highest p-p-priority project we were wa-working on."

"It is. But she decided a break from it would be beneficial. Tell you what, I'll talk to Ms. Brown and see if she will let you assist her with the testing."

"You'd—you'd do that?"

"Sure. At this point a new pair of eyes might see something we're missing."

"Th-thanks."

Wade waited until Casey had walked off and then he opened Linda's file and printed out another copy of the polymer formula.

*****

The man took the umbrella out of his drink and twirled it in his fingers. This was the first time, in several weeks he could relax. He planned to take full advantage of it. He leaned back in the deck chair and looked out across the pristine waters. He closed his eyes and took a deep breath of the salt air. He was trying to decide what he wanted for lunch when the phone on the table chirped. "Yes?"

"All work on the polymer has been halted."

The only outward sign of the man's irritation was the broken umbrella he dropped on the table. "This is only a minor setback. Since that is the nature of the business, there is no reason to worry."

"I don't like it."

The man shifted the phone to his other ear. "What's not to like? You have a secure job that pays decent and I pay you very well. What do you care how long it takes? You are raking in money either way."

"The longer I stay here, the more likely I am to be caught."

"Oh stop whining and don't call me again until you have something useful to report."

He stood as the model strolled up the deck. She held out her hand. He took it and placed a lingering kiss on her lips. She smiled a lazy smile and stretched out in the deck chair he had just vacated.

"After last night, I wasn't expecting to see anyone before the photo shoot."

"You probably won't see anyone else."

He squatted down beside the chair. "Well then, what say you and I go ashore and see what kind of trouble we can get into."

She merely smiled.

He stood and held out his hand. "I'll have you back in plenty of time for the photo shoot. No one will even know you were gone."

She took his hand. "Let's."

CHAPTER 15

Darrel glanced at his watch. He had been sitting for an hour. The man in the car looked like he was working the crossword puzzle. Evidently he wasn't planning on leaving anytime soon.

He drummed his fingers on the steering wheel. When he realized what he was doing, he stopped. Maybe he needed to take some time off, get away and take himself through training again. Impatience was costly in a game of cat and mouse.

His stomach rumbled. He looked towards the restaurant and back at the man. Why should he sit in the parking lot of a restaurant and be hungry? He pulled his out phone and Peter Burk's card fell out. He set it on the seat. He accessed the internet, pulled the number for Manny's and dialed it.

"Manny's."

"I would like to order a Manny sandwich to go please."

"Is there anything special you would like on that, Sir?"

"No, but I would like a glass of tea."

"We can have that ready in fifteen minutes. Your name, please."

"Darrel Foss."

"Contact number?"

Darrel gave her his cellphone number and hung up. He picked up the card and looked at the number written on the back. Might as well do something useful while he waited. If Jason could steer some qualified people his way, it would speed the hiring process. He punched in the numbers.

"Burk Security, Jason Perdue speaking."

Darrel closed his eyes. Of all the Jason's on the planet, this one had to be Perdue. The one human being on the face of the earth that knew his darkest side; knew what he was capable of. He gently closed the phone. It was time to seriously think about taking the duffle bag option.

Laughter drifted towards him. Linda and Penny were exiting the restaurant. He looked at the man in the silver compact. The man laid the paper down and watched the women as they walked toward the Ford. Darrel grunted.

He turned his phone's camera function on. Stepping out of the car, he held the phone up like he was dialing. He zoomed in on the license plate of the silver compact and snapped a couple of pictures. He slid the phone into his pocket and started toward the restaurant. As he passed the silver compact, he turned and nodded at the man sitting there, then walked on. The windows were tinted so he didn't get a good look at the man.

"Darrel!"

Darrel turned and saw Penny waving at him. He changed directions and stopped in front of them. He looked at Linda but she refused to look at him. He asked Penny. "What are you doing here?"

"We just finished eating. I wish we had known you were coming, you could have eaten with us."

Darrel caught a jerky movement out of the corner of his eye and smiled. Linda was shaking her head.

"That would have been nice. It's not every day I have the chance to be seen with two lovely ladies." He reached up and brushed the cheek under his blackeye. "Although, I don't know if you would want to be seen with me."

Linda's eyes got big and she quickly looked at the ground.

Penny laughed. "It gives you a roguish air. I think it suits you."

"What do you think, Ms. Brown? Does it make me look roguish?" He didn't know why he was pushing Linda. Well, to be honest that wasn't exactly true. He wanted her to look at him. There was something about those eyes. She looked up with narrowed eyes and he smiled.

"I am sure, Mr. Foss, that you do not need me to tell you how handsome you are with or without a black-eye. And, I'm also sure that you *don't* have to appear roguish for the ladies to fall at your feet."

"Lin!"

*****

Penny had a funny look on her face. Darrel was grinning from ear to ear. Linda closed her eyes as what she'd said replayed in her mind.

She had just told Darrel Foss he was handsome enough to have women falling at his feet. And had there been the tiniest sound of jealousy to it?

She squared her shoulders and stuck out her chin. In a voice that would have frozen a lake she said, "Penny, we need to go or we will be late for our appointment." She nodded at Darrel. "Please don't let us keep you from your lunch, Mr. Foss." She grabbed Penny's hand and started dragging her towards the car.

*****

Penny looked over her shoulder and shrugged at Darrel. He was still grinning from ear to ear and motioned that he would call her. She nodded. When they reached the car, she jerked away from Linda. "What's with you?"

"Get in the car."

"Not until you tell me what's going on. I have never known you to be so rude before."

Linda glanced at Darrel. "Please, just get in the car."

Penny slid into the car. She waited until Linda had shut her door. "Okay, what gives?"

"Start the car and get us out of this parking lot."

"But..."

Linda looked at her. "Don't argue, just do it."

"Okay! Okay." Penny started the car, backed out and headed for the exit.

Linda leaned her head against the car seat and groaned. "Did I just tell Darrel Foss, to his face, that I thought he was handsome?"

"In a round about way."

"And did I just say that he had ladies falling at his feet?"

Penny laughed. "In a round about way."

Linda sighed. "What is it about that man?"

"What do you mean?"

"Every time I'm anywhere near him, I seem to make a complete fool of myself."

Penny patted her on the shoulder. "Really, Sis..." she chuckled. "It's not that..." she started laughing, "ba-a-ad."

Linda rolled her eyes. "You're not very convincing."

"Sorry. But you're acting like you have a crush on Darrel Foss and I think it's cute."

"Cute! You think making a complete fool of myself in front of a colleague is cute!"

"No-o-o. It's just that I have never seen you act this way before. Not even in high school. You kept your nose buried too deep in a beaker to notice any of the boys."

"This isn't high school and I'm not sixteen. I have to work with the man and it's not like I can completely avoid him." Linda crossed her arms. "Although, I'm going to do my best to; starting right now."

Penny pulled into the salon's parking lot and cut the engine. "Linda, it really wasn't that bad."

Linda cut her eyes at Penny.

Penny held up her hand. "No, really. It surprised me because I have never known you to behave the way you do around Darrel. I doubt he noticed."

"Not notice? That man notices everything."

"He seems like a really nice guy to me and I don't think he would intentionally embarrass you at work." Penny grinned, "Although, he *does* look roguish with that blackeye."

Linda groaned.

"Oh, quit feeling sorry for yourself." Penny started fluffing her hair and spoke with a southern drawl. "We have a whole afternoon of pampering ahead of us."

*****

The silver compact pulled out behind Penny's car. So far, the watcher had been content to harass the Brown's in small ways. But if something happened to jeopardize the watcher's mission...

Darrel rubbed the back of his neck. He'd feel much better if he was with the ladies but Linda had looked happy until she saw him. He sighed. It would be better if he kept his distance.

He sent the picture of the license plate to Karen then dialed her number. "I will be out of the office for the rest of the day. I just sent you two pictures of a license plate. Email those to Peter Burk at Burk Security."

He reached in his pocket and came up empty; Peter's card was still on the seat of his car. He went to the car and got the card. He dialed the circled number and then put in 'darrel211'. Next, he called the cellphone number on the front of the card. It went straight through to voice mail.

"There is a watcher. I'm e-mailing two pictures of a license plate. If you can trace the owner of the car, I would appreciate it.

Only have general description of the driver; mid thirties, medium build, brown hair. Am tailing him. Will get a better description. Call cellphone with questions."

He went in Manny's and gave his name. The girl handed him a sack and a glass of tea and then took his money. He walked to one of the tables and sat down. He pulled out his pen and pad then dialed Penny's number.

"Hello?"

"What is your itinerary?"

"No, definitely not that. Keep looking."

"What?"

"Sorry, I wasn't talking to you. Let me call you back in about ten minutes."

"Ten minutes."

The phone went dead. Darrel smiled. From the sounds of things, the Brown women were shopping. He would be surprised if Penny remembered to call.

CHAPTER 16

Darrel leaned back in the chair and took a long drink of tea. He glanced at his watch. It had been twenty minutes. As he picked up his phone, it rang. "It's been twenty minutes."

"Sorry. Finding just the right hair style took longer than I thought. What did you want?"

"Just was wondering what you ladies are up to."

"Why? Did you want to tag along? Think before you speak. I am very good at detecting lies."

Darrel paused. Penny *was* sharp and he didn't want to scare her. He just wanted to know where they were. "I'm free for the rest of the afternoon and thought I might join you if you were doing something interesting."

Penny laughed. "I don't know many men who would enjoy an afternoon at the spa."

"Neither do I."

"That's what I thought. NO!"

Darrel tensed. "What is it?"

"You let her finish. We did not go through all of this for you to back out now."

"What?"

"Oh, sorry. Linda is getting a new hair style and halfway through, she wants to change her mind."

Darrel heard the distinct sound of scissors. "She's cutting it?"

"Yep."

Darrel pictured all that lovely hair falling to the floor. "Why?"

Penny sighed. "Men. She wanted a new 'do' that's why. And, she decided to go short and donate it."

"Well, I guess it's okay. It *is* for a good cause."

Penny snorted. "Like you would have any say."

Darrel laughed. "It didn't hurt to voice my opinion. Listen, I *would* like to spend more time with both of you."

"Really?" Penny's voice sounded suspicious.

"Really. I enjoyed last night and would like to know both of you better. I wouldn't want to intrude, though. And, I'm sure you don't want a roguish looking man hanging around you all afternoon. It might cramp your style."

Penny laughed. "What style? Besides, I'm not blind. It's not really me you want to spend time with."

"Don't read more into this than there is."

"Don't worry, I'm not."

"Penny."

Penny laughed. "I'll see what I can do to help the cause. We'll be here for at least another hour..."

"And where is 'here'?"

"Beauty Bootcamp. We're going to Chaz Boutique when we leave here. If we don't find what we're looking for there, we'll decide then. Let me see. Do you like..." Penny paused "...on second thought, that was a really good sandwich you had last night. Want to buy a girl supper and bring it over about sixish?"

"I don't know. Linda seemed to be enjoying herself until she saw me."

"That's just embarrassment because of the shiner. Besides, you'll be *my* guest. She will have nothing to say about it."

"I'll be there, then. Anything special either of you want on your sandwich? Mama Dona's has a wide selection."

"We're both pretty basic. A club sandwich will do fine."

"Got it."

"Oh...and some croissants if it's not too much trouble."

"Be there at six." Darrel closed the phone and looked at his watch. Karen's first interview should be over. He called her.

"Hey, Boss. What's up?"

"I need the address of 'Beauty Bootcamp'. It's a salon..."

"I know what it is, Boss. I go there. 1111 North Fourth."

"Did you get those pictures to Peter Burk?"

"Yes, Sir."

"Let me know if you get a reply"

"Sure thing and Boss, if you're thinking about a new look, biker dude would suit you."

Darrel chuckled and hung up. He picked up his tea and went to the car. 1111 North Fourth wasn't far and since lunchtime traffic had thinned, it wouldn't take him long to get there.

Darrel eased down the street in front of Beauty Bootcamp. The silver car sat in the parking lot, empty. He pulled in and parked four spots away. He scanned the area and finally spotted the man standing in the shadows at the corner of the building. His fingers itched to walk over there and use some friendly persuasion to find out why he was following the Brown women.

But, he would wait and see. This watcher was small potatoes. Professionals didn't harass the target; they just got the job done. If he took this guy out now, someone else would just take his place. The next one might be a professional. Until he found out who was behind this, it was better to go with this guy

*****

"Come on, Sis. It really does look good."

Linda didn't want to open her eyes. She had set through the shampoo, haircut, and style without once looking in a mirror. Now she was afraid of what she would see. Her hair hadn't been above her shoulders since she was eight.

"Oh, forevermore." Penny poked Linda in the side.

Linda jumped and opened her eyes. What she saw in the mirror surprised her. She sat forward. Soft curls brushed her cheek and tickled her chin. She couldn't believe it.

Penny bent down beside her and looked in the mirror. "See, I told you."

She looked at Penny then back at herself. They really looked liked sisters now. Although Penny would always be drop-dead gorgeous, at least she didn't look like the ugly duckling anymore. The curls softened her strong jaw line and made her face seem more...feminine.

"So, what do you think?" Tabatha asked.

"It's...amazing. How in the world did you get my hair to do this?"

Tabatha laughed. "It wasn't that hard. Your hair has a natural curl. All we had to do was cut all that weight off."

"Can I make it look this good?"

"Sure. Wet it, tousle it and let it dry."

"I can handle that."

"Penny said you often wear it pulled back because of work. All you need now are some comb clips like this." Tabatha pulled the hair up off the sides of her face and fastened it with the comb.

Linda bowed her head; hair still brushed her check but it didn't fall into her eyes. She looked at the mirror again. Who knew a haircut could be so transforming?

*****

The phone rang and Darrel jumped slightly. He kept his eyes on the man leaning against the outside wall of Beauty Bootcamp. "Yes?"

"The car is a rental. Registered to Adam Smite. No known Adam Smite at that address. Working on a real name."

The door opened and Penny walked out.

"They're coming. Thanks for the info."

"Darrel, the polymer has military applications."

Darrel whistled. "That ups the ante." He snapped the phone shut and watched as the ladies crossed the street. Linda glanced in his direction and shock rippled through him. With a snip of scissors, she had gone from classic beauty to stunning.

The man came out of the shadows and hurried across the street. He bumped into Linda, stopped like he was apologizing and hurried across the street. By the time he got to his car, he was laughing and tossing some keys into the air.

Darrel gripped the wheel until his knuckles turned white. It took all his will power to not take the man out right then. He took a deep breath and slowly lifted each finger off of the wheel.

When the ladies pulled out of the parking lot, he cranked the car and waited for the silver sedan to pull out behind them. It didn't. Instead, it leisurely backed up, went to the exit and turned in the opposite direction. Darrel glanced in the direction the ladies had taken then pulled out behind the sedan.

He followed until it stopped in front of a seedy motel that advertised rooms by the hour. He had never been in this part of the city before but he knew its reputation. No surprise the man had business here. It was the nature of the business that worried him. Anything from a mugging to a hit could be brokered here for the right price. Military interest in the polymer put the whole situation in a different light. Peter said the polymer could bring big bucks on the black market. That made it worth killing for. So until Linda perfected the polymer and it became public, he was going to be her constant shadow.

CHAPTER 17

Linda held the dress against her and looked in the dressing room mirror. "I don't know, Pen. This is a little over the top for me, don't you think?"

Penny gave an exaggerated sigh. "I thought we agreed I would pick the outfit and you would wear it twice before you decided it wouldn't do."

"Where would I wear something like this?"

"I don't know. Maybe one of the swank parties at Cy-Rac." Penny shrugged. "Maybe on a date."

"A date! I don't think so."

"Why not?"

"Men don't date women like me."

"Oh? What kind of women do men date?"

"The pretty ones. The ones that have it all together. Like you."

"How would you know? You've never given a guy a chance to ask you out. You didn't in high school and you don't now."

"That just kept me from having to wonder why no one ever asked."

"Did you ever think, my oh-so brainiac sister, that you might intimidate the guys just a little?"

"No."

Penny laughed and put her arm around Linda. "You do, believe me. But, that is about to change." Penny stopped. "By the way, I haven't exactly had the masses knocking down my door to ask me out, either."

"That's only because you have been so focused on finishing this last semester that the guys probably didn't think it would do any good to ask."

"Isn't that what I just said about you?"

Linda paused. "I guess it is. I always thought I wasn't pretty or interesting enough for the guys to want to go out with."

Penny turned Linda back toward the mirror. "Sis, you are beautiful; always have been. And, you are interested in other things beside science."

"Like what?"

"You are a 'Three Stooges' aficionado and still laugh at every movie even though you've probably seen them a hundred times. You like to hike and ski. You even have a passing acquaintance with a surfboard."

"That's true but those are everyday things; not the kinds of things that make you interesting."

Penny sighed. "How you can be so smart and dumb at the same time? You know, there were several guys that wanted to date you in high school but were too intimidated to ask."

"Name one."

"Barry Monteg."

"Barry Monteg? The bluest eyes ever paired with a dimple and mischievous smile Barry Monteg?"

"The one and only."

"And how would you know that?"

"Because he asked me if I thought you would go out with him. I told him to go for it."

"You never told me that."

"That's because Monica got her claws into him before he had a chance to ask you out. After that, it was all over for poor Barry."

"Ouch. That's a little harsh, don't you think. I mean the boy did have a choice."

"Not with *her* claws in him."

"M-e-o-w."

"Oh, alright." Penny huffed. "It's just that I had such high hopes. If anyone could have gotten your nose out of the beakers, it was Barry Blue-eyes."

"Thank you for never telling me. The fact that he wanted to ask me out but went straight to Monica would have reinforced what I already thought about myself." Linda laughed, then sobered. "Wait, what do you mean it's going to change?"

Penny tilted her head to the side. "I think we should get a few separates so you can make several outfits. It wouldn't hurt to wear something else besides the standard suit to work, either." Penny turned Linda toward the dressing rooms. "Try this on while I look around."

*****

The watcher hadn't left the motel since entering it. Darrel glanced at his watch; 4:30 pm. He had a date with two beautiful ladies and he couldn't be in two places at once. The choice was obvious.

He started the car, did a u-turn and headed back across town. He pulled out his phone and punched in Karen's number.

"Hey, Boss."

"How did the interviews go?"

"Good. I marked two off the list—pending your approval, of course. I sent you the files with my notes."

"I may be late getting to the office in the morning, is there anything that needs to be rescheduled?"

"You have a meeting with Mr. Cage at 10:45am to do the final walk-through of the security system."

"I should be there by then. You know how to get hold of me if you need me."

"Yes, Sir."

Darrel looked at his reflection in the rearview mirror. He was looking slightly unkempt and this morning's hasty wash down in the exec's restroom had worn off during his stakeout at the motel. Three minutes under a hot shower and a fresh shave would be just the thing. If he called his order in to Mama Dona's, he would have plenty of time to freshen up. Plus, it could have the added benefit of not having to field any of Mama's questions or pointed remarks about buying croissants two days in a row. He parked, got out and called.

"Mama Dona's."

"I need two club sandwiches on white bread, one turkey on rye and six..." Darrel thought about Linda's penchant for croissants "...make that twelve croissants with extra honey butter."

"We have some croissants coming out of the oven in about twenty minutes, if you would care to wait."

"That's fine."

"Name?"

"Foss."

The voice on the other end of the line perked up. "Mr. Foss, sorry I didn't' recognize your voice. I'll have everything ready when you get here."

Darrel stepped into the shower and let the hot spray wash some of the tension out of his neck. He quickly shampooed his hair and showered.

He grinned when he looked in the mirror. His shiner was turning purple, green and yellow. He looked at it from right and left angles. Nothing would ever help his looks but at least it gave him an interesting quality. He shaved and toweled his hair dry.

He looked at the suit thrown across the bed and shook his head. He glanced in the closet. Showing up in jeans and a t-shirt might be too casual. They wouldn't have been home long by the time he arrived so Linda would probably still be in her work clothes. He pulled on a pair of khakis and a polo shirt. He looked neat and clean, which was the best he could hope for.

Mama Dona was standing at the counter when he walked in and Darrel sighed. "Mama, how are you today?"

Mama put her hands on her hip. "What happened to your face?"

"An accident."

"Looks pretty intentional to me."

"It was more a case of mistaken identity."

"Hmm." She said something to the girl in the kitchen window and then turned back around. "The croissants were a hit with the pretty lady, yes?" She took the bag and box from the window and set them on the counter. "I brushed these with honey butter as soon as they came out of the oven. That should really impress the lady...but three sandwiches?" She patted his check. "Three makes a crowd, you know."

"Mama..."

She held up her hand. "No, don't try to change my mind. I know what I know." She wagged a finger at him. "Bring her here to meet me so I can see for myself if she is good enough for you. Soon, before you are too far gone to recover."

Darrel shook his head. No matter what he said, Mama wouldn't change her mind. The best way to handle this was retreat. He put chips and three root beers on the counter. Mama put the items in the bag and rang up his purchase. He paid, started out the door and then stopped. "Do you have fancy or spicy mustard?"

"Mustard? You?" Mama held up her hand again. "Do not bother. It is also to impress the lady." Mama walked over to a shelf, picked up a small jar and set it on the counter. "If the lady likes mustard, she will love this."

Darrel paid for the mustard and beat a hasty retreat before Mama could make any more observations. Inside the car he looked at the box of croissants. Was he trying to impress the lady? He shook his head. The real question was *could* he impress the lady. He hadn't cared about what anyone thought of him in years but suddenly, it was important that Linda like him.

He snorted. It would take more than a dozen croissants dripping honey butter. Women like Linda didn't date rough-edged men like him. Plus, he would never fit into her life. He enjoyed things like hiking, camping, snow skiing or boogie-boarding at the beach. She was all about dinner parties, grand openings and premiers. He shuddered at the thought of being trussed up in a tux.

He pulled into the driveway. This was as close as he would ever get to being a part of her life. Keeping her safe was one thing he *could* and *would* do: whatever it took.

Darrel got out of the car and looked around. Everything appeared normal so he got the food, walked to the door and pressed the doorbell. After ringing the doorbell several times, he heard movement and wasn't sure what to expect, especially if the ladies were still trying to locate Linda's keys. When the door finally opened, he almost dropped the food.

CHAPTER 18

Linda smoothed the skirt of her gown and sighed with pleasure. She had never had anything so beautiful. Penny was right; she did look good in it. It seemed to shimmer when she moved and made her feel like a little girl playing dress up.

She swept her hair up, fastened it with one of her new combs and studied the effect in the mirror. Her head felt much lighter and her hair was certainly easier to fix. She should have cut it sooner.

She picked up her new earrings and was fastening one when she heard the doorbell chime. She looked at the clock: 5:58 pm. Walking into Penny's room she asked, "Did you call for take-out?"

Penny glanced up. "Ohh la la. You look fabulous."

The doorbell chimed again and Linda asked, "Take-out?"

Penny got a closed look. "Sort of. Would you mind getting it while I finish dressing?"

"What you really mean is that you want me to pay."

"No-o-o, it's already paid for." Penny shooed her out of the room as the doorbell chimed again. "Don't keep him waiting and put on your shoes so you won't have to come back upstairs."

"Yes, Ma'am." Linda put her other earring on, slid into the sandals and gingerly headed out the door. The sandals were the latest rage. They also had three and a half inch heels and made her feet look slender and her legs look long. But they were going to take some getting used to. The doorbell chimed again. "Oh, hold your horses," Linda mumbled.

She looked at the stairs. There is no way. She slid the sandals off and picked them up. She started down the stairs and had to stop. The slim skirt of the gown was causing her to put both feet on a step before she could go to the next one. Maybe she wasn't made for this dress-up stuff. She had never seen Penny have this trouble. Sighing, she hiked her skirt and took the stairs two at a time.

Linda jerked the door open. "Sorry to keep you waiting..."

*****

Darrell swallowed hard. Linda was wearing a deep bronze gown that highlighted the gold in her eyes. Dangling earrings caught the light and sent it flying in a dozen different directions. Her hair was swept up in a comb and strappy sandals hung from her fingers.

"Uh, hi!"

"Hi, yourself." She glanced at the box and bag. "Don't tell me; you're the delivery boy."

Darrel nodded.

"By all means come in then."

Penny called, "Is that Darrel?"

Linda raised her voice, "Yes."

"Do I smell croissants?"

Linda looked at him and raised an eyebrow.

Darrel nodded.

"You do. Now get down here." Linda crossed her arms and cocked her head at Darrel.

"I'm sorry if this is an inconvenient time. Please, don't let me keep you from getting ready to go out."

*****

"What?" Linda looked confused. She glanced down and sighed. She had done it again. The quintessential wallflower all dressed up with no where to go. "I'm not getting ready to go anywhere. We're spending a quiet evening at home. It was Penny's idea to..." Linda cut her eyes at him. "You were supposed to be here at six?"

He nodded.

She looked at the packages in his hands. "I'm sorry. Take those to the kitchen while I get Penny." She turned toward the stairs and mumbled, "That girl has some explaining to do."

Linda hurried up the stairs. She jerked the comb out of her hair and flung it and the offending sandals into her room as she walked by. She stepped into Penny's room and put her hands on her hips. "What is that man doing downstairs?"

"Bringing food?"

"Penny Brown, don't get smart with me. You know exactly what I'm asking." Linda threw her arms in the air. "And what was your idea: 'Sis, let's dress up tonight and eat at home'. You did this on purpose, didn't you?"

"Answer me this. Did he have to pick his jaw up off the ground when you opened the door?"

"Don't try to cha..." Linda grinned. "He did look a little shocked."

"I'll bet it was more than a little. I *really* wanted to be there when you opened the door but you know what they say about three being a crowd."

"Penny," Linda sighed. "Darrel is a nice looking man and he does have the most gorgeous liquid brown eyes..."

Penny snapped her fingers and waved her hand in front of Linda's eyes. "Earth to Linda."

Embarrassed, Linda laughed. "...but we don't really know anything about him."

"Now wait just a minute. We know he is kind, considerate, compassionate a*nd* he seems to be smitten with you."

"You think so?"

"I know so."

Linda shook her head. "Still, I have to know if he loves God as much as I do before I even allow myself to *think* about him like that, much less get serious about him."

"I know, Sis, but we won't find that out unless we get to know him."

"That's true but after yesterday, I already *really* like him. I'm afraid that by the time we get to know him, it will be too late."

Penny puffed out a breath. "I hadn't thought about that. I'm so used to the people we know loving and living for God. He just seemed so...right." She walked over and hugged Linda. "I'm not throwing in the towel yet." Stepping back, she used her southern drawl and said, "I mean, *honey*, there's a good looking man downstairs and he brought croissants. I suggest we go downstairs and enjoy both."

Linda laughed and locked arms with Penny. "It is croissants."

*****

Darrel grinned as Linda walked away. So, Penny hadn't told her he was coming. Maybe, if he was very quiet, he could hear what was said upstairs. It was a good bet Linda's voice would be loud enough to carry.

He was hard pressed not to laugh when she stopped, hiked her skirt and headed up. About half way up she turned around and raised an eyebrow at him. He kept eye contact as he backed up. When he reached the kitchen door, he grinned at her. She scowled back at him. He laughed, walked into the kitchen and set the food on the counter.

Seeing Linda standing there ready to grace a Hollywood premier had definitely been a shock to his system. And he had thought putting his suit back on would make him overdressed. Compared to Linda, his crisp khakis and polo shirt did make him look like the delivery boy.

Suddenly he smiled. He rummaged through the cabinets until he found what he was looking for. He sat dishes on the counter and pulled three towels out of the drawer. He laid one on the counter, tucked one in his belt and used the other one to wipe off the china and crystal. Taking the items to the table, he laid the placemats down and then arranged the glasses and silverware. He couldn't find any candles but he did find two large flashlights so he sat those in the middle of the table with the light pointing towards the ceiling and turned them on. He put the mustard on one plate and the packets of mayonnaise on another, put a knife on each plate and sat them in the middle of the table.

The flashlights made it less than elegant but it wasn't' too bad for such short notice. What it really needed was some kind of decoration around the lights. He closed his eyes and reviewed the rooms he had walked through last night. There had been a wreath made of old flowers hanging on the garage wall.

He stepped into the garage. Penny's car was the only one there. He grunted. That was why the ladies were not frantic about the keys. It was a good bet Linda didn't even know they were missing.

He took the wreath inside, slid it over the flashlights and stepped back. It wasn't the Ritz but it would do. He picked up the other towel, laid it across his arm and took up a position just outside the kitchen door.

He could hear murmuring and it sounded like the ladies were coming. He looked toward the stairs and froze. There, sitting right in the middle of the desk, was Linda's keys. He couldn't remember if the keys had been there when he came in the door. She had been the only thing he could see.

He checked the door. Unlocked. He silently locked it. He was slipping. Especially if the guy had come in while he was in the kitchen or the garage. He reached the bottom of the stairs just as the ladies reached the top. He looked up and smiled.

"Could you lovely ladies do me a favor?"

They both started down the stairs and Penny said, "Sure."

"Go back upstairs and do some more of whatever it is you do to look so lovely. I need a few more minutes to finish my surprise."

"What surprise?" Linda asked.

"If I told you, it wouldn't be a surprise." Darrel smiled and waved a hand at them. "Shoo."

"Uh, I don't know if I like being ordered around in my own home." Linda grinned at him. "But, I do like surprises." She took Penny's arm. "Shall we?"

Penny laughed. "I think we shall."

Darrel waited until the ladies turned the corner and then he pulled out his knife and headed for the garage. A quick sweep satisfied him that no one was in there. He looked through the other downstairs rooms and didn't see anything. He made a mental note to ask Penny if anything had been disturbed. He sheathed his knife, put the towel across his arm again and went to the bottom of the stairs.

"Okay, I'm ready."

Darrel watched as Linda and Penny came around the corner and down the stairs. They were laughing. A deep satisfaction settled around the region of his heart. It was good to see his ladies happy.

Darrel looked at the keys on the desk. God have mercy on the person that tried to harm either one of them because *he* wouldn't.

CHAPTER 19

When they reached the bottom of the stairs, Darrel bowed slightly. "Ladies, allow me to show you to your table." He turned toward the kitchen and Linda and Penny followed. As they walked in the door, he turned off the lights. The bright glow from the flashlights lacked the atmosphere of candles but both ladies oohed and aahed anyway.

At the table, Darrel pulled out a chair and motioned for Penny to sit down. Then, he moved to the other side and motioned for Linda to sit down.

When Linda sat, he jerked the chair back slightly. She grabbed the seat to keep from sliding out of it.

Linda turned around and he leaned into the chair like he was pushing for all he was worth and made faces like the strain was hurting him. When he turned like he was going to put his back into it, she stood and the chair jumped forward. With a grunt, he and the chair slid into the table.

While Darrel righted himself and the chair, Linda tapped one foot as a smile played around the corners of her mouth. He smoothed back his hair, patted his brow with the towel and in a droll voice said, "Thank you so much for your help." He scooted the chair closer to the table and motioned toward it. "Let's start a little closer to the table, shall we?"

Linda put her hand on her hips and cocked her head. "What?"

Darrel put a forced smile on his face. "Really, it's no trouble. At La Bella Brown, service is our pleasure." He motioned toward the chair.

Linda flicked her head. "Of all the nerve. Don't expect a tip from me, Mister."

Darrel gave a long-suffering sigh. "Of course not." He waved at the chair. "Please, *sit* so we can get started."

"Well, I never!" Linda twitched her skirt and sat.

Darrel shoved the chair up to the table and murmured, "much better". He stepped to the side of the table, smoothed his hair back and laid the towel across his arm. He bowed slightly. "My name is Darrel and I will be your server tonight. Would you like to start with an appetizer? We have flaky croissants swimming in honey butter." Darrel put his fingers to his lips and kissed them. "Deliciouso."

Penny grinned. "What else is on the menu?"

"I don't care what else is on the menu," Linda said. "I want a croissant."

Darrel looked at Penny, "And you?"

"I'll take one, too."

Darrel went to the counter, picked up the two saucers with the croissants and put them in the microwave.

Linda drummed her fingers on the table. "And after that little display, Mister, mine better be sa-wimming in honey butter."

Darrel grunted and waited for the microwave to ding. He carried the saucers and the extra honey butter to the table. He sat the saucers in front of the ladies. Breaking open Linda's croissant, he smeared a large portion of the honey butter over it. He laughed when she smacked her lips. He sat Penny's in front of her, handed her the knife and was surprised when she caught his hand.

Penny smiled at him then closed her eyes. "Father, thank You for bringing Darrel into our lives..."

Darrel jerked. God hadn't brought him into their lives. Some faceless, nameless lowlife scum had.

"...We have a lot of friends but You have brought us someone who slid into our lives like he has been here forever. Bless him as he blesses us. And, thank You for this good food we are about to eat. Amen."

Linda echoed, "Amen".

Darrel cleared his throat and stepped back. He went to the refrigerator and got out two bottles of root beer and two bottles of water. Setting the bottles inside a basket, he walked back to the table and presented the basket to the ladies. In a cheesy Italian accent he asked, "Could I interest you in a fine root beer? It's at least two months old." He put his fingers to his lips, "aged to perfection." He pointed to the water. "Or perhaps you would prefer a bottle of our finest water. Taken from a spring high in the Colorado Mountains at just the right moment to insure the freshest taste."

"No slush?" Linda asked

"Afraid not."

Linda sighed. "What a shame. What culinary masterpiece is following our appetizer?"

"That would be one of Mama Dona's club sandwiches."

"Water for me, then."

Penny nodded. "Me too."

Darrel poured water into the glasses, placed the full bottle on the table and stepped back. "Give me a yoo-hoo when you're ready for the sandwiches."

Linda licked her fingers. "You might as well bring them now. This croissant won't last long."

Darrel bowed. "Your wish is my command."

Linda laughed. "Oh, please."

Darrel clicked his heels. "Two sandwiches coming up."

By the time he got back to the table, the croissants were gone. He stopped and looked pointedly at Linda's empty plate, then Penny's. "Alright ladies, this is how it's going down. I'm going to ver-r-r-ry gently set the sandwiches on the table in front of you and back away. Please refrain from eating until my fingers are well clear of the table."

Both ladies gasped.

Darrel pasted a fake smile on his face. "Your condiments are well within your reach. I know this is a high-class joint and I'm supposed to be waiting on you hand and foot but for my fingers' sake, you can do it yourselves." He slid the plates onto the table and quickly stepped back. Then walking backwards, he wiggled his fingers in front of his face until he bumped into the counter. "Let me know if I can throw you anything from across the room. I'm not coming any closer until the food is gone."

Penny snickered and Linda bowed her head but her shoulders were shaking.

Darrel stopped backing up when he got to the refrigerator. He raised his voice, "I see you aren't eating yet. Is there a problem with the food?" He asked a little louder, "Do you require anything else? Maybe another kind of sauce?" He pulled the ketchup and salad dressing out of the refrigerator and held them up. "We have these fine dressings. I will lob them to you if you want them."

Penny started laughing. Linda finally gave up and joined her.

"You—have—got—to stop," Linda sputtered.

"Please, I am only trying to make your dining experience at La Bella Brown enjoyable," he lowered his voice, "and leave with all my fingers."

"Stop it!" Picking up her napkin, Linda dabbed at her eyes.

Darrel bowed. "Your wish is my command. I am only here to serve."

While the ladies fixed their sandwiches, Darrel got a sandwich bag and the tongs and put them in his back pocket. "You ladies need anything else?"

"Not me," Penny said.

"Me either," Linda echoed.

Darrel headed for the back door.

"Where are you going?"

Darrel stopped and looked at Linda. "I thought I'd take a quick look outside while you ladies eat."

Linda looked at him like he had lost his mind. "Whatever for?"

Penny's eyes were huge. "Yeah, what for?"

Darrel looked at the ladies. What could he say that would satisfy them? He thought about the window behind his back. That needed to be fixed right away. "It's what I do, remember. I *am* in security. If I'm going to make a recommendation on what kind of security system you need, I need to look around."

"Security system?" Linda looked at Penny. "We decided to get a security system?"

Penny shrugged. "It wouldn't hurt. Teddy is leaving for college in a few weeks and I would feel much better having one."

*****

Linda looked back and forth between Penny and Darrel. Suddenly the light atmosphere vanished and an undercurrent, she didn't understand, swirled around them. Both of them seemed to be holding their breath waiting for her response. So, maybe trying to set her up with Darrel wasn't the only reason Penny had invited him over. She and Penny were definitely going to have a heart-to-heart talk when he left.

Linda nodded. "That's true"

It seemed like the whole room took a deep breath.

"But it can wait. I, for one, am not going to let this sandwich sit uneaten while I traipse around outside getting this lovely gown dirty so I can look at doors and windows."

"That's okay because you aren't going. You're going to eat." Darrel walked back to the table and waved his hand around. "That's what all this is for."

Linda stood. "I'm going to do what?"

"Eat." Darrel wagged his head. "You are going to eat."

Linda jerked back like she had been slapped.

"Uh oh," Penny said. "I'm going to take my sandwich and..." She didn't bother finishing. She just grabbed the sandwich and fled.

Linda put her hands on her hips. "I know you didn't just tell me what I'm going to do in my own home, again."

"I'm perfectly capable of walking around the house and making an assessment without you."

"I *suppose* you are but nothing is happening in *my* home without me being a part of it." Linda threw up her hands. "Men!" She started to walk off but Darrel grabbed her arm.

"Men? What is that supposed to mean?"

She huffed. "We were having a perfectly good evening and you had to go and ruin it with some macho thing. This walk through could have waited until after we ate. It would have been nice to sit down and eat together like family. We haven't done that in a long time."

*****

Darrel stilled when she said like family. Penny had said he had slid into their lives like he had been here forever and Linda just said she wanted to eat like family. He did a quick search of Linda's face and a small tendril of warmth wrapped itself around his heart. She meant every word.

Linda started to turn and he stilled her with a touch of his hand. "Wait."

"What for?"

Darrel smiled. "I apologize. It never crossed my mind that it would matter whether I ate with you or not."

"Why ever not?"

Darrel waved at her, "Well, you're..." Then he waved at himself, "and I'm..."

Linda held up her hands. "What?"

Darrel pointed back and forth between them. "It's obvious you are leagues above..."

"What?" Linda put her hands back on her hips. "Are you calling me a snob?"

"Uh, no..."

"Because you better not be. I'm not the one having the problem."

Darrel pointed at her again. "But you're just so..."

"I'm so what?" Linda looked down at her shimmering gown then up, her eyes narrowed. She got in his face. "Is this about clothes? I'll have you know, Mister, this is the first evening gown I have ever owned. *I* thought it looked nice but if you're going to make an issue of it, I can go upstairs right this minute and change." She threw up her hands. "How about some jeans or maybe sweats? Would that make you more comfortable?" She walked off mumbling.

"Linda, wait."

*****

Linda stopped mid-stride as a frisson ran through her body. This was the first time Darrel had called her anything but Ms. Brown and the sound of her name wrapped around her like a warm blanket.

"Please don't change on my account. You are right, the gown is perfect and you look gorgeous. If you and your lovely sister would allow me to join you for supper, I would be most honored."

Linda sighed. It was that Regency thing again. It wasn't so much what he said but how he chose to say it: If they would *allow* him, he would be *most* honored. How could a girl resist that? Or stay mad at him? She turned around. "Of course we want you to eat with us."

"Then let's eat." Darrel grinned. "Only don't ask me to seat you again." He wiped his brow. "Once was enough."

Linda laughed.

*****

The man standing in the shadows crushed the cigarette until it fell in pieces from his hand. He'd had plans for these two tonight and this fellow was fast becoming more than a nuisance. Since the Brown woman had started running with him, she had called a halt to work on the polymer. He needed to do something about it but he wasn't sure what. He pulled out another cigarette and lit it. Victor would know what to do. Only Victor wasn't here because he got himself killed in a bar fight in Jamaica.

He pulled out his phone. His fingers hovered over the keys. Should he call the boss and ask? Or, should he take care of this himself? After all, the guy was just Head of Security at Cy-Rac. He snorted. The high and mighty fall just like everyone else.

The fellow needed to be taken out so that Brown woman would start working on the polymer again. She had to finish and it was his job to make sure she did. He slid the phone back into his pocket, pulled the gun out of his waistband and smiled.

CHAPTER 20

Darrel glanced at his watch; 9:00 pm. Where had the evening gone? He looked at Linda and Penny and knew. It had been a very long time since he had relaxed and enjoyed himself. He paused. That wasn't exactly true. Last night hadn't been relaxing but he had definitely enjoyed it.

He looked at the keys on the desk. He hated to change the happy mood but he really needed to get those keys. It was doubtful but they might be able to pull a finger print off of them. He waved towards the desk. "I see you picked up your keys."

Linda looked toward the desk and nodded. "I did but that's not them. When we got here, I couldn't find them. I thought I dropped them in my purse but we were so intent on getting out of the building I wouldn't swear to it. That's my spare set."

Darrel closed his eyes. It was going to be another long uncomfortable night. He stood and stretched. "Well, ladies, I have certainly enjoyed myself but I think it's time I left. I don't know about you but I'm tired."

Penny stood. "I am, too. I think I'll go on up." She walked over to Darrel and kissed him on the cheek. "Thank you...for everything."

Darrel smiled. "You are most welcome." They stood in silence until Penny started up the stairs. He turned to Linda, "When do you..."

"I really appr..."

They both laughed.

"Sorry, what were you saying" Linda asked.

"Lovely ladies first, I insist."

"I just wanted to add my thanks to Penny's. This has been a very relaxing day for me. I appreciate you bringing supper *and* entertaining us."

When Linda smiled, a tingle ran across his skin. It would be so easy to pull her close and kiss her. For just a fraction of a second, it looked like she was leaning toward him and his arms started to reach out on their own. Then she stilled and took a step back. He willed his arms back to his sides.

*****

Linda hadn't been expecting the look in Darrel's eyes. She really *could* see him kissing her senseless and had almost put thought to action and leaned into him. She felt the heat rise in her face and looked at the floor.

What was it about this man that made her...she sighed. It was his eyes. Looking into them, she imagined possibilities that were totally impossible. It was the way he treated her—she felt cherished. He had seen her at her worst and helped her retain her dignity.

When he touched her cheek, she gasped and looked up. He smiled and bowed.

"My Lady, anytime I can be of service, you have only to call."

And, it was the Regency thing. How was she supposed to resist a package like that? Smiling, she curtsied. "Thank you, Sir. I will keep your kind offer in mind."

Darrel laughed. "On that note, I think I better go."

"Wait." She put a hand on his arm. "What were you going to say earlier?"

"Oh, just wondering what you ladies had planned for tomorrow. It is Saturday. I could come over to do the walk through for that security system."

Linda dropped her hand. The cold intrusion of reality made it plain that kissing her was the last thing on his mind. "Tomorrow would be fine. What time?"

*****

Darrel searched Linda's face. She sounded...disappointed? A tiny ray of hope lodged itself in his heart. Maybe there was... He mentally shook himself. He could not go there. "What time do you get up?"

"We're usually up by eight."

Darrel calculated how long it would take him to go home, take a shower, change, get pastries and get back here. "About 9:00 then?"

"Works for me."

"I'll bring pastries."

"Not for me. I have croissants and I'm not going to let them go to waste."

"What about..."

Linda held up her hand. "I will handle lunch. You have already fed me two nights in a row. Now get. I need my beauty sleep."

Darrel looked at Linda's face. No amount of sleep could possibly make her more beautiful than she was right now. He stepped out the door. "Lock up." He raised his hand when she would have spoken. "Humor me on this, okay?" She nodded and he stood there until he heard the click of the lock.

He stepped back and looked at the house. Linda had assumed he would eat lunch with them. He smiled. Not once had she made him feel like he didn't belong in her world. Or that who he was or what he looked like made any difference. The more he learned about Ms. Linda Brown, the more he liked. Spending time with her would be an easy habit to fall into.

He shook his head. She didn't know him like he knew himself. If she ever did, that would be the end of that and his heart might not recover. Definitely better to never let it get started.

He got in the car, pulled out of the driveway and went around the block. At the corner of her street, he turned off his lights and slowly pulled into the driveway of the house next door. It was for sale and empty. He set in the silence and studied the front of Linda's house until he knew every shadow.

It would have been better if he could have changed into dark clothes but since the watcher might show up any time, that was out. Getting out, he shut the door with a soft click then walked down the side of the house until he stood at the kitchen window. The faint glow from the appliances illuminated the whole area. This window had to be covered.

Next, he walked around the house and looked under the bushes. The shadows were too deep to see anything so it was really a useless endeavor. If the watcher had left another calling card, finding it would have to wait until morning.

Darrel walked to the far edge of the back yard and sat down against a tree. He could still see most of the house. The overhanging branches provided some cover and helped to mask his light colored clothing.

Satisfied, he set his watch to beep in twenty minutes then leaned his head back against the tree. He didn't know if it was worry about the Brown women or not getting much rest last night but he felt drained. And this was only his second long night. There was a time when he could have gone days on two hours of sleep.

He let the silence envelop him. It was never quiet in his neighborhood. A constant mix of car horns, sirens, loud music and yelling voices made up his usual lullaby. There was a peacefulness here he wished he could bottle and keep with him forever.

He caught the flicker as the last light went off in the house. He felt a squeezing in the region of his heart. Before yesterday, he had often seen Linda at work but never interacted with her. And now... How had these women gotten under his skin so quickly?

Penny said God brought him into their lives. He shook his head. No way. God wouldn't want someone like him mixed up in their lives. He paused. Then again, there had been times in the Old Testament when God had used the ungodly to help his people. He could see that in this situation. After all, he did have the skills they needed. He saluted toward the heavens. "I will do my best."

His watch beeped and he reset it. Standing, he stretched and moved towards the house. Hopefully there were no late night window watchers. He didn't need someone calling the police because they saw him snooping around the house. He chuckled softly. That would not earn him any points with the ladies.

Staying in the shadows, he did a slow sweep around the house. He didn't see anything but then he hadn't expected to. If the watcher was smart, he would wait until the neighborhood was all tucked safely in their beds and had had time to reach the deep sleep stage. Then even if someone thought they heard a noise, they would attribute it to the neighbor's cat and go back to sleep. It was suburbia.

Darrel stood in the shadows and studied the sky. Linda and Penny acted like God was a part of their everyday lives and not someone they visited on Sundays. He had never met anyone like them.

He had never doubted there was a God. Even as a child, he had recognized the natural things surrounding him could not have just happened. In Sunday school he had heard the creation story and although not exactly sure where he stood on it, he was more inclined to believe it then evolution. He believed what experts called evolution was actually the decaying effect of sin and not natural selection. After all, God had said that if man ate the fruit he would die. Man had eaten and things had been dying ever since.

God was definitely out there. He had just never known anyone that actually believed God was close to them. Wouldn't it be amazing to have the God that created the universe be your friend? Darrel shook his head. It would never happen for him, he had lost that chance a long time ago. The beep of his watch surprised him.

He was about to turn the corner in front of the garage when he caught the flicker of a cigarette out of the corner of his eye. Instead of stopping, he walked out into the light and across the front yard. He made a show of studying the windows and then went to the door like he was checking to see if it was locked. He scanned the road. In essence, making sure he was very visible. He looked around and could still see the cigarette's glow.

Darrel grunted. Definitely an amateur. Or...very arrogant. That could be good. Or it could be bad. Darrel stepped around the corner and back into the shadows. The next move was up to the watcher.

*****

The man shook his head. Amateur. Didn't even have enough sense to stay out of the light. He took a long drag on his cigarette and flicked it into the street. This was going to be too easy. And, this guy was Chief of Security at Cy-Rac? He snorted. Maybe he should apply for the job when it became vacant. He could handle it in his sleep. He walked to his car, got in and pulled out onto the road. There wasn't anything else he could do here tonight but at least the trip back hadn't been wasted. He lit another cigarette and smiled. Now he knew the kind of guy he was dealing with.

*****

Darrel saw the glow arc and drop into the street. He smiled. One more piece of evidence. He listened as the watcher walked away and waited until he heard a car start.

He stayed in the shadows as the car drove slowly by the house. When the watcher passed, he lit another cigarette and the flare briefly illuminated the man's face. Darrel wouldn't swear in a court of law but he was ninety-nine percent sure it was the same man that had been following the ladies today.

He stepped out into the light. The watcher already knew he was here so he didn't have to worry about hiding his movements.

He stood there until the taillights disappeared around the corner. Then he took his pen and rolled the cigarette butt into a piece of paper. Tomorrow he would see about getting it to Peter.

He leaned against the house. He could go home now. It was doubtful the man would come back again tonight. Sighing, he eased further back into the shadows. He wasn't going anywhere and he knew it.

CHAPTER 21

The phone rang and he looked at the number. The only evidence of the man's irritation was the slight crease between his brows. The whiny phone calls were becoming more frequent and he was fast losing patience with them. Nothing had gone smoothly since his best man had gotten killed in Jamaica trying to rescue his idiot of a partner.

He quietly sighed to himself. Victor must have deflected a lot of the annoying bits of the business because since his death, it seemed he was surrounded by fools. Not one was capable of making a rational decision on his on.

He looked at the group of men sitting with him. "Please excuse me, gentleman, I must take this." He smiled. "Business."

One of the older men laughed. "By all means, take it. We are more than willing to wait while you make more money."

He walked a few feet away and answered the phone. "This had better be good."

"It's Scranton, Sir. He's been made."

He sighed. "Who made him?"

"Darrel Foss, Chief of Security at Cy-Rac."

"What did Scranton do?"

"He's been hanging around Ms. Brown's house and tailing her wherever she goes. He's also been entering the Brown house and moving things around to have fun with the ladies, lurking in the shadows of the parking garage making just enough noise to spook Ms. Brown. It was one of these incidents that put him on Foss' radar."

The man ground his teeth. Scranton was fast becoming a liability. "What do we know about Foss? Is he a threat or competition?"

"I'm looking into that." The caller paused. "Scranton *is* right about one thing; Ms. Brown has halted all work on the polymer since Foss entered the picture.

"Is this going to be a problem?"

"I don't know, Sir but since our main objective is the completion of the polymer, it could be."

He sighed. "Then do something to get Scranton and Foss to chase each other. Maybe if both of them leave Ms. Brown alone, she will finish."

"Yes, Sir."

The man pocketed the phone. The polymer should have been finished by now. Garth Brown had been a brilliant man and his daughter was only slightly less brilliant. That, he believed, had more to do with experience than intelligence. He was beginning to wonder if the hold up was intentional. He knew from his man on the inside that Ms. Brown had been working night and day to finish the polymer to honor her father. He really didn't care why she finished it, he just wanted it finished. His outlay on this venture had already been substantial and if he hadn't known that this particular product would be worth millions on the open market, he would have abandoned it several months ago.

He looked at the men sitting on the deck of his yacht. They were sipping mixed drinks and greedily eating the shrimp cocktails he had provided. They were laughing; the atmosphere open and relaxed. He smiled. Relaxed men tended to make on the spot decisions because they were in a good mood.

He paused. Maybe this Foss interruption wasn't such a bad thing. Ms. Brown might get better results if she loosened up and had some fun. It was true that all work and no play made for a dull boy.

He motioned to the bikini clad girl standing beside the group to come over. "Bring out another round of drinks and less food this time."

The girl nodded and left.

He had already entertained several of these men on his yacht and had plenty of material to use to bring down their house of cards if he needed to. But, it wouldn't hurt to get more. By this afternoon, every one of them would be drunk and more than willing to do things they would never do sober.

He joined the group. "Sherri is going to bring out another round of drinks. Do you gentlemen want anything else?"

The men looked around at the sunbathing women, all in varying degrees of undress and shook their heads.

"Good." He sat down and turned to the man on his left, "Now, Senator, what were you saying about that appropriations bill?"

CHAPTER 22

The sound of a car starting next door pushed its way into Linda's consciousness. She groaned and rolled over. The clock read 4:30. What nut was out and about this early on a Saturday morning? She rolled back over and let her eyes drift shut. Next door? Her eyes popped opened. That house had been vacant for two months. Why would someone be there at this time of the morning?

Knowing it would be useless to try and sleep until she investigated, she got up and walked down the hall to Teddy's room. She would be able to see the road from there. Opening the door, she stopped in surprise. The room was neat and clean. Not being allowed into Teddy's inner sanctum, she had just assumed it would be a disaster area. She laughed at herself. He was a Brown and they were notorious neat freaks.

She got to the window in time to see a dark car with its lights off ease out of the driveway next door and head down the road in front of their house. She ran down the stairs and out the front door but the car was already at the corner. All she saw was the taillights come on and disappear as it turned. What in the world had it been doing next door and why were they driving with their lights off?

There had been something familiar about the car. She closed her eyes. After several seconds, she shook her head. No, she couldn't remember where she had seen it before. She turned and looked at the house next door. Nothing looked out of place but she wouldn't know for sure unless she checked it out. She looked at the shadows surrounding both houses and shivered. Did she really want to know bad enough to find out?

What she *wanted* to do was call the police and have them check it out. But what would she tell them? Uh, a dark car pulled out of the driveway next door and drove away with its lights off. Right.

She didn't have a make, model or license plate number. Plus, there could be a perfectly good reason for that car being there. If she called the police and it was nothing, she would feel like a fool. Sighing, she went back in the house to get a flashlight.

Linda stopped at the walkway between the houses and peered into the darkness. She turned on the flashlight and started to walk between the houses, then stopped. Maybe she should turn on the kitchen light. It would light up most of the walkway and definitely make her feel better.

She chuckled. This was her neighborhood. She would be fine. She shone the light into the walkway and crossed over to the other house. It was a carbon copy of theirs, except it was reversed so that their kitchen windows faced one another. She started with the garage and walked around the house. Nothing looked out of place but it wouldn't hurt to call the realtor and let them know someone had been there.

She stopped at the kitchen window and gasped. She could see everything in the kitchen and some of the living room. Granted there wasn't much to see in the empty house but still. She turned and walked over to their house. The view was the same. Standing there in the dark, she felt a shiver run up her spine. They needed to put up curtains.

Linda saw a light come on across the street. Suddenly, she realized she was standing there in her bare feet and pajamas and grimaced. She was going to have to go to the front door to get in. She could just hear the neighborhood grapevine wondering why she had been seen outside at that time of the morning in her pajamas.

She stepped into the house and closed the door. Sometimes living in suburbia was not all it was cracked up to be. Still, she had grown up in this neighborhood; played on these streets. She would like that kind of freedom for her kids, too. Immediately, a picture of a dark haired boy and girl came to mind. The little girl had her wavy hair and the little boy, her stubborn chin. They both had liquid brown eyes like their father and his slow lazy smile.

Whoa! Linda stepped back trying to distance herself from the image. Where had that come from? She had always wanted children. A boy and a girl. Well, maybe two boys and a girl. But they had always been vague, far off future thoughts in her head. This image was so clear, so real she felt like she could touch them. She closed her eyes but the image was imprinted on the back of her eyelids and wasn't going away.

She groaned and sat down on the couch. She had been fussing at Penny for trying to set her up with Darrel because it might make things go farther than she could handle. She put her hand in her hands. She was already in too deep. Had been since she had looked into those eyes.

"Lord, what am I going to do? I don't know anything about this man except that he has been kind to Penny and me. I love You and anyone coming into my life to stay, needs to love You too. It's important to You and it's important to me. I'm afraid, though, that my wayward heart has already given itself away because I really, *really* like Darrel Foss a lot."

She sighed as silent tears slid down her face because her heart, once given, was going to be very hard to get back.

*****

Darrel wiped the fog off the mirror and grimaced at his reflection. His hair was all over the place. His black-eye was now a sickly looking green and yellow and his five o'clock shadow looked more like it was ten. No two ways about it, he looked rough.

He was feeling a little rough, too. Even with a couple of hours sleep on his couch, every muscle ached and his eyes felt like they were full of sand.

He washed his face and slicked back his hair. Today was going to be another long day. At least it was if he had his way. Linda had indicated she expected him to be there for lunch. He was going to shoot for supper, too.

Darrel stopped and stared at his reflection in the mirror. "You idiot. You know all the reasons you can't pursue that line of action. You need to get in and out today. It's a simple walk through. You should be done in an hour, tops. Don't stay for lunch. Don't stay for supper."

"But..." his heart said.

"But what?" he asked.

"You know you want to stay."

He crossed his arms. "Yeah, and I'd like for there to be world peace but that ain't happening either."

Suddenly, Darrel shook his head and chuckled. He was arguing out loud with himself. Not a good sign. He wiped his face, toweled dried his hair, and put on jeans and a t-shirt.

He pocketed his cell phone and slid the knife into its holder, then took one last look around the apartment before heading out the door. What he needed was coffee: a lot of coffee. That meant stopping at Mama Dona's.

Darrel stopped in front of the deli. Maybe Mama wasn't here this morning. He loved her dearly but sometimes she could be a little too motherly. He was looking rough and she wasn't going to let it slide without a comment. He snorted. Mama was always here this early and if he wanted coffee, he might as well face the music. Taking a deep breath, he walked in.

"Good morning, Mr. Foss."

Darrel winced at the way the girl's voice carried. "Morning."

He had barely gotten the word out when Mama came through the door with a burrito in her hand. "Good morning," Mama looked up and stopped mid-stride, "what is wrong with you? You look like something the dog drug in and the cat chewed up."

Darrel smiled. "Good morning to you, too and, might I say, that *you* are looking lovely this morning."

Mama dimpled and waved a hand at him. "Go on with you and don't think you can change the subject on me." She put her hands on her hips. "It is this lady, no? If this is how you are going to be, maybe she is not so good for you. You should bring her by so I can see for myself. If you can not get rid of her, I can."

"I'm fine. It is the lady *but* this is work related. I'm doing my job and it has meant a few late nights." He shrugged. "That's all."

Mama patted his check. "No, that is not all but I will not impose." She looked at the girl behind the counter. "Get his coffee." She started back to the kitchen, stopped and turned around. "Do you need anything for the lady?"

Darrel smiled at the not so subtle question. "No, Ma'am. She is having croissants for breakfast."

"See, I knew." Mama looked at the girl. "Get him some fresh honey butter."

*****

Linda did not want to open her eyes. It was Saturday morning so she shouldn't have to. She rolled over and kept rolling until she hit the floor with a thud. She opened her eyes and realized the couch was on her left and the coffee table on her right. She chuckled. At least Darrel wasn't here to see this one.

She quickly sat up and glanced at the clock: 8:15. Darrel said he would be here at 9:00 and he was an on time guy. She stood and stretched. If she set the coffee to brew, she could get a quick shower and be ready at 9:00. Especially, since it was a t-shirt and jeans kind of day.

She went into the kitchen and stopped cold. Fear welled up within her until it burst out in one single word. "Penny".

CHAPTER 23

Penny jerked awake as the scream ripped through the air. She pushed back the covers and stumbled out of bed. For one second her feet felt like they were sinking in quicksand and refused to obey her command. Another scream rent the air, galvanizing her into action. She ran into Linda's room; empty. She raced down the stairs. The living room was empty so she went straight to the kitchen. She slid to a stop beside Linda and turned to look where she was pointing. A man was standing at the big kitchen window with a set of keys dangling from his fingers.

"Call 911."

Without taking her eyes off the man, Penny sidestepped until she reached the phone. She picked it up and eased back to Linda. Dialing 911, she handed the phone to Linda. "You talk to 911. I'm calling Darrel."

Linda took the phone.

"911, what is your emergency?"

"There is a man standing outside my kitchen window with my set of keys to my house." She paused. "I have no idea." She shook her head. "No, I don't know him. Have never seen him before in my life." She paused again. "Right now, laughing." Linda paused again. "YES, he's threatening us. I told you he had a set of keys to my house. Why would he be standing there unless he was going to use them?" Linda shook her head again. "No, I don't know how he got them. Look, I don't mean to be rude but are you sending someone or not?"

*****

Darrel's phone rang. He looked at the number and smiled. Maybe the ladies decided they wanted something besides croissants for breakfast. "Hello?"

"Where are you?"

The fear in Penny's voice was a living thing. He could feel its force over the phone. "What's wrong?"

"There is a man standing outside the kitchen window holding Linda's keys in his hand."

The watcher had come back. Darrel shook his head. It didn't make sense. Now the ladies could identify him. "Have you called 911?"

"Linda's on the phone with them right now."

Darrel put his foot down and the car shot forward. "Is he trying to get in?"

"No."

"What's he doing?"

Penny's voice caught. "L-laughing at us."

Darrel ground his teeth. This slime had just stepped over the line. It didn't matter if *they* did send someone else in his place, this man was going down. Darrel heard the sirens ahead of him. "I can hear the police sirens. I'm turning into the subdivision now."

Silence.

"Penny?"

"Yeah?"

"Is the man still there?"

"No. He left as soon as we heard the sirens."

Darrel sighed. He wasn't sure whether it was from relief or aggravation. For the ladies' sake, he was glad the guy was gone. But he would have loved to have gotten his hands on him. Darrel paused. He *did* know where the guy was staying, so it *could* be arranged.

He slid to a stop behind the police car. Linda stood in the front door talking with an officer. She looked lost. The urge to protect her was so strong that he had to steel himself not to rush up to the house and wrap her in his arms. He took a deep breath. Right now he would only complicate things with his presence. But, he did need to talk to the police before they left. Something he would rather not do in the ladies' presence. "Penny?"

"Yes?"

"I'm right outside. I'm going to talk to the police before they leave and then I'll come in, okay?"

Penny walked to the door and moved past Linda and the policeman. She came straight to his car, opened the door, sat down and said, "Okay."

Darrel reached across the seat and took her hand. "It's going to be alright. You know I won't let anything happen to either of you, right?"

"I know you'll try but you can't be here twenty-four seven."

"No, but I can arrange for someone to be. I've already talked with Peter Burk and he has offered to help."

"I don't know that I'd feel any safer with a stranger in the house."

Darrel had to smile. He was still essentially a stranger. "We'll figure out something, don't worry." He glanced at the house. Linda and the policeman were walking towards the car. "I'm going to talk to the police. You can stay here as long as you want."

Penny nodded so he got out.

When Linda and the police officer reached the car, his arms opened by themselves. Linda walked straight into them and laid her head on his shoulder. He could feel the tremors running through her body. She held onto him like she had no intention of ever letting go. He knew, in that moment, there was no going back. His heart belonged to this lady for good.

He looked at the policeman. "Sir, if I could have a moment of your time?"

The man nodded.

"Linda, I need to talk to the policeman. Why don't you wait in the car with Penny then we'll go into the house together."

Linda stepped back. "Okay."

Darrel waited until she was in the car then he turned to the policeman and held out his hand. "Darrel Foss."

"Vickers."

Darrel looked at Linda and Penny. "Let's head toward your car."

Vickers turned and started walking toward his cruiser. "Do you know what happened?"

"Yes Sir, Penny called me while Linda was on the phone with 911."

"Do you have something to add?"

"Yes." Darrel rubbed the back of his neck. "I'm the Chief of Security at Cy-Rac Industries. Linda Brown is Head of Research there. Cy-Rac has just installed a new security system and we were working with the cameras when we spotted Ms. Brown in the parking garage. She became agitated upon exiting her car. I wouldn't have thought that much about it but I had the sensation someone was watching me that morning, too. When I reached the parking garage elevators, she burst out of the stairwell and almost knocked me down.

Long story short, I escorted Ms. Brown home and talked with Penny. Penny believes someone has been in their home several times and has moved objects around just enough so they would know it."

"Neither one of them said anything about that. I checked and there hasn't been a report filed from this residence."

"I did ask Penny if they had called the police."

"And what did she say?"

"She slouched down and started fiddling with her hair and said 'Uh, officer, I know that newspaper was sitting on the end of the couch instead of in the middle like it is now and this notepad was a quarter of an inch further this way."

Vickers smiled. "I get the picture. What else?"

"I walked the perimeter and found a cigarette butt under the bushes in front of the kitchen window. I also found an identical one at Cy-Rac's parking garage."

"Where are they now?"

"I gave them to Peter Burk of Burk Security. He is having them analyzed." Darrel stopped.

"And?"

This is where it could get sticky in a hurry. "Look, I might as well lay it out for you. I believed Penny, so I started looking around. I spotted the watcher." Darrel grunted. "It wasn't that hard. He keeps making idiot moves like this one."

"So, you knew that someone was stalking the Brown women, had evidence to the fact and did not contact us?"

"That about sums it up."

"Why didn't you file a report?"

"I just learned Ms. Brown is working on a polymer the military is interested in. I don't need to tell you what complications can come with something like that. I have been told this particular project could be worth millions." Darrel grunted. "Like I said, this guy is an amateur. Easy to spot. Easy to keep up with. If he is taken out of the equation, whoever wants the polymer might send someone more professional, less easy to spot. I wasn't willing to take that chance."

"That's really not your decision to make even if you are Chief of Security at Cy-Rac Industries. This should have been reported as soon as you realized this man was stalking the ladies. We would not have ignored that kind of proof." Vickers shook his head. "Is there anything else we need to know?"

"Yes. I had Burk Security run the license plate of the car this guy was driving. It came back a rental registered to an Adam Smite but there was no record of an Adam Smite at the address listed." Darrel sighed. "Yesterday, I tailed him while he tailed the ladies. At one point he pretended to bump into Ms. Brown and walked away with her keys."

Vickers frowned.

Darrel held up his hand. "Wait, there's more. I continued following him expecting him to come to the house or try to get to Linda's car. Either way, I would have had solid proof against him. But, instead he went to a motel. I waited until 4:30 pm when I had to leave to make an appointment. He never left. I knew he had gotten those keys for a reason and I expected him to return to the house last night so I staked the place out."

"And did he come?"

"Yes, but I made sure he knew I was here and he quickly left." He looked at the car again. "My only thought was keeping him away from the ladies."

Vickers shook his head and handed Darrel a piece of paper. "Write your name and cellphone number plus the name and address of the motel. We'll check it out. A detective will be contacting you today. He will want a statement and all the evidence."

Darrel nodded. "Of course."

Darrel waited until Vickers drove off before he walked back to his car. Linda and Penny met him on the lawn.

"What was that all about?" Linda asked.

"We were just talking about the investigation."

"What investigation?" Linda frowned. "This just happened."

"I just wanted to make sure they took this seriously."

"They better." Linda shuddered. "I won't forget that face for a long time."

*****

The man pinched the bridge of his nose. If he had to hear one more whiny voice today, he was not going to be responsible for his actions. "What now."

"The police are involved."

He closed his eyes. "How?"

"Scranton stole the Brown woman's keys, showed up at their house this morning and stood there laughing at them while they called the police."

"And you know this how?"

"I was watching him."

"Did it not occur to you to stop him?"

"Sir, he has no idea who I am and I prefer to keep it that way. His stupidity got his last partner killed. I'm not ending up the same way."

"Do the police have him?"

"No, he left before the police arrived. But, the ladies will be able to ID him. Foss knew the name of the motel Scranton is staying in and now the police know. If he is not already in their custody, he will be soon."

The man stared out across the snow tipped mountains but he didn't see any of it. How much did Scranton know? Victor had known a lot and Scranton had been his partner. Just because of normal everyday conversation, he could know more than he realized. And ,Scranton being Scranton, the police would quickly find out all he knew. The man shook his head. "Scranton has become a liability."

"What do you want me to do, Sir?"

"Deal with it. I am in the process of choosing a replacement for Victor. This is your chance to step into that spot.

"Yes, Sir."

CHAPTER 24

"I like this one." Penny said.

"Could it be because it is just like the one that is on the door now?" Darrel asked.

"Is it?"

Linda walked over and looked at the package. "Yes, it is. It might not use the same key but that thought would always be in the back of my mind so I suggest we get something totally different." She looked at all the packages hanging on the wall. "Who knew there were so many to choose from? Do we want to shake things up and get something daring? Or quirky? Or should we stay with something simple?"

"Simple," Penny said.

"I definitely vote for simple and something on the same basic design since I will be installing them," Darrel said.

"Good plan. Why don't you pick out three or four that fits your criteria and we'll choose from those."

Darrel scanned the packages and pulled three: one gold, one silver, one antique. "Okay ladies, choose."

When they started discussing the merits of each one in minute detail, he looked at his watch. They had already been in the store for over an hour and right now, it didn't look like they were going to be leaving anytime soon. He started to speak when his phone rang.

"Darrel."

"Mr. Foss, this is Detective Seth Acers. I'm calling about the incident at the Brown residence this morning."

"Yes, Sir."

"I am going to need you to come in as soon as possible and make a statement. I also want all the evidence you have collected to date."

"I'm not sure who has the cigarette butts but I'll find out." Darrel paused. "Would it be possible for me to come in tomorrow and give my statement? I was planning on changing the locks on the Brown's house today. Carpentry is not my thing and it might take me awhile."

"Be there by 9:00 am tomorrow or I'll have you picked up for interfering with an investigation."

"Yes, Sir."

Darrel watched as Linda laid the gold knob aside and Penny picked it up and put it back beside the other two. He shook his head.

"Ladies, I don't mean to sound impatient but you spent an hour choosing the perfect curtain rod and curtains." He pointedly looked at his watch and then back at them. "It's just a door knob. You will not change the fate of the world by choosing one over the other."

Linda scowled at him. "We both have to live with the choice and we want it to be right."

Darrel sighed long and loud. "It's not like you have to live with it forever. It *is* possible to get different door knobs if you decide you don't like the one you pick."

Linda put her hands on her hip. "But if we take the time now, we won't have to do that."

"Ladies, I implore you, have mercy on a man. My stomach is knocking on my backbone and I would really like some lunch."

Linda looked at her watch. "It hasn't been that long since breakfast."

"For you. If my memory serves me correctly, I was taking measurements and looking for tools while you ladies munched on warm croissants." He sighed again. "The very thought makes my mouth water."

Linda scowled. "Now I know you got that honey butter this morning when you picked up something to eat."

"Yes, I did and managed two bites before..." Darrel grimaced. "It's still on the console of my car."

Penny put her hand on Linda's arm. "Sis, I say we take pity on the guy. After all, he is going to be working most of the afternoon."

"Okay." Linda put the gold and silver door knobs back and got another antique one. "Is there anything else we need? I don't want to have to come back because we forgot something."

Darrel looked through the buggy. "I think we have everything."

"Let's go find you something to eat then."

When they got to the checkout line, Darrel got his wallet out.

Linda put her hand on his arm. "What are you doing?"

He looked at the wallet in his hand then back at Linda. "Uh...habit?"

Linda laughed. "Flimsy, but I'll let you slid on that." She paid for the items and picked up the bags.

Darrel took them out of her hand. "At least let me do this."

"Works for me. Where are we going to eat?"

"What are you ladies in the mood for?"

"We are supposed to be feeding you, remember?" Linda said. "What are you in the mood for?"

Penny hooked an arm through Linda's and one through Darrel's. "You two quit being so polite to one another. First we need to decide if we want to sit down and eat or get it and run."

Darrel looked at his watch. Allowing an hour each for the doors and the kitchen window, it could be early evening before he was through. "I would rather sit but I think we had better run. I want to be done before dusk."

Penny nodded. "Run it is then. How far are we from Mama Dona's?"

"Across town."

"Oh, man. I really would like to see what other kinds of sandwiches she has."

Linda pulled out her phone. "We could always call for takeout."

"I'd rather get something on the way so I have a chance to eat it before we get home," Darrel said.

Linda stopped. "What do you mean get it eaten before we get home? You make it sound like we wouldn't let you eat once we got home."

"Well," Darrel said, "That does seem to be the pattern. I missed lunch two days ago and then someone," he looked at Penny, "ate more than half my supper that night. And as I stated earlier, my breakfast burrito is still on the console of my car."

"I don't think we interrupted any of your meals yesterday, now did we?"

"I did get to eat supper last night," Darrel wiggled his fingers, "but I had to watch my fingers at all times."

Linda crossed her arms. "Oh, stop whining. The point is, you ate."

"Yes, I did. It's the interval between then and now that is the problem." He thumped his chest. "Big man; need sustenance."

Linda laughed and patted his arm. "Poor baby. We'd better get that food before you starve. We can't have you falling out on us. You have too much work to do. Besides, as big as you are, we would just have to leave you where you fell."

*****

Linda tilted her head to one side and studied the kitchen curtains. "That's much better, don't you think?"

Darrel grunted. "A little too frilly for my taste but you have to live with it."

Penny swatted his arm. "It's much better than what was there this morning."

Linda shivered. "That's true."

"I can just about guarantee you won't have that problem anymore," Darrel said.

Linda frowned. "How can you guarantee that?"

"The police are involved now and this guy knows it. If he has any sense at all, he won't be back. So, I think I'm safe in saying that you won't be seeing him again."

"I sincerely hope so," Linda said.

He put an arm around each of the ladies. "Well ladies, I hate to leave all this fun we're having but I'm tired and I have some errands I need to run before I call it a night."

Linda shrugged off his arm and cocked an eyebrow at him. "Yeah, right. You're just trying to get out of cleaning up"

Darrel looked around the kitchen. "Clean up?"

Penny rolled her eyes. "All the dust you generated when you put in the doorknobs and hung the curtain rods has settled on everything."

Darrel stepped back. "Whoa. Nobody said anything about having to tie on an apron and dust." He raised his arms in the classic bodybuilders pose. Deepening his voice he said, "I have done the manly stuff. I'll leave girly stuff for you."

Both ladies crossed their arms and cocked their heads at him. He started laughing. "Seriously, I had some business come up this morning that I have to take care of tomorrow and I need to get everything together."

Penny huffed. "So inviting you to church is out."

"I don't know how long it will take." Darrel shrugged. "Besides that old saying 'the roof would cave in' certainly fits me."

"Why would you say that?" Penny asked.

"Let's just say I have done some things in my past I'm not proud of."

"So? We all have. Nobody's perfect." Linda said. "That church has stood for thirty years without the roof caving in because a sinner walked in the door. I don't think you're going to be the one to make it fall."

Darrel jerked slightly. He knew in his heart he was a sinner. Knew that God didn't want to have anything to do with him but hearing it said out loud was a little disconcerting. And, it reinforced the fact that he would never fit into Linda Brown's world.

"Still, I wouldn't want to be responsible for your church falling down so I think I'll pass." He picked up the drill and screws and went into the garage.

Darrel sighed. Linda hadn't followed him, hadn't tried to get him to stay or pressed the going to church thing. It was for the best. He knew that but he wanted—was beginning to need like the air he breathed—the life he saw these women living. He walked back into the kitchen. "When's your brother getting home?"

"Sometime tomorrow night," Penny said.

"Either one of you have plans to go out?"

Both ladies shook their head no.

He didn't know if he would be able to get back to watch the house until late tonight. With the watcher still out there, he didn't like it. "I'd just feel better knowing you were both home tonight."

"Don't worry about us, we'll be fine."

Without thinking, Darrel wrapped his arms around Linda and pulled her close. "*I* would feel better if I was camped out on your couch."

*****

So would I, Linda thought. She wanted more than anything to ask him to stay. Maybe get some takeout. Maybe watch a movie. But, he wasn't interested in God so it would be better if he left. She rested her head on Darrel's shoulder for just a moment and then stepped back. Putting her hand to her forehead she sighed dramatically. "But just think of the scandal."

Darrel snorted. "Seriously, you have my number. If anything happens, call. I don't care what time it is."

"We will. Now, get out of here."

Darrel saluted. "Yes, Ma'am.

CHAPTER 25

Darrel glanced at his phone. One message. DNA: both street butts belong to same person. House butt too contaminated. Garage butt belongs to someone else.

It could mean nothing. A lot of people working at Cy-Rac towers smoked. But they weren't supposed to smoke on Cy-Rac property and he had never caught anyone breaking that rule. He rubbed the back of his neck. It was that nagging feeling. He was inclined to believe there were two watchers. That was the assumption he was going to work from, so there was no way he was going to leave the ladies alone.

He slowly reached in the car and got Peter's card. As much as he wanted to distance himself from his old life, he needed help. What was happening to Linda and Penny was bigger than his issues. Slowly, he dialed the number.

"Jason Perdue."

"Perdue, this is Darrel Foss."

"Hello, Darrel."

"Did Mr. Burk tell you what is going on?"

"Yes."

"I need backup. Tonight, if it is at all possible."

"Male or female?"

"It doesn't matter. I just need someone who can handle the job."

"Give me thirty minutes and I'll call you back."

The line went dead. Darrel shook his head. Jason had never been one to waste time. Next, he tried calling Peter and got his voicemail.

"Peter, Darrel. The watcher showed up at the Brown residence this morning. They called 911 so now the police are involved. I told the police what I knew and they want the cigarette butts for evidence.

I have to give a statement tomorrow and would like to give them a time frame for getting the evidence. Since the DNA results suggest there might be a second watcher, I called Jason and requested backup."

He got in the car and pulled into the driveway of the house next door. He would stay until someone else took over. Hopefully, the ladies would think he had left for the night. He could see the street and the kitchen window from where he sat and that would have to do. It was too early to make regular checks around the whole house. Since the neighborhood was still wide awake, it would be a miracle if no one called the police because his car was sitting in the driveway of the vacant house.

He put his head back and closed his eyes. He was tired, very tired. He *could* blame it on the fact that he had missed sleep. He *could* blame it on not being used to the long hours or lack of food. Other people would accept those explanations but he couldn't. He had deliberately kept himself in shape in case he ever had to get back in the game.

This weariness had seeped into his bones. It *had* to be a mind thing. The Brown women had him longing for things he couldn't have and a feeling of despair kept trying to push its way in. His usual antidote for whatever ailed him had been to pick up and move on: new places, new people and new jobs to learn had always buried the despair. But until this issue with Linda was settled, that was not an option.

His phone chirped. "Darrel."

"Address?"

"1617 Elmwood in the Briarwood Addition."

"Be there in forty-five minutes. You can fill me in on the particulars when I arrive."

The phone went dead. Darrel rubbed his forehead. He had a headache starting behind his eyes. Seeing Jason again wouldn't make it any better. Especially since the last time they had been face to face, he had been holding a gun to Jason's head.

*****

The young man sucked in a breath as he read the report. He didn't know how A'alia got his information but it was always reliable. He looked at the paper again and read the one line that meant more than any other; 'his code name was Ghostman'. One bullet, two kills. And then, like his namesake, he had vanished into the jungle

It had been a blessing, in a way, that the old man had died. Yes, life had become much more difficult when his family had been evicted from their palatial home and thrown into the camps. He laughed bitterly. It had made him the man he was today.

The only thing he regretted was that his father's death had been so easy. He should have suffered like he made everyone around him suffer. But his brother... Sweet Phillipe, had not deserved to die for his father's sins.

He set the paper down and picked up the knife lying on the table in front of him. He ran his fingers lovingly across the blade and slowly smiled. The contact of the cold steel made him feel...powerful. He balanced it on the tip of his finger, flipped it and slashed the air in front of him.

It had been his intention to get Foss to chase Scranton but his brother's murderer had to pay for what he had done. He slashed the air a few more times.

In his youth, he would have confronted Ghostman, fought him and let him lay where he died. He wanted nothing more than to slit the man's throat but eight years in the camps had matured him, toughened him; taught him patience and how to fight. He flipped the knife and caught it. The time would come when he could fight blade to blade with Ghostman. But not now, now required patience. The young man smiled. But there were ways he could make him suffer.

*****

Linda walked back into the kitchen and sat down at the table. She put her head in her hands. "Father, what have I gotten myself into? Darrel doesn't want anything to do with You and I can't live without You."

Did he actually say he didn't want to have anything to do with Me?

"Not in those words, no."

Than don't put words in his mouth. Pray for him that he will have ears to hear the truth because it is the truth that will set him free.[1]

Linda nodded. "Father, I come before you right now in the name of Jesus. I speak over Darrel that his ears will be open to hear Your truth. I ask that someone he respects comes across his path and speaks Your word in such a way that he can receive it into his mind and heart and find the freedom that only comes from You. Amen."

"Amen."

Linda jerked upright. Penny opened her arms wide and she walked into them.

"It's already too late, isn't it?" Penny asked.

Linda stepped back and nodded. "And I don't understand it." She got a paper towel and wiped her eyes. "I'm a scientist. I don't believe it's possible to form a lasting attachment just by eye contact." She threw up her hands. "And yet, here I am."

Penny started laughing. "You're talking about love at first sight, right?"

Linda nodded. "I want a relationship like Mom and Dad's. One built on respect, compatibility and friendship. One that is going to last." Linda sighed. "But the first time I looked into those eyes, I was lost."

"It's true Mom and Dad had all that," Penny said, "but they also had that look. I've always believed I would know when the right man came along because he would look at me the way Dad looked at Mom."

Linda smiled. "They did have that look. It always seemed like in that moment, as far as they were concerned, no one else existed."

"I really miss them."

"Me too," Linda said. "Especially on days like today." She hugged Penny. "What say we call for some takeout and see if we can find an old movie on TV."

"Sounds like a plan to me. What do we want to eat?"

"Chinese," they said in unison.

Linda shook her head. "I think, little sister, that we are getting in a rut. Instead of watching TV, why don't we talk. We haven't done that in a long time."

"I'd like that."

*****

Darrel looked at his watch as the black SUV pulled into the driveway. Right on time. He waited as Jason got out and walked over to him. It was all he could do to stand still and let him come.

Jason stopped about three feet from him and crossed his arms. "Darrel Foss. It's been a long time."

Darrel nodded. "Look, lets' get this over with. How do you want to play this out?"

Jason shrugged. "It's your gig. You call the shots."

Darrel cocked his head. "I'm not talking about the Brown women and you know it. If there's anything you want to do, do it so we can get on with this case."

Jason smiled. "You know you're leaving yourself wide open."

"I know."

"And you won't retaliate?"

"No."

"Or resist?"

Darrel sighed. "Just get it over with."

When Jason walked up to him and stared into his eyes, Darrel stared back. Jason knew a lot of ways to *really* hurt him. He braced himself for whatever was coming and waited while Jason, ever so slowly, raised his arms.

Jason laughed and threw his arms around Darrel. "Man, it is good to see you."

Darrel stood still as Jason hugged him and when Jason let go, he stepped back. "That's it?"

"That's it."

"Even though the last time we saw each other I...?"

"That was not the last time I saw you. I was there for every step of your evaluation." Jason clasped his shoulder. "I wanted to make sure they understood the depth of the problem and not just sweep you under the rug. You were a good Marine and deserved to be treated fairly."

Darrel felt himself relax. "So we're good?"

"We're good. We can catch up later. Right now, bring me up to speed."

"There has been a man watching Linda Brown. Not sure how long but I came into the picture two days ago. We believe he has entered the Brown home on numerous occasions and moved things around to harass them. Yesterday, I made him while he was following them. He stole Linda's keys. I staked out the place last night and he showed up. I made myself visible and he left. I left around 4:30 am. At approximately 8:20 this morning, he showed up at their house and stood at the kitchen window with her keys in his hand."

Darrel shook his head. "Frankly, I don't understand his behavior. It's almost like he wants to be caught." Darrel shrugged. "I don't consider him a threat but the DNA results from cigarette butts I recovered suggest there might be a second watcher. I can't be here twenty-four seven but somebody needs to."

"Description."

"I've only ID'd one watcher. Mid-thirties, medium build, brown hair. Smokes a lot so he's easy to spot."

"If he comes back, do I engage?"

"No. Since the police are already involved, call them and just keep the guy from bothering the ladies."

"Will do. Anything else I need to know?"

"Ms. Brown is currently working on a polymer that has military interest."

Jason whistled.

"Exactly."

*****

Linda slid on her fuzzy slippers, stepped to the door and looked up and down the hall. When she realized what she was doing, she chuckled. The new locks were in and the house was locked down tight. There was no way someone was going to be lurking in the hall. She started to head for the stairs but stopped. Rolling her eyes, she went back into her room and looked out the window. The backyard was empty.

She went into Penny's room and glanced out. The left side walkway was empty. Next, she went into her father's room. She could see part of the backyard and right side walkway: both empty. She went into Teddy's room, looked out the window and stilled. An SUV and dark sedan were parked in the driveway of the house next door. She studied the sedan. She was almost positive it was the same one that was parked there this morning. And, like this morning, there seemed to be something familiar about it. But in the gathering dusk, it looked like half the other dark sedans sitting in driveways up and down the street.

It could be the realtor. They did have to be flexible for a prospective buyer. But...with everything that had happened today, it would be better to be safe than sorry. That meant finding out who was out there. She took a deep breath and headed downstairs.

Penny met her at the bottom of the stairs. "I ordered the food. You're going to get this, right?"

Linda smiled. "Of course. I knew supper would be on me."

"You know I'll buy next weekend when I get paid."

Linda sighed dramatically then rolled her eyes. "Like I haven't heard that before."

"Hey, you are the big-time Head of Research. You can afford it."

Linda stopped and looked at Penny. It was true. God had blessed her with a job that gave her financial freedom. Cy-Rac Industries had been under no obligation to offer her the position. "That is very true." She laughed. "Praise God for that blessing."

Penny smiled. "Amen to that. Especially since I haven't decided what kind of law I want to practice. You might be supporting me for a while."

Penny held up her hand when Linda started to speak. "We'll discuss it over supper. I want to get changed before the food gets here."

"Okay."

CHAPTER 26

Linda looked out the window. Both vehicles were still there but now two people stood beside them. From their build, it looked like men. She turned on the front door light and both of them glanced in her direction then went back to talking. She didn't want to go over there but she didn't want to call the police, either. If it was just the realtor and she went over herself, she would look like a nosey neighbor. If it was the realtor and she called the police, she would look like a nut-case. But if it wasn't the realtor, she could be putting herself and Penny at risk by not calling the police.

She needed advice; Darrel's advice. She hated to call him because he would probably insist on coming back. Linda rested her head against the windowpane. Who was she trying to kid? She wanted him to come back. It felt much safer...she felt safer with him in the house.

She walked over to the desk, picked up Penny's cellphone, then walked back to the window. She scrolled down and found Darrel's number. Her finger hovered over the call button. She looked out the window one more time and pressed the button. The phone began to ring and she saw one of the men reach into his pocket, take out a phone, glance at it and then at their house.

"Penny?"

Linda looked at the phone in her hand and out the window. That man was supposed to have left over an hour ago.

"Penny?"

Linda hung up the phone and jerked open the front door. Why was someone who couldn't stay for supper standing in the driveway of the house next door?

*****

Darrel saw Linda come out the front door and head their way. He looked at Jason. "Uh oh, busted."

She stopped in front of him and crossed her arms. "Why are you still here? I thought you had too much to do to stay for supper." She threw her arms out. "Yet, here you are."

Darrel was hard pressed not to smile. Linda's hair was pulled up into a bright purple scrunchie and she had changed into a pair of faded blue sweats and the ugliest orange slippers he had ever seen. "Uh..." He closed his mouth. What could he tell her?

Linda crossed her arms again. "What? Does Mr.-Always-have-the-answer not have one this time?"

Jason held out his hand. "Jason Perdue, Ma'am."

Linda looked at him and blinked. She took his hand and pumped it once. "Linda Brown." She turned back to Darrel. "Well?"

Jason cleared his throat. "Darrel, given the circumstances, it might be better to take this inside."

"It would." Darrel waved toward the Brown house. "If madam is so inclined, we will go inside to discuss this."

"Madam is so inclined." Linda poked Darrel in the chest. "But don't think that Regency act is going to smooth things over this time."

When Linda turned and headed towards the house, Darrel looked at Jason. "Regency act?"

*****

Linda stood in the doorway and tapped her foot until they got there. Then she stood aside and motioned them in. She waited until they were inside and gently closed the door. She raised her hand when Darrel started to speak. "First things first. Penny and I have called for Chinese takeout. Would either of you like to order something?"

"Orange chicken for me," Darrel said.

"Pepper steak, please."

Linda dialed the restaurant. "Linda Brown. Has our order left yet? Good, please double...no, make that triple our order. Thank you." She hung up the phone and looked at both men. She walked up to Jason and held out her hand. "I'm sorry I was so rude. Please tell me your name again."

Jason shook her hand. "Jason Perdue, Ma'am."

She motioned toward the couch. "Mr. Perdue, please make yourself at home." She turned to Darrel. "You, on the other hand, can feel as uncomfortable as you want to."

Darrel grunted.

Linda crossed her arms. "Do you have something you want to say to me? An explanation, maybe?"

"Let's wait for Penny. I only want to have to do this once."

"O-kay." Linda walked to the bottom of the stairs. "Penny, get down here."

Penny came around the corner with her slippers in her hand and headed down the stairs. "Is the food already here? That was fast."

"No. Darrel's here and he wants to tell us why he was standing outside our house when he was supposed to have left over an hour ago."

Penny's face paled and she turned to Darrel. "What's wrong? Are..."

"Wait," Darrel put his hands up, "if you'll just come this way," he started backing up and motioning for them to follow, "I'll tell you."

Linda cocked her head. "Don't you think you're in enough trouble without the sarcasm?"

Darrel sighed. "You have no idea."

Linda and Penny sat on the couch and looked at him. "Okay," Linda said, "spill."

Darrel looked at Jason.

Jason raised his hands in mock surrender. "Hey, I just got here. This is your ops."

"Ops?" Linda looked at both men. "What do you mean by ops?"

Darrel sighed again. Anyway he approached it, Linda was not going to make this easy. "First, let me ask: Penny, have you said anything to Linda about what has been going on?"

"No. We were planning on talking tonight."

Linda turned to look at Penny. "What's been going on?"

"Well..." Penny shifted on the couch. "Little things have been happening around the house like the pillows being in the middle of the couch instead of on the ends. My pens and notepads being moved. One of the drawers on my desk being left slightly open. The other night, when we were going through the house, your bunny was sitting on the end of the bed instead of propped against the headboard like it usually is. And sometimes..."

Linda cocked her head. "Sometimes what?"

Penny shrugged. "Sometimes, when I come in, it feels like someone has just left the house."

Linda paled. "Why didn't you tell me?"

"Tell you! When? You—were—never—HOME!"

Linda jerked like Penny had slapped her.

Penny took her hand. "I'm sorry. I didn't mean to yell. It just that you have been so focused on work that even when you are physically here, you aren't here. *And* you've been so stressed; I didn't want to add to it with my foolish fears."

"I would not have thought your fears were foolish," Linda said.

Penny smiled and swiped at the tears on her cheeks. "Oh please, admit it. Until this morning, you would have thought my fears were foolish."

"No, I wouldn't have. I have been seeing things hiding in the bushes and feeling like someone was watching me for weeks." Linda put her arm around Penny and pulled her close. "If you had said something, I would have called the police then." She looked at Darrel. "So, you knew all this?"

Penny pulled away. "Well, yes, I told him. I have been praying and praying for help." She smiled. "When I came home the other night and saw Darrel sitting in that ridiculous chair holding your hand while you were asleep, I thought he might be the answer. So," she shrugged, "I told him."

Linda asked Darrel. "So, that's why you have been spending all this time with us?"

"Yes. Uh, wait...no," Darrel held up his hand. "Wait, let me finish. The day I brought you home I did a sweep outside and found a cigarette butt under the bushes at the kitchen window. Not that big of a deal. Someone in the house could smoke. But when Penny told me she thought things were being moved around the house, it made me...concerned."

Darrel stood and started pacing. "I went back to work, swept the parking garage and found another cigarette butt." He sighed. "With the lights already off, that corner was in darkness. You wouldn't have noticed anyone standing there but a person standing there could have seen you." Darrel rubbed the back of his neck. "So, technically, your actions brought me into this. What I found made me stay."

"What did you find?" Linda asked.

Darrel sighed. "Someone has been following you."

Both ladies gasped.

"And, evidently, coming into the house and moving things around to frighten you."

"Well, they did a good job," Penny said.

"Wait," Linda said. "How was he getting in? I had those keys up until yesterday afternoon."

"That first night when I checked, I found two downstairs windows that were not locked." Darrel looked at Penny, "Has anything been moved since that first night?"

Penny cocked her head at him. "N-o-o-o."

Linda stared at Darrel. "When did you find out someone was following us?"

"Not us, you. There is no evidence that anyone is following Penny." Darrel knelt and took Linda's hand. "When you left the building yesterday, I followed you and caught the guy."

"If you caught him," she asked, "why was he standing outside my kitchen window this morning?"

"Made would be a better word. I spotted him, got his license plate number and a general description and sent the information to Peter Burk at Burk Security."

"Why not the police?" Linda asked.

"Mr. Burk is in security and he has ties to Cy-Rac Industries. Besides, I didn't have any solid evidence to give the police."

Linda jerked her hand out of Darrel's. "Seeing the guy following us wasn't evidence enough?"

"Yes, but..."

"But what?" Linda asked.

"I didn't want to spook him." Darrel said.

"You—didn't want to spook *him*?" Linda said. "But, it was okay to let him spook us?"

"NO!" Darrel took a deep slow breath and sat down beside Linda. "This guy is an amateur. If you hadn't been so preoccupied with the polymer, you would have spotted him right away."

Linda scooted closer to Penny. "How did you know I was working on a polymer?"

"Penny told me. When Mr. Burk told me that the military was interested, it changed the whole game."

"What do you mean?" Linda asked.

"Anything that has potential military applications means big money on the black market. It's safe to assume the guy following you isn't a stalker."

Linda crossed her arms. "That still doesn't explain why you didn't stop him as soon as you knew who he was *and* what he was doing."

"This guy is not a professional...".

Linda interrupted. "And how would you know that?"

Darrel wiped all emotion from his face and moved to within an inch of Linda's. He purposely made his voice cold and flat. "Because, I *am* a professional. If it had been me, you would never have known I was there until I got what I wanted or you—were—*dead*."

As one, Linda and Penny moved away from him.

Darrel stood. "Look, it will take precise timing to steal the polymer formula between the time you perfect it and go public with it. This guy is incapable of that. That means someone else is calling the shots. That's why I left him alone. I was hoping he would lead me to his boss."

Darrel clinched his fist. "If I had taken this guy out, they would have sent someone else. The next guy might be a professional and I might not spot him until it's too late." He knelt in front of Linda and looked into her eyes. "I just couldn't take that chance."

CHAPTER 27

He was telling the truth. She could see it in his eyes. "That still didn't give you the right to not tell me what is going on."

Darrel sat back on his heels. "I could give you ten or twenty reasons for not telling you but I doubt you would think any of them good enough."

"That's true." Linda said.

"Let me see if I have this straight," Penny said. "You're saying that even if the police put this guy in jail, this isn't going to stop."

"Correct," Darrel said.

"Then what will stop it?" Penny asked.

Darrel stood. "Linda has to finish the polymer. This won't end until Cy-Rac goes public with it."

Linda jumped up. "What do you think I have been trying to do? According to the numbers, it *should* work but for some reason the polymer doesn't hold together under extreme pressure."

"Maybe it's time to bring someone else into the mix. A fresh set of eyes might help." Darrel said.

"I've been thinking the same thing. It's just that..." Linda paused. It was time to admit the truth. "I am so paranoid about someone stealing the formula that I haven't been willing to allow anyone to help me."

"That is very evident," Darrel said. "Was your father working on the formula by himself or was it a department project?"

"Actually, Wade Waters was working with him," Linda replied.

"What?" Penny stood. "You mean to tell me that you have been ignoring us and killing yourself over this stupid polymer when this Wade person already knew more about it than you did? He might have finished it by now."

Linda sighed. "With my head I know that but...I just didn't know who to trust."

"What do you mean?" Penny asked. "We are talking about people you work with everyday. Why would you *not* trust them?"

Linda shrugged. "I...I don't know. I just know that it's my job to keep someone from stealing the formula." Her shoulders slumped. "I just don't know how I know."

"Obviously, your father trusted Wade," Darrel said. "Why don't you?"

Linda shivered. "There's just something about him that doesn't mesh."

"Mesh?" Darrel asked.

"The persona he projects doesn't fit the way he acts. Everything about the way he looks is perfect: too perfect. Armani suits, Gucci shoes, a very expensive leather briefcase, a laptop I would give my eyeteeth to be able to afford and hair so stiff it wouldn't budge in a hurricane."

Linda held up her hand when Darrel started to speak. "That speaks of a self-assured, take charge, be in front man. Yet, he takes a backseat to everybody. He always promotes others and never himself. He has impeccable credentials. He was the perfect candidate to replace my father as Head of Research at Cy-Rac. I'm pretty sure they approached him about the position but he turned it down. Why?"

"Have you looked at his file?" Darrel asked.

"No," Linda answered.

"Let's check his file first thing Monday morning and then decide how to proceed."

The doorbell rang. Darrel motioned for them to stay on the couch. He and Jason moved to the door. Darrel looked through the peephole. It was the delivery boy. He motioned Jason away from the door and then opened it. He pulled his wallet out and felt a hand on his arm.

"Oh no you don't. I'm paying for this," Linda said.

"Ms. Brown?"

Linda smiled. "Casey?"

Casey ducked his head. "Yes, M-Ma'am."

"When did you start delivering Chinese?"

'T-t-this is my f-first day," Casey answered.

"Aren't we paying you enough at the lab?" Linda asked.

"Oh, yes M-M-a'am. I...uh...there's t-this...uh...r-red Mu-Mu-Mustang and...uh..." Casey shrugged. "I-I-I'm just t-trying to r-raise some extra ca-cash."

He sounded so much like Teddy she smiled. She waved at everybody and said, "Everybody, this is Casey and he works in the lab at Cy-Rac."

Casey nodded. "Hi."

"Okay," Linda said. "Everybody ante up so we can help Casey get that Mustang."

She looked in her wallet. She had two twenties and a hundred. She slid the hundred out. God had been good to her; she could afford to be good to someone else. She took the money everyone was holding out. "Penny, why don't you take the food into the kitchen?"

"Gladly." Penny took the food and headed for the kitchen.

Linda put the money in Casey's out stretched hand. "I would ask you to join us, but since you're working, maybe some other time."

Casey stood mute and seemed to be in a trance. She looked the direction he was staring and she saw Darrel.

"Casey?"

"What!"

Linda jumped. She looked at Darrel and then back at Casey. "Is something wrong?" she asked.

Casey blinked his eyes. He looked at the money in his hand and stuffed it in his pocket. "Nah, nothing's wrong." He smiled. "Like you said, some other time." Turning, he walked off

Linda shut the door. That was odd. Totally un-Casey like. She paused. Or was it? She really didn't know him that well. Maybe Darrel knew him better. "Darrel?"

When he didn't answer, she turned around and the living room was empty. Hah! They had deserted her in favor of the food. She didn't blame them, it did smell good. She walked into the kitchen. They were seated at the table and in the process of filling their plates.

"You could have waited."

Darrel picked up the orange chicken. "I learned quickly that in this family when it comes to food; if you snooze, you lose."

"Excuse me," Linda said.

"Oh, don't try to act all innocent for Jason's sake." Darrel smiled. "Jason, these ladies may look sweet and kind but when it comes to food, if they can't steal it, they'll bite your fingers off trying."

Linda put her hands on her hips. "I know you didn't just say that in front of God and everybody."

Darrel held his hands up and started wiggling his fingers. "The truth's the truth."

Penny poked Darrel. "But that's not true and you know it." She looked at Jason. "It's *not* true."

"This is from the person who was going to eat my *whole* sandwich until I stared her down." He looked at Jason. "Then she graciously offered to let me have half," Darrel shook his head, "of my *own* sandwich!"

"Well, it was a *big* sandwich so it didn't hurt for me to share. But if I'd known how good it was..." Penny grinned. "It might have been another story."

"And the fingers?" Jason asked.

"Listen," Darrel said, "if either of these ladies asks you to pass them food, it might be safer to throw it at them and not let your fingers anywhere near their mouth."

Linda's eyes narrowed. "Stop."

Darrel smiled and leaned toward Jason. "Trust me on this."

Penny ducked her head and started laughing.

"Re-al-ly," Linda said. "You—have—got—to—stop." She turned to Jason. "Mr. Perdue ...please don't...take...anything this man..." She glanced at Darrel and he wiggled his fingers again. She gave up, put her head down and started laughing.

"Well," Darrel sat back, "I believe that corroborates my statement."

Linda held her hand up. "Stop!" She turned her back to Darrel and took several deep breaths. "Honestly, Mr. Perdue, don't believe anything this man says."

"I don't' know, Ma'am." Jason picked up his plate and pushed his chair away from the table. "I've never known Darrel to lie."

"See," Darrel said. "The man knows the truth when he hears it. Now that he has been warned, can we *please* eat?" Darrel looked longingly at his plate. "I would really like to eat this while it is semi hot."

"I agree." Penny held out her hands. "Let's say grace."

Jason scooted back to the table and sat his plate down. He took Penny's and Linda's hand. "I would like to pray."

"Please do," Penny said.

Darrel cut his eyes to Jason. Did he intend to ridicule the ladies or was he trying to schmooze them? Darrel studied Jason's face and frowned. Jason really wanted to pray. What in the world could have made Jason Perdue go all religious? When Penny grabbed one hand and Linda grabbed the other, Darrel closed his eyes.

"Father," Jason said, "I'm so glad You brought Darrel back into my life."

Darrel's eyes popped open and looking across the table he saw Jason smiling at him. Jason winked and then bowed his head.

"And for introducing me to Linda and Penny. I look forward to them becoming my friends. Your word says You will lead and guide us and give us wisdom. Lord, we are going to need it in the days to come. We open our ears and eyes to receive that wisdom and act on it. And, thank You for this food and the fellowship around this table. Bless this food to the health of our bodies for when we are healthy, we are better able to live for You here on this earth. Amen."

Linda and Penny echoed, "Amen."

Jason picked up his chopsticks. "Now, which one of you lovely ladies wants to tell me why you'd be inclined to eat my fingers?"

CHAPTER 28

"So what's the game plan?"

Darrel rubbed the back of his neck. "It hasn't changed. The safety of the ladies is our first priority. The only difference is now we won't have to sneak around *them* to get it done."

"What are you two discussing?" Linda asked.

Darrel smiled. "Nothing major. I have to get going. If it's at all possible, I'll come back later tonight and relieve Jason." He put his arm around Linda. "Get some sleep. We've got some long days ahead of us."

Linda leaned into Darrel. She really didn't want him to go. Jason Perdue might be everything Darrel said he was but he wasn't Darrel. She looked into Darrel's face. He had been running on very little sleep himself for several days now but none of it showed. If anything, he was more handsome today than when she had first looked into those eyes. If only he *could* stay. She gave him a quick hug and stepped back.

"We'll be alright. Surely, that guy isn't stupid enough to come back tonight. If Jason is really the bad guy you say he is..." she grinned at them and went into a karate stance. "Wha-a-a." She swayed back and forth. "He should be able to stand out front, do a couple of those fancy moves and scare the guy off."

Jason laughed.

Darrel snorted and pulled Linda into a hug. Even knowing everything that was going on, she was still able to laugh about it. The strength in this woman amazed him. "Woman, you are crazy."

Linda laughed and hugged him back.

Without thinking, Darrel leaned down and quickly kissed her. She instantly stilled in his arms. He immediately leaned back. Her eyes were big and luminous and she was looking at him like...like... Oh man, he had better go before the temptation to properly kiss her overwhelmed him.

He gently stepped back. "I really have to be going." Opening the door, he quickly scanned the area then looked at Jason. "Don't hesitate to call."

Jason nodded.

Darrel walked to the car, got in and started it. He took a deep breath and backed out of the driveway. When he drove by, he glanced at the house. Linda was standing in the door with her fingers pressed to her lips.

*****

Linda watched until the lights of Darrel's car disappeared around the corner then she stepped back in the house and shut the door. She had never expected her first kiss to be like that. In her daydreams, it had always been a little more...dramatic. She pressed her fingers to her lips again and smiled.

"Ms. Brown?"

Linda turned and smiled. "Mr. Perdue."

"Jason, Ma'am."

"Jason, call me Linda. So, have you known Darrel a long time?"

"Yes and no. I met Darrel when we were both in the military but I haven't seen him in years."

Linda pursed her lips and tapped the side of her cheek with her fingers. "Interesting." She smiled. "Let me get a blanket and pillow for you. Then you and I need to talk."

*****

Darrel turned the car off and rested his head on the steering wheel. What in the world had he been thinking? He tried to remember and couldn't. That was the problem, he hadn't been thinking. She had been right there in his arms and he had just...in front of Jason, too. And, that look. She had been surprised; definitely surprised. But so had he and too chicken to stick around and give her time to react. He sighed. All he could think about was doing it again and again...and again.

He sat up. He needed to focus on the job at hand. Focus—he could do it. Had been trained to do it. He took a deep breath and stepped out of the car. First, he needed to get his report ready for tomorrow's interview with Detective Acres. Second, he needed to contact Peter to see if they had learned anything new about Smite. Third, he needed to make sure the cigarette butts were on their way to the police.

He started to open the door to his apartment when a whisper of wind reached him. He looked to his right. The door at the end of the hall clicked shut. The last tenants had trashed that apartment and it was vacant for repairs. Why would someone be going in there this time of night? It could be a homeless person crashing for the night but... He shook his head. He couldn't ignore it; not with everything that was going on. He eased down the hall hoping the natural noises of the old building were enough to mask his footsteps.

He quietly opened the door and let it swing free. The room was empty. The bathroom door was open; the inside clearly visible. The apartment was set up like his so he stepped in and hugged the wall until he reached the bedroom door. Crouching down, he stepped into the room and immediately to his right. The closet door was open. The room was empty but the window was open and he could hear footsteps racing down the fire escape.

He walked to the window and glanced out. The guy...or girl was almost to the street. It would be a waste of time to give chase. By the time he got down to the street the guy, wearing dark jeans and a hoodie, would have merged with the rest of the dark figures that roamed these streets at this time of night.

Darrel closed the apartment door. It *could* be a homeless person or a reckless kid looking for something easy to steal. But, he had very publicly stuck his nose into Linda's business and now someone had just fled his apartment building.

He walked back to his apartment, started to open his door and stilled. The tape was broken. Had it been broken the first time he walked up? Or had someone been in his apartment while he was chasing the other guy? The guy on the fire escape could have been a decoy. He shook his head. He had been so caught up in the memory of that kiss he hadn't looked at the tape. He studied the lock and grunted. There were faint scratches around the keyhole.

He got his handkerchief and turned the knob. When the door swung open, he closed his eyes. They had just upped the ante. The man he knew as Adam Smite was lying on the living room floor in a pool of blood. His gun was on the floor beside the body. Checking for a pulse was useless. The neat little hole between Smite's eyes said it all. There was no sign of a struggle, so Smite had probably known his killer. They might have come in together.

Darrel pulled out his phone and dialed 911. Just as the operator said 911, he heard feet racing up the stairs. Raising his hands, he turned around as two policemen with drawn guns stepped into the hall. Darrel could hear the emergency operator saying "what is your emergency?"

"Officer, I just came home and found a dead man in my apartment. I'm on the phone with 911 right now. Would you talk with them?"

"Put the phone down, put your hands behind your head and step away."

Darrel set the phone on the floor, put his heads behind his head and stepped back.

The older man said, "Kidd, see if he's telling the truth."

The young officer got the phone, "Officer Kidd."

Darrel looked at the policemen and at Smite. Very neatly done. The police would take him to the station while they corroborated his story and the forensic team gathered evidence. At some point, they would know he didn't kill Smite but even so, he could be tied up with this investigation for the next several days.

He grunted. If they thought this would effectively leave Linda without protection, someone hadn't done their homework. Of course, he had only called Jason in a few hours before but surely they knew he wouldn't let his ladies go without protection.

"Alright, put your hands on the wall and spread 'em."

Darrel smiled. The older policeman still had a gun trained on him. It looked like a scene from a low budget action movie but since this was very real, he slowly turned, put his hands on the wall and spread his legs.

"Kidd, pat 'im down and cuff 'im."

As Officer Kidd started to pat him down Darrel said, "I have a knife strapped to my right leg."

Officer Kidd finished the pat down and then raising Darrel's trouser, took the scabbard and knife off of his leg. He slid the knife out and whistled. "This is a beaut. What are you doing carrying it?"

"I am Chief of Security for Cy-Rac Industries. I carry a knife instead of a gun."

"You do know that we can arrest you for having this on your person."

"Yes, Sir. I do."

Officer Kidd laid the knife on the floor. He reached up and pulled Darrel's right arm down and put on the cuffs. Then he pulled Darrel's left arm down and cuffed it. Officer Kidd picked up the knife and walked back to stand beside his partner.

"Alright, turn around—slowly."

Darrel turned and looked at the man's name tag. Decker.

Officer Decker holstered his gun and said, "Kidd, check the dead guy and call it in."

They waited while Officer Kidd bent over Smite and checked for a pulse.

Darrel heard the squawk of the radio.

"Officer Kidd. We have an 11-44 at..."

"Now, tell me what happened," Decker said.

"I got here about five minutes before you did. I started to enter my apartment when I saw the door at the end of the hall close and I went to investigate."

"Do you investigate every door that closes around here?"

"No Sir," Darrel said. "That apartment is being renovated and empty at the moment. I thought it strange that someone would be going in there at this time of night."

"Find anything?" Decker asked.

"Nothing inside. The window to the fire escape was open and when I looked out, someone was rapidly descending towards the street."

"Description?"

"Dark hoodie, dark pants, slim; maybe a 150 pounds." Darrel shrugged. "He was already too far away to get a good look."

Decker grunted. "Then what?"

"I came back to my apartment and found the tape broken."

Decker interrupted. "The tape broken?"

"Yes, Sir. If you will look just about five inches below the doorknob there is a piece of tape on the door and one on the door jam."

Decker looked at the door and then at the door jam. "You always this paranoid?"

"Yes, Sir."

Decker shook his head. "Alright, finish."

"It was too much of a coincidence that someone left the building via the fire escape of an empty apartment right before I found the tape on my door broken. When I opened the door and saw the body, I immediately dialed 911. Then you showed up."

"You didn't check to see if the man was alive?" Decker asked.

"No, Sir. It was obvious that Smite was dead."

Decker's pen stilled and he looked at Darrel. "So you know the deceased?"

"Not really." Darrel sighed. "Both myself and this man are part of a case Detective Seth Acres from precinct 1023 is working. If you will call him, he will confirm my story. I have an appointment with him tomorrow to discuss it."

Decker grunted. "So, you didn't enter the apartment?"

"No, Sir."

"When was the last time you were in the apartment?"

"I left around 7:30 am."

"Where were you all day?" Decker asked.

"I was helping friends with some home improvements."

"What time did you leave their place?"

"Around 8:30 pm."

Decker looked at his watch and noted the time. "Name and address."

"Linda and Penny Brown, 1617 Elmwood."

"They will corroborate your story?"

"Yes, Sir. Please contact Detective Acres and tell him what happened. He needs to know right away."

Darrel closed his eyes as the full impact of Smite's death hit him. There *was* a second watcher and he didn't know who it was. And, unlike Smite, this one would kill for what he wanted.

"Officer Decker, I really need to make a phone call. Linda Brown's life could depend on it."

CHAPTER 29

"So, Jason, you work for Burk Security?" Linda asked.

"Yes, Ma'am."

"Doing what?"

"I'm an instructor for the training division," Jason answered.

"Instructor? What do you teach?"

"Basic stuff, Ma'am."

Linda laughed. "I can see getting information out of you is going to be like pulling teeth."

Jason smiled. "Sorry, that's the SEAL training. You don't leave it behind just because you leave the Navy."

"So you and Darrel were in the Navy?"

"No, Ma'am. Darrel was a jarhead but we were stationed together."

"A jarhead?" Linda asked.

"A Marine. We call them jarheads; they call us squids," Jason laughed, "and they definitely aren't terms of endearment."

Linda cocked her head. "Mr. Perdue, why don't we cut to the chase?"

Jason smiled. "Ms. Brown, what would you like to know?"

Linda sighed. "As much as you can tell me."

Jason paused as if weighing his words. "Darrel was a Marine sniper; one of the best. He is trained in the art of war and there's not a better man to have on your side in times like this. You can trust him. He'll be the last one standing when it's all said and done"

"That's not much."

"No, Ma'am but it's enough."

"At least," Linda said, "now I know Darrel isn't..." Linda put her head down.

"Ma'am, Darrel knows what he's doing."

Linda wiped her eyes. "I'm sorry; it's just that today I found out someone is really out to get me. Well, not me but the polymer. And..."

Jason's cellphone rang and he looked at the number. "Excuse me. I better get this. Hello."

"The watcher's dead. There is another watcher and I believe he killed this one to try and get me out of the way. Get the ladies out of the house, now."

"Can you stay on the line?" Jason asked.

There was a pause and Darrel said, "I can."

"Linda, I need you and Penny to pack enough clothes for a couple of days and be back down here in fifteen minutes."

"What..."

"Please," Jason said, "don't ask; just do."

Linda nodded and headed for the stairs.

Jason could hear Darrel laughing when he picked up the phone.

"She actually did it?" Darrel asked.

"Yes."

"Man, I'm going to have to get your secret. She double and triple questions everything I ask her to do."

"Details?"

"When I got home, I found the watcher dead. A single shot between the eyes with my gun."

"Convenient," Jason said.

"That's what I thought. Thank goodness, so does Detective Acres. Especially since I can prove I was with the Browns all day. The police are releasing me on my own recognizance when they get through with me. I don't know how long that will be so I don't know when I can relieve you."

"Don't worry about that. I'll take care of your ladies." Jason heard the ladies on the stairs. "They're coming. I'll keep in touch."

Linda sat her tote bag down. "Are you going to explain?"

Jason held up his hand. "Let me make a phone call." He dialed the number. "Cass, sorry to disturb you so late but I need a favor. I have a couple of ladies who need a place to stay tonight." Jason waited. "No. I didn't think about that. Don't worry, we'll go somewhere else." He nodded his head. "If you're sure. Thanks. We'll be there in about thirty minutes."

He looked at Linda and Penny. "We're going to Cassie's. She's a colleague of mine. Once we get there, I will explain everything. Right now, I need you to do exactly what I say and not argue or ask questions. Okay?"

Linda and Penny nodded.

"Good. I want you to make it seem like you're still here. Leave a few lights and the TV on; maybe put a book and the remote on the coffee table; move the pillows and throw the afghan back like you just got up." Jason pulled out his gun and the ladies gasped. "I'm going to make sure everything is locked up tight."

As Jason walked away, Penny asked, "What's going on?"

Linda shook her head. "I don't know. We were talking and his cellphone rang. Then he said for us to pack some clothes and get back down here."

Penny grabbed Linda's hand. "This just got a lot worse, didn't it?"

"It looks like it." She squeezed Penny's hand. "Let's pray."

Penny nodded.

"Father, You know exactly what's going on. Penny and I both dwell in the secret place of the Most High so we know that we live under the shadow of the Almighty. Your word says that when we call upon You, You will answer us. You will be with us in trouble and deliver us. You promised to honor Your word above Your name so we declare that You are our refuge, our fortress; our trust is in You. Father, thank You for bringing Darrel and Jason into our lives in our time of need. And thank You for Your keeping power. Amen."

Penny echoed. "Amen."

*****

Darrel rubbed his wrists. They still had a faint red mark from the handcuffs. "What's next?"

"They're through with the body," Acres said. "Look around and see if anything was taken."

Darrel walked into the apartment. The TV was still there. He checked the kitchen cabinet, the closet and glanced in the bathroom. "Nothing's missing."

Acres grunted. "You been here long?"

"Two years."

Acres looked pointedly around the room. "This gives a whole new meaning to the word minimalist." He walked over to the case sitting on the counter and picked up the bag beside it. "This a replica?'

"No. My great granddad was the sheriff of a small town in New Mexico and that was his gun."

Acres shook his head. "A genuine Colt Peacemaker. I bet if this baby could talk it would have some wild stories to tell."

"I don't know. I gather the town was pretty peaceful and I know my great granddad died of old age."

Acres sighed and put the gun down. "This doesn't look good."

"I know," Darrel answered. "So, where do we go from here?"

"*We* are going to the local station and *you* are going to give your statement. Then *we* are going to go to the precinct where you are going to give your statement again." Acres spoke to officer Decker and then motioned for Darrel to follow him. "You were with the Brown's most of the day?"

"Yes. I installed new door locks on the front and back doors and put up curtains at the kitchen window. That pretty much took the whole day."

"I'll send a patrol car to their house."

"Don't bother. The Brown's have already been moved. Officer Decker allowed me to call the man staying with them. He knows what he is doing and will get them to a safe place."

Acres rubbed his forehead. "You *really* need to let us handle this. My superiors were not too happy about the fact that I didn't haul you in earlier." He chuckled. "They are definitely not going to be happy now. I have no idea when you will be allowed to leave once we get there. I don't even know if they will let me to take your statement." Acres pulled Darrel's cellphone from his pocket. "So-o-o, if there is anything you need to settle, you need to settle it before we get to the car."

Darrel took the cellphone. "Thanks." He dialed Jason's number.

CHAPTER 30

Jason pulled into the driveway and hit redial. "Cass, we're here." He turned to the ladies. "I don't think anyone followed us but we're not taking any chances. Make sure you have everything in your hands when you step out of the vehicle. We all exit to the left side and stay close. Everybody moves together."

Jason waited while the ladies stepped down and then he moved them up the driveway. When they were almost to the door, he spoke into the phone. "Open the door."

Linda smiled when the door swung open and no one was standing there. It was just like a scene from some low-budget movie. Penny bumped into her back and she felt the tension crawl up her spine. Only this wasn't a movie. This was reality: their reality. Their lives had changed drastically when that man showed up at their kitchen window this morning.

Jason waited until they were both inside. "I'll do a perimeter sweep and give the knock when I'm ready to come back in." He shut the door without waiting for a reply.

"Why don't I show you where to put your things?"

Linda jumped and spun around.

The woman standing before her smiled. "Sorry, I didn't mean to startle you." She held out her hand. "I'm Cassandra Unger but you can call me Cassie."

Linda started to shake her hand but Penny pushed past her and said, "But you're so beautiful."

Cassie just looked at Penny.

Linda poked her. "Pen!"

Penny jumped. "Oh, that was rude. I apologize. It's just that Jason said you were a colleague and I assumed you work with him in security."

"Pen, that wasn't much better. Your assumptions are showing. A woman can be beautiful and work in security," Linda held out her hand. "Why don't we start again? I'm Linda Brown and this is my sometimes not so tactful sister, Penny."

Cassie shook Linda's hand and smiled. "That's okay. I get comments like that more times than you'd expect. Especially in this day and age." She shrugged and smiled at Penny. "I do work with Jason but not in security. I teach beginner's Tae Kwon Do at his dojang."

"Dojang?" Penny asked.

"That's the term applied to a Tae Kwon Do school. I know you've heard the term dojo."

Penny nodded.

"It's basically the same thing." Cassie picked up both of their bags. "Let's get you settled."

*****

Jason scanned the street one last time and rapidly knocked three times on the door. He counted to five and then rapped three more times. The door swung open, he stepped through and shut it. He caught movement out of the corner of his eye and turned. Linda was standing there with her arms crossed.

"Okay, Mr. Cloak and Dagger, it's time to talk."

Jason laughed. "Darrel warned me about you. Can I at least get something to drink before you start grilling me?"

"There's a glass of tea on the coffee table. I suggest you make it quick because there are three ladies who want to know what's going on." Linda cocked her head. "And they want to know now."

Jason smiled. "Thanks for doing this on such short notice, Cass." He motioned toward Linda and Penny. "This is Linda Brown and her sister, Penny."

"We introduced ourselves," Cassie said.

"Linda is Head of Research for Cy-Rac Industries. They are currently working on a project that the military is interested in."

Cassie whistled.

Jason nodded. "Precisely. A few days ago Cy-Rac security became aware someone was following Linda and harassing both of the sisters. Darrel Foss, Chief of Security and an old friend of mine, has been keeping tabs on the Browns and the watcher. This morning the watcher showed up at the Brown's house with a set of Linda's keys he had stolen the day before. I received a call from Darrel that he found the man dead in his apartment when he got home."

"Dead!" Linda and Penny exclaimed in unison.

Jason went on like he hadn't heard them. "He asked me to move the ladies to a safe place. You were the first person I thought of."

"Uh, hel—lo." Linda waved her hands. "The ladies are sitting right *here* and would like to be in on this conversation."

"Okay, speak," Jason said.

Linda raised an eyebrow. "I don't handle sarcasm well."

Jason smiled. "So I've noticed."

Linda's eyes narrowed. "Can we focus on the part about Darrel finding a dead man in his apartment? Did he call from jail? Is he hurt?"

"Whoa," Jason held up his hands. "I can only tell you what I know."

"Speak," Linda said.

Jason shook his head. "Darrel is right about you. I could almost pity the man." Jason held up his hand when Linda would have spoken. "To answer your questions. When Darrel arrived home, he found the watcher dead from a single gun shot wound to the head and his gun laying on the floor beside the body. The police arrived almost immediately."

"So, of course, the police think Darrel did it," Linda said.

"Actually, no." Jason said. "Acres believes it's a little too coincidental that the same guy who was at your house this morning was found dead in Darrel's apartment this evening. Plus, he has you to back up his alibi. So, they are going to release Darrel on his own recognizance after they take his statement."

Linda sat back. "That's a relief." Then she sat back up. "But if the man is dead, why did you whisk us out of the house? Shouldn't everything be okay now?"

"Remember, Darrel was concerned that there might be more than one watcher." Jason said.

"Yes. Does he *know* someone else is watching me?" Linda asked.

"No, he doesn't know but after tonight he's pretty sure," Jason said.

"Why?" Linda asked.

"Darrel knows *he* didn't kill this guy. He thinks another watcher is trying to get him involved with the murder investigation so he won't have time to guard you."

Linda smiled. "They don't know Darrel very well, do they?"

"No, they don't," Jason agreed.

"Wait. Did you say the guy had been killed with Darrel's gun?" Penny asked.

"Yes," Jason answered.

"But he doesn't carry a gun. He said so. He carries a knife," Penny said.

*****

Linda gasped. "A knife!"

"Yeah, a big ugly one. Scared me silly when he pulled it out the other night," Penny laughed. "Especially since it had red sticky stuff all over it."

"Just because he doesn't' carry a gun, doesn't mean he doesn't own one", Jason said.

Penny cocked her head. "Why would he choose to carry a knife over a gun?"

"You'll have to ask him." Jason said. "Now, I think there is one more question that needs answering before I take off."

"Take off? Where are you going?" Linda asked. "Aren't you supposed to be guarding us?"

"That is part of the answer to the last question which was 'why did I have to whisk you out of the house'." Jason didn't know a way to tell Linda and Penny what they needed to know without scaring them. He cleared his throat. "Darrel is concerned about what this other watcher might do once he believes he has Darrel safely out of the picture."

"You mean Darrel thinks he might try to hurt me?" Linda asked.

"No," Jason sighed, "at least not at first. If he could get you and your research, he might take you to another lab somewhere for you to finish the polymer. Then, he would kill you."

"Kill me?" Linda took a deep breath and slowly let it out. "Why now?"

"Why now what?" Jason asked.

Linda shook her head. "My father has worked on the polymer for several years and started the testing phase before he died. Why now? Why wasn't this happening to him?"

"Do you know it wasn't?" Jason asked.

"I...don't." Linda looked at Penny. "Did Dad ever say anything to you about anything like this?"

"No," Penny said.

"Nothing may have been going on. The work on the polymer may not have drawn public attention until your father's death." Jason said.

Linda sighed. "Well, they can forget it. I don't care what they did to me; I would not finish the polymer for them."

"I believe you," Jason said. He leaned over and put his hand on hers. "But would you do it for Penny's sake?"

Linda jerked her hand back. "What do you mean?"

"These people don't fight fair. They would think nothing of torturing Penny if they thought it would accomplish their goals. Darrel is worried they might try to grab both of you while he is out of the picture. That's why he wanted you away from the house. That's why I have to go. He can't watch the house; I can. If they show up there, I can at least identify them so we'll know who we are dealing with. You will be safe here with Cassie. She knows what she's doing."

Jason stood. "Cass, walk me to the door."

When they reached the door Jason said, "If you can just let them stay tonight, I will find some place else for them tomorrow."

"They can stay until Monday morning," Cassie said. "I sent Hope to stay at her cousins and she is over the moon. They are older and will spoil her terribly. Auntie Dana will drop her off at daycare Monday so that's all set."

"Thanks," Jason said. "Cass, I trust your judgment and if at any time you think you're in danger, get the ladies in the car and call me. We'll decide where to go from there."

CHAPTER 31

Darrel walked out of the police station and looked around. He dialed Jason's number.

"Hello."

"I'm out. Where are you?"

"I'm headed to the Brown's house."

"Nothing's happened, has it?" Darrel asked.

"No," Jason said.

"Where are the ladies?"

"With a friend," Jason said. "Meet me at the Brown's and we'll talk."

"I'm on my way."

Darrel pulled into the driveway of the house next door and stepped out. Every light in the Brown's house was on. He scanned the area but didn't see Jason. The front door suddenly opened and Jason walked out. Darrel headed toward him.

"Good call," Jason said.

"What do you mean?"

"The place has been trashed. The furniture has been slashed and there's nothing left on the shelves. Drawers are open and the contents are scattered everywhere. There is not a room in the house that hasn't been tossed." Jason paused. "And unless there was more than one perp, he must been watching the house. He would have had to get here right after we left to have time to do that much damage."

Darrel walked in the door, looked at the devastation and then at Jason. "Called the police yet?"

"No. I decided to do a quick sweep to make sure no one was here."

"You touch anything?"

"The light switches. The front doorknob." Jason said.

Darrel got his phone and dialed Acres' number.

"Do you know what sleep is?" Acres asked.

Darrel snorted. "You're still at the station, aren't you?" Darrel heard a deep sigh.

"Yes, but I had high hopes of getting home before sunrise."

"Sorry, not gonna happen. Someone has trashed the Brown's residence."

"Particulars?" Detective Acres asked.

"Wait." Darrel handed the phone to Jason. "He wants particulars."

Jason took the phone. "I arrived at the house about..." Jason looked at his watch, "...fifteen minutes ago. From the outside, everything looked normal. I started a perimeter sweep and found the kitchen window shattered. I entered the house through the window and did a sweep. Whoever trashed the place was already gone."

"Did you touch anything?"

"Just the light switches and the front doorknob, Sir."

"Let me talk to Darrel again."

Jason handed the phone back to Darrel. "I'm going to do a closer inspection of the outside."

Darrel nodded and said into the phone, "Yes?"

"Where did you get him? He sounded like he was filing a military report."

"Ex-Navy."

Detective Acres grunted. "I'll get a team headed your way. What about the Brown's?"

"They were not here and have not been apprised of the situation yet."

"Good. Keep it that way. After our team gets through, we'll bring them in to see if anything has been taken. I'll be there in about twenty minutes."

Darrel pocketed his phone and then balled his hands into fists. Why the sudden violence? Cy-Rac had been working on this polymer for several years and not once had there been a whisper of a security problem surrounding the research. The most nagging problem was that the only *known* person with interest in the ladies was lying in the city morgue.

He looked around the living room. The destruction looked more like an act of rage than someone looking for research. He stepped out onto the stoop. What if Linda had been here? What if he hadn't called Jason because there was bad blood between them?

His mind started filling with images. Penny running but not able to get away. Linda screaming in terror as her assailant drove a knife into her body time and time again. His chest constricted and it felt like all the air was being sucked out of his body. A hand touched his shoulder and without thought, he turned toward the hand, grabbed it and brought his arm, elbow out, up and over to ram his assailant's face.

"Hey!"

Darrel blinked and Jason's face came into view. He let go of Jason's hand and stepped back. Suddenly his legs wouldn't hold him and he went down with a plop.

Jason knelt in front of him. "What is it?"

"I could have lost her." Darrel blinked rapidly. "If I had been too stubborn to call you, I could have lost her."

Jason sat down beside him and stared at the street. "She is something, isn't she?"

Darrel smiled. "She is."

"It's easy to see how you feel about her. How does she feel about you?"

Darrel shook his head. "Doesn't matter. As soon as this is over, I'm outta here."

"Outta here. Why?" Jason asked.

Darrel leveled a stare at Jason. "You, of all people, know why." He looked forward. "What's done is done. I can't go back and undo the past."

"That's true, but ..." Jason stopped as sirens filled the air.

They both stood as the first patrol car stopped in front of the house.

A policeman got out and came toward them. Taking out his pad and pencil he asked, "First on the scene?"

"Me," Jason answered.

"Show me what you found."

Darrel sat down again as Jason and the officer walked away. He shook his head but couldn't shake the image of a knife repeatedly plunging into Linda. He wiped his hand across his face. "I don't know what I would have done if something had happened to her. Thank You, for keeping her safe."

Darrel jerked upright and looked around. Had he just said that out loud? And, had he really just thanked a God he didn't believe cared about people's everyday struggles for keeping Linda safe?

Darrel paused. Yes, he had and it had been as natural as breathing. He looked up at the sky and then down at himself. No bolts of lightening. He was still alive. The Almighty God of Heaven hadn't struck him dead for daring to speak to Him. Maybe, Linda was right. Maybe the roof of the church wouldn't fall in if he stepped inside.

Jason and the officer came around the side of the house just as Detective Acres pulled in the driveway. They both switched direction and headed for his car, so Darrel joined them.

"What do we have?" Detective Acres asked.

"Perp or perps entered the building through a bay window in the kitchen," the officer shook his head. "That's a lot of damage for one person to inflict in such a short time."

Detective Acres looked at Jason. "How long were you gone?"

"We left approximately ten minutes after receiving Darrel's call."

Detective Acres grunted. "Of course, we don't know the exact time the house was entered." He looked at the officer. "Opinion?"

"It's pretty bad, Sir. I would say that the perps intentionally inflicted the damage. They didn't toss this place looking for something to steal. I would have to wait for the Browns to confirm it but I'd bet nothing has been stolen."

Detective Acres nodded. "Talk to any neighbors who are still awake. Maybe they saw or heard something. If not, we'll canvas the rest of the neighborhood in the morning," Detective Acres paused, "and make sure I have a copy of those notes on my desk first thing."

The officer nodded and walked away just as the forensic van pulled up.

Detective Acres followed the forensic team into the house. He stopped abruptly and whistled. "Does the whole house look like this?"

"Yes," Jason answered.

"This *was* intentional." Detective Acres leveled a look at Darrel. "We need to take a closer look at this whole case, start to finish." He waved his hand around. "Let's step outside and let the forensics work."

*****

A slow smile spread across the face of the young man in the shadows. It was all he could do not to laugh out loud. He had been right; Linda Brown was the way to get to Darrel Foss. He softly chuckled and stepped deeper into the shadows. "The suffering has only begun, my enemy."

CHAPTER 32

Linda groaned as a loud ringing assaulted her ears. Surely it wasn't time to go to work. She tried to hit the snooze button but her alarm clock wasn't in its usual place. She moved her hand around the table but couldn't find it. She finally managed to open one eye and saw Penny asleep in a twin bed across the room.

Since the annoying ringing had stopped, she rolled onto her side. Maybe it wasn't for her. Suddenly her eyes popped open and she looked across at Penny, then around the room. This was definitely not her room. The rising sun was just peeking in the window and cast a rosy glow on everything. Pink ballerinas danced around the border in an orderly fashion. A pink and purple boa was thrown across a paste jewel tiara on the dresser. She smoothed her hand down the princess bedspread she was lying under and smiled. It had been a long time since she had been in a room this...girlie.

The door opened and a disembodied voice said, "Sorry to wake you but there has been a break-in at your house. The police need you to see if anything's been stolen."

The memories of last night came rushing back. Darrel saying he found their harasser dead. Jason whisking them out of the house. Cassie kindly taking them in. Sitting up, Linda pushed back the cover. She got up and shook Penny.

"Get up."

Penny yawned. "It can not *possibly* be time to get up yet."

"Cassie just said that..." Linda turned and looked at the open door. "Oh no."

Penny moaned. "Wah-at?"

Linda paused at the door. "Get up. Our house was broken into."

Linda walked into the kitchen. "Cassie?"

"Before you ask any questions," Cassie handed Linda a cup of coffee, "drink this. It'll help."

Linda took a sip of the rick dark brew and grimaced. "Whew! That is strong. Do you drink this stuff all the time?"

"Yes," Cassie smiled. "My husband got me hooked on it."

"You're..."

Cassie held her hand up. "That's another story for another time."

Penny walked into the kitchen rubbing her eyes. "Did you say a break in?"

Cassie poured a cup of coffee and handed it to Penny. "Drink this." She looked at Linda. "Now, to answer your question. Your house was broken into last night sometime between when you left and when Jason got back."

"What?" Penny exclaimed. "Why didn't they call us right away?"

"The police wanted to wait until their forensic team had gone through the house. They are finishing as we speak and want the two of you to come see if anything is missing."

Linda sagged. "I just *don't* understand why all this is happening now."

"The workings of a criminal don't often make sense to us." Cassie pointed at their coffee cups. "Either of you want yours to go?"

"Please," Linda said. "Just add a little water to mine."

Penny handed over her cup. "Same for me."

Cassie began pouring Linda's coffee into a styrofoam cup. "Get your things. This has changed the dynamics of the situation. Jason will want you to stay somewhere more secure until they figure out what's going on."

Linda and Penny nodded.

*****

Darrel watched as the sky begin filling with the rosy glow of morning. It was usually his favorite time of the day. He leaned up against his car and closed his eyes. He felt the car move and heard a sigh. Opening one eye, he looked at Jason. "You look as tired as I feel."

"It's been a long night."

"So it has," Darrel said, "Do you think we're getting old? I remember several occasions when we closed down every bar in town and made it to muster the next morning with no ill effects."

"We were *a lot* younger then," Jason shook his head, "and a lot dumber."

Darrel chuckled. "True." He pointed at the house. "Your opinion?"

"I don't know." Jason paused. "How long has her father been dead?"

"I'm not sure. I can check the records. Why?"

"Do you know how he died?" Jason asked.

"Plane crash. He and Linda were headed to a conference in Pennsylvania in a chartered plane when they hit bad weather and crashed."

"Does anyone know for sure the weather caused the crash?"

Darrel sighed in frustration, "It never crossed my mind to check into it."

"Maybe we should. This might not be the first time these people have tried to harm the Brown family. Since Linda and Mr. Brown were in the plane together, they both might have been targeted. And, if the plane crash wasn't an accident, there might be something there that could point us toward who is doing this."

Jason's phone rang. "Hello."

"We're almost there. How do you want to do this?"

"Cass, drop the ladies off and go. Don't get out of the car in case we need your services again."

"Okay," Cassie said.

Jason put up his phone. "They're almost here."

"I'm worried about Linda."

"What do you mean?" Jason asked. "She seems like a pretty tough lady to me."

"She is. She has to be," Darrel said, "or she wouldn't have made it this far. Since her father's death, she has been pushing herself to perfect this polymer. My guys tell me she is often waiting for them to open the building and sometimes sleeps there all night. She's not resting, not eating and it is causing havoc with her health, both mental and physical."

Darrel smiled and pointed at the faded colors surrounding his eye. "She did this when I tried to wake her up from a nightmare. Penny says they're almost a nightly occurrence now. Linda is holding on through sheer determination." He waved at the house. "What if this pushes her over the edge?"

"Darrel, Linda is not holding on by sheer determination. At least not from what I've seen. She is standing strong in her faith." Jason put his hand on Darrel's shoulder, "It will get her through."

Both men turned as a car pulled into the driveway. Linda got out, glanced toward the house and started walking in their direction. She walked up to them and waited until Penny joined them. "Are they ready for us?"

"I'll let Detective Acres know you are here," Jason said.

*****

Linda looked at Darrel. "Does it look like anything is missing?"

"It's hard to tell," he answered.

"What do you mean?" Linda asked. "I know you haven't been in the house that many times but you are so observant surely you would know if something big was missing. Is the TV there? How about the stereo?"

Darrel held up his hand. "What have you been told?"

"That the house was broken into and the police wanted us to see if anything had been stolen," Linda said.

Darrel sighed. "The house is trashed."

"Trashed! You mean like the movies kind of trashed?" Linda asked.

Darrel nodded.

Linda turned and headed for the door with Penny close behind her.

"Wait!" Darrel called.

Linda ignored him and kept walking. She stepped in the door and gasped. The living room looked like a tornado had ripped through it. The TV and stereo lay on the floor smashed beyond repair. The desk, coffee and side tables had their legs broken off; their tops scarred with deep groves. The couch had been slashed repeatedly. And her grandmother's chair...

Linda picked up one of the chair legs. This chair had survived two generations of children. She closed her eyes and shook her head. 'Why!" Whirling around, she shook the leg at Darrel. "Why would anyone *do* this to us? This—is—totally—uncalled—for! How dare they think they can come into my home and do this."

*****

Darrel blinked at Linda's tone. She stood in the middle of total devastation but was she hysterical over the destruction? Over someone invading her home and violating her space? He had expected her to be. Had been ready to comfort her, calm her but once again the lady had surprised him. She didn't even look close to falling apart. As a matter of fact if the person responsible was standing in front of her, she would probably hit him with the chair leg. He felt a smile tugging at the corners of his mouth.

"Not the reaction you were expecting, was it?" Jason whispered.

Darrel shook his head.

"Told you, she's one tough lady."

"I'm beginning to see that," Darrel quietly replied.

"What are you two whispering about?" Linda demanded.

Darrel crossed his arms. "You."

"Quit whispering then." Linda pointed at Penny. "We're through meekly doing whatever you say. From now on, we are in on every decision or we don't make a move."

Darrel held his hand up. "Whoa, Lady. In the first place, I don't recall you meekly doing anything I've said. You're very good at questioning everything. Second, remember we're on your side."

Linda closed her eyes and took a deep breath. In a calmer tone she said, "I know but I have been living in abject fear for the last six months. Jumping at every shadow. Cringing at every sound. That stops right now. I refuse to be a victim anymore." She looked around the living room. "I just hate that it took this to bring me to that point. It's time to be proactive. So what do we do first?"

"The first thing I need for you to do is search the house and see if there is anything missing."

Linda jumped at the voice behind her and spun around.

Detective Seth Acres smiled and held out his hand. "Detective Acres.

Linda shook his hand. "Linda Brown."

"Sorry we had to meet under such trying circumstances." Acres smiled. "Right now, I need for you to look around and see if anything was taken. Then, I need you to promise to stay wherever Darrel puts you. Otherwise we will have to take you into protective custody ourselves while we look into this."

"Detective Acres, I'm not promising anything right now," Linda said. "I won't just sit back and wait on something else to happen. Wait on someone else to do something."

"That's exactly what you are going to do. We don't need another civilian," Detective Acres looked at Darrel, "sticking their nose in our case."

Linda put her hands up. "I'm sorry but..."

"Wait," Darrel said. "We all want the same thing. I agree with Detective Acres. The first thing to do is walk through the house and see if anything is missing. Then together we can decide our next step." He looked at Linda. "Agreed?"

"Agreed," Linda said.

He looked at Penny. "How about you?"

"I... I...," Penny looked around her and sighed, "I'm good with whatever Linda decides".

CHAPTER 33

The young man hit redial. The boss was not going to like this.
"What now!"

He winced. "The Brown house was trashed last night."

"And I care because?"

"It could indefinitely halt all work on the polymer."

"Surely someone else is capable of testing the polymer."

"Only one other person has worked on the polymer, Sir and
she hasn't allowed him to help since her father died."

"Either get her to let him test the polymer or test it yourself. I
did not hire you to give me excuses. I hired you to get results."

"Yes, Sir."

"The next time I hear from you, it had better be good news."

"Yes, Sir."

"Get rid of that phone as soon as you hang up. I will send you
a new one through the regular channels."

The phone went dead. The young man gently put the phone
on the table. How had everything gone so wrong? This really should
have been a cut and dried job. He grunted. It had been until
Scranton showed up.

If the boss wanted to point the finger at someone, he needed
to point it at himself. He's the one who brought Scranton into the
mix. If Scranton hadn't acted like an idiot and let himself get caught,
the Ghostman wouldn't have been brought into it. And if the
Ghostman hadn't been brought into it, things could have gone on
and on forever just like they had been: one boring day after another.
This current mess wasn't his fault and he wasn't about to take the
blame for it.

He looked down at the phone. Everything within him stilled.
The boss had said he would send another one through regular
channels. He had gotten *this* phone from Victor right before he died.
As far as he knew, there were no other regular channels.

He shook his head at his stupidity. It wouldn't do any good to hit redial. The boss would have destroyed his phone as soon as they hung up. He had just been very...neatly...fired.

He slowly rolled his hands into a fist. After all this time. After all his effort. After all the demeaning, petty work he had put up with! Day after day of STUPID BORING PEOPLE! The boss had the nerve to fire *him*?

Reaching out, he knocked the phone off the table. It slid across the floor and hit the wall with a very satisfying thump. He cocked his head. The boss *had* said to get rid of it. He walked over and with his toe, pulled the phone away from the wall. He stood on it and twisted it back and forth...nothing. Kind of like the dead-end job he had been working at Cy-Rac: still there but totally useless now.

Picking the phone up, he threw it at the wall. It hit and then bounced across the floor. Walking over, he picked it up and looked it over...nothing. Kind of like his life at the moment: full of nothing.

He stilled. The boss was a very powerful man and could black-list him. If that happened, he would *never* get this kind of work again.

He shuddered. Just the thought of having to actually *work* at a place like Cy-Rac for the rest of his life... He started violently shaking his head. No... No... NO! He couldn't let that happen. Wouldn't let that happen. Raising his hand, he slammed the phone face down on the table repeatedly until he smashed his finger between the table and the phone. When he jerked back his hand to throw the phone at the far wall, a single sheet of white paper slid off the table and gently floated to the floor.

Dropping the phone, he picked up the paper. Slowly, a smile spread across his face. He was fired. He laid the paper on the table, took out his knife and cut a small sliver off the page. He was free. Now, he could revenge the death of his brother. With great care, he cut the page into small pieces until only one word remained: Ghostman.

The young man flipped his knife and went into a fighting stance. He weaved back and forth slicing the air. He could see the knife plunging into Ghostman's heart. Could feel the rush of blood flowing over his hand as he twisted the blade deeper. Could see the shock on Ghostman's face the split second he realized he was dying.

He drove the tip of his knife into the small piece of paper and twisted it around and around until it was shredded. A low rumble started in the depths of his chest then he threw back his head and laughed. The day had finally come.

He stilled. That would be very satisfying but would it be enough? No. He shook his head. No, no. The Ghostman had to suffer before he died. He tapped his finger against his cheek and then slowly smiled. Linda Brown must die first.

*****

The man sighed and pinched the bridge of his nose. Life had *definitely* gotten more complicated since Victor's death. Even though he hadn't admitted trashing the Brown's house, Valdez had done it. And by doing so, he had crossed the line. The idiot had stirred up a hornet's nest by going after Linda Brown.

He knew about Ghostman's connection to Valdez's family. But it was Ghostman's connection to Linda Brown he was concerned with. He only knew the Ghostman by reputation but if he had to choose between Valdez and Ghostman, his money would be on Ghostman.

He sighed. Because Valdez couldn't control his desire for revenge, one of the government agencies would step in. Cy-Rac was a priority company on the Homeland Security list and this had been a deliberate act against Cy-Rac's Head of Research.

He leaned back in his chair and looked out across the ocean. He had put a lot of money and effort into this particular project but it was obviously time to cut his losses. Standing up, he threw the phone as hard as he could and watched as it splashed into the ocean.

Now, to get rid of his one loose end. He studied the prepaid phones lined up in his briefcase. Who did he want to be now? Günter Rutgers? Oliver Wendell? Chavez Arro? Beauregard Hampton III? He smiled. Being a 3rd sounded very refined. He picked up the phone and punched in a number.

"State your business."

"New name; new game."

"What can I do for you?"

"I need a package delivered."

"Name and address."

He supplied both.

"Conformation in the usual manner?"

"Yes."

"The package will be delivered upon receipt of the shipping and handling fee."

He punched the number into the phone. When it connected, he moved the required money into the secure offshore account. He picked up his juice and looked out across the serene waters. Now, what account was he going to charge this expense to?

CHAPTER 34

Linda watched as Darrel nodded and Detective Acres got in his car. Detective Acres had wanted to talk to Darrel privately. She snorted. Much as she loved that man, she wasn't about to stand around... Much as she loved that man? Linda sighed deep within herself. She did; there was no denying it. She was totally, irrevocably in love with Darrel Foss.

She loved everything about him. He was gentle but there was an undeniable strength surrounding him. He was good at taking charge and backing off when he needed to. He had walked into her life and without hesitation, plunged himself into the middle of it. He treated her like she was the most precious woman in the world. She had come to respect his opinion and couldn't imagine her life without him.

"I knew you'd be waiting."

Linda jumped. "You have got to quit sneaking up on me."

Darrel looked around. "You watched me all the way from the car. I wouldn't exactly call that sneaking."

She could feel the heat rising in her face. "Uh, my mind was elsewhere."

"That's understandable."

She waved towards the road. "So, are you going to tell me what that was about?"

"Detective Acres expects the FBI or NSA to take over this investigation by Monday or Tuesday," Darrel said.

"Why?" Linda asked.

"Because Cy-Rac is a high profile company and the polymer has military applications..."

"Everybody keeps acting like the polymer is the next big military weapon." Linda threw her hands up. "It's just a polymer."

"Doesn't Kevlar use a polymer in its makeup?" Jason asked.

Linda jumped at the sound of Jason's voice. She cut her eyes at him. "Yes, Kevlar does use a polymer in its makeup but so do most things."

"Still, think about how Kevlar changed the face of war on foreign soil and here in the city streets." Jason paused, "Linda, were you aware the military was interested in the polymer?"

Linda frowned. "Not really."

"I find that odd since you are Head of Research and took over your father's work. Shouldn't that information come with the territory?"

Linda nodded, "It should and to be truthful, it probably did but I haven't read all of Dad's notes on the polymer..." She took a deep breath. "Since his death, I have solely focused on the formula."

"Why is that?" Jason asked.

"I DON'T KNOW!" Linda put her hand over her mouth. She looked at Jason. "I'm sorry. But I really don't know and it's so frustrating. All I know is that I have to protect the polymer at all cost."

Darrel put his arm around Linda and pulled her close. "It's okay. We'll figure it out. Why don't we go inside and decide on a course of action."

"No." Penny started shaking her head.

"No?" Darrel asked.

"I can't... I don't think... No."

"I'm with Penny. Since we are going to have to live somewhere else while the house is being repaired, I say we just walk away. We could go to a hotel."

"A hotel would be a logistic nightmare," Jason said.

"I agree," Darrel answered.

"I'd rather not stay in a hotel. I don't mean to make a lot of trouble but redoing the house could take a while. I would rather not spend the next month or so living out of a suitcase," Penny said. "Plus, Teddy is coming home tonight. A hotel suite for the three of us could get expensive. Do you think we could find a house to rent on a month by month basis?"

Darrel turned and looked behind him and then looked at Jason.

Jason nodded. "That would work. It's definitely close. We'd be able to keep an eye on the place and the ladies at the same time."

Darrel smiled. "It would make moving a lot easier."

"What would make moving easier?" Linda asked.

Darrel pulled out his phone and punched in the number of the realtor listed on the sign. "Hello, I am calling in regards to the house at 1619 Elmwood in the Briarwood Addition. I would like to put a non-refundable retainer on the house under the condition that we can move in right away."

"What..." Linda said.

"I realize that but this is an unusual circumstance. Yes, I understand. Would twenty thousand be sufficient?"

"Wait!" Linda said. "I don't have twenty thousand dollars for a non-refundable retainer."

"No Ma'am, I meant *right* away," Darrel said. "Bring the key right now and I will have a check waiting for you."

Linda grabbed Darrel's arm. "What are you doing? I don't have that kind of money."

"Thank you. I will be waiting." Darrel shut the phone.

"What—did—you—just—do? I told you I don't have the money for that," Linda said.

"That's okay. I do," Darrel said.

"W*hat*?" Linda asked.

"We need a place. I have the money. You can be here to oversee the repairs on the house. Since we'll be right here, we can keep watch over you and the house." Darrel shrugged. "Everybody wins."

"That is not the point," Linda said. "I thought we agreed that Penny and I were going to be in on *all* the decisions from now on."

"This really wasn't *that* much of a decision," Darrel said.

"Darrel, you just put a twenty thousand dollar non-refundable retainer on a house you don't intend to buy." Linda crossed her arms. "I would say that's a pretty big decision."

Darrel looked at Linda. She had just called him Darrel instead of Mr. Foss and he liked the way it sounded.

"Well?" Linda asked.

"Uh...," Darrel saw a bright red sedan coming their way, "...that is probably the realtor. I had better write that check." He turned and headed for his car.

"Wait, we haven't finished discussing this." Linda said. She followed Darrel to his car. By the time she got there, the realtor was standing beside Darrel with the keys to the house. When he ripped the check out of the checkbook, she grabbed his arm. "Don't do this until we talk about it."

Darrel looked at the realtor. "Excuse us."

The realtor nodded.

Darrel took Linda's arm and moved off a few feet. "Let me do this. Honestly, I have the money. The house is in good shape and it is in a good neighborhood. I've never invested in residential property before but I'm fairly sure this is a safe investment. If nothing else, I should be able to get my money back."

Linda crossed her arms. "You mean to tell me that you have twenty thousand dollars just lying around in case you come across something to invest in?"

Darrel laughed. "No, not just lying around. This particular twenty thousand has been in a CD earning interest for the last two years. But yes, I do keep money 'lying around' so I can invest it when the opportunity arises."

"Really." Linda looked at him and then gave his car a pointed look. "You don't look like you have that kind of money."

Darrel felt a twinge of irritation and something else deep within his heart. He had thought she was one of those rare people that didn't judge a person by how expensive their stuff was. Crossing his arms, he asked "What is 'that kind of money' supposed to look like?"

Linda shrugged. "Most people..."

"I am NOT most people. Nor will I ever be." Darrel held up his hand when Linda started to speak. "Later. Right now we have to get you and Penny settled."

"Uh, wait!" Linda called but Darrel didn't stop. "What in the world?"

"I think your assumptions are showing."

Linda whirled around. "What?"

"Your assumptions; they're showing," Penny said.

"What are you talking about?" Linda asked.

"Lin, just because Darrel doesn't wear Armani suits and drive a BMW doesn't mean he doesn't have money. He doesn't strike me as the kind of guy that cares about things. He seems more into people and helping them."

"I know that," Linda said.

"But you just told him that he couldn't possibly have money because of how he looks and what he drives."

"What?" Linda said. "No, I didn't. I said..." Linda stopped. "I did, didn't I?"

"Yes, and from the look on his face, it hurt."

"Oh no." A tear spilled onto Linda's check. She brushed it away but two more quickly followed and then two more.

Penny wrapped her arms around Linda. "We'll get it straightened out. Right now let's just go with what the guys want to do, okay?"

Linda nodded.

Penny looked at their house and sighed. "I say we go back in the house, bawl our eyes out and get that over with."

*****

Darrel saw the first tear slip from Linda's eye and it took all he had to stand still. By the time his ladies started for the house, he was shaking from the effort. When they walked in the front door, he fell back against the car. Everything in him wanted to go to them, enfold them, shelter them...her from this whole sorry mess. But he wouldn't. Linda had given him the perfect opening to quietly withdraw from their lives. He had to take it.

He closed his eyes. He had just been deceiving himself when he had thought there was a chance, however slight, he could fit into Linda's life. She had always been out of his reach. And that whole God thing put a huge gulf between them. He would stay in the background until this whole mess was over. Then, he would take the duffle bag option.

Darrel sighed. For some reason that no longer sounded appealing. The thought of leaving...starting all over again in a new job...meeting new people... He shook his head. He *had* to leave. Out of sight—out of mind, right? He grunted. He could go to the ends of the earth and Linda Brown would never be out of his mind.

He looked toward the house and saw Jason headed his way. Shaking himself, he stood. They had things to do. He pulled out his phone and punched in a number. "Gino."

CHAPTER 35

Linda watched as Darrel and Gino took the last mattress across the yard. With two phone calls, Darrel had bought a house and moved all their belongings—the ones that were left—into it. He had directed the workers, helped move things, hung sheets for curtains, checked the locks on every window and door. He had been everywhere but in her immediate vicinity. It was amazing how he managed to avoid her even when she was doing her best to bump into him.

"Ms. Brown?"

Linda jumped.

"Sorry," Jason said. "We have all the heavy stuff moved so Gino is sending his guys home. Will you and Penny make a last sweep of the house and make sure we didn't miss anything?"

Linda nodded and started in the house. She stopped. "It's almost noon. I hate to send those guys away hungry."

"It's okay. They are eager to get home. Besides, they will be generously compensated."

Linda glanced across the yard and saw Darrel shake one man's hand and give him an envelope. "Make sure they know how much we appreciate their help."

"I will." Jason saluted and walked off.

"I can't believe they got everything moved so quickly," Penny said. "Those men certainly know how to get things done."

"Yes, he does."

Penny smiled. "What's he doing?"

"Paying them." Linda crossed her arms. "Something I should be doing. They *have* been working for us."

"Don't you dare. This is his 'ops'..." Penny sighed. "Can you believe our life has become an 'ops'?"

"No. And things aren't going to get better any time soon." Linda groaned. "Pen, I don't know how to fix the polymer."

Penny wrapped her arms around Linda. "Let's ask God for the wisdom."

"I have been."

"Then its time you asked for help. Why don't you talk to that Wade guy first thing tomorrow?"

"I guess I'm going to have to."

"Is there anything else?"

Linda and Penny jumped at the question. Linda whirled around. "You have *got* to quit sneaking up on us."

"Hey," Jason grinned. "I made a lot of noise when I came in the kitchen door. Are you through?"

Linda sighed. "We haven't even started."

"Started what?" Penny asked.

"Making sure everything we need is moved," Linda said.

"If it's not moved by now, it can wait. Besides we're right next door. If we've forgotten something, we can come get it."

"True," Jason said. "But let one of us know first. We are going to set up a few booby-traps around the house—just in case. If you ladies will step outside, I'll get started.

Linda nodded and walked out. She stopped at the edge of the yard and stared at their new home.

"You can't keep avoiding him," Penny said.

"I'm not avoiding him; he's avoiding me."

"Then ambush him."

"I've already tried several times." Linda crossed her arms. "He is very adept at evasion."

Penny laughed. "We'll think of something. Let's get settled in."

*****

Darrel watched as Linda and Penny crossed the yard. Maybe moving them into the house next door wasn't the best idea. He rubbed the back of his neck. Occupying the same house with Linda Brown was not going to be easy. This thing could end tomorrow or it could drag on for days.

When he heard the front door open, he quickly stepped out the back. It wouldn't hurt to see if Jason needed help. He stopped. Who was he trying to kid? Jason didn't need help. He started to open the door to go back inside and stopped. Shaking his head, he walked toward the back fence. Stopping just out of sight of the kitchen, he sat down and rested his head in his hands.

Weariness stole over him. The last few days were beginning to catch up with him. Trying to avoid Linda wasn't helping. Raising his head, he looked toward the house and smiled. She was good. Not as good as him, but good. It had taken some fancy footwork to evade a couple of her attempts to corner him. Something he couldn't let happen. If he ever once looked into those eyes...he shook his head.

"What are you doing back here?"

Darrel jerked.

Jason laughed. "You've got it bad."

"What?"

"For as long as I've known you, I have never been able to sneak up on you. This is the third time today."

Darrel grunted. "Maybe I'm getting old."

"N-o-o. Your mind is somewhere else." Jason smiled. "Right now, I would bet it is trying to find an excuse not to go back into that house."

Darrel stood. "Since this has turned into a 24/7 protection detail, we are going to need help. I need sleep and so do you. I don't want anyone to get past us because we're tired."

Jason crossed his arms and cocked an eyebrow. "I'll let you slide this time but you can't avoid this discussion indefinitely. At some point you are going to have to face what happened."

"We need to concentrate on the mission."

"Okay. What do you want to do?"

"I'm hungry, I need sleep and I need to get some things from my place. I'm leaving to take care of all that. You are the one who knows people. Get help."

"How many?"

"One bodyguard for each family member 24/7."

"Okay. Any special request?"

"I trust your judgment." Darrel started walking toward the front of the house, stopped and turned around. "Erik Vaughn is in town."

Jason whistled.

"Precisely. We can call him in, if it comes to that." Darrel turned to go.

"You're not saying goodbye to the ladies?"

Darrel kept walking. "I'll leave that to you."

"Chicken."

Darrel looked over his shoulder and smiled. "Bwak, bwak."

*****

Linda watched as Darrel got into his car and drove off. "See what I mean?"

"He'll be back," Penny said. "We'll get him then."

"We?"

"Of course. I'll get him talking and you can sneak up from behind."

The door opened and Jason walked in. "Are you ladies settled in?"

"In, yes; settled, no." Linda crossed her arms. "What now?"

"First we set a few ground rules. From now on, neither of you ladies answers the door; period, no argument. I prefer you don't answer your phones, either. We are bringing in help so you will have someone with you at all times. You are never to leave the house without your bodyguard even if you are just going across the yard. Stay away from the windows, eat and shop at places you always frequent and where you know the people..."

"In short," Linda said, "clear everything we do outside this house with you first."

Jason grinned. "I knew you were a smart lady."

Linda rolled her eyes. "Okay, so what *now*?"

Jason shrugged. "You hungry? I'm hungry. Order lunch. That Chinese we had was good." He smiled. "I have some calls to make so when the food gets here, let me know and I'll get the door.

CHAPTER 36

Darrel pulled in the driveway and turned off the car. He looked at the food sitting on the seat beside him and back at the house. He should have called first. It was 6:30 pm; they had probably already eaten. He hunched his shoulders. Four hours sleep on his couch had helped but he still felt... He didn't know exactly how he felt. Well, that wasn't true either. The woman was driving him crazy. She dogged his every step and *refused* to leave his mind.

He shook his head and looked at the house. Not only was he mixed up in the life of a beautiful woman, he was a home owner. Never in a million years would he have imagined that. The odd thing was, it felt right pulling up in the driveway with supper. He sighed and pulled out his cellphone. "I'm here and coming in."

"Roger that."

Darrel scooped the packages off the car seat and headed across the yard. He knocked on the door three times. When it opened, he stepped in the door and then to the right. The door shut and he heard the bolt slide home.

"The man of the house with supper."

Darrel turned and saw Linda standing at the base of the stairs. Arms crossed, head tilted to one side with one eyebrow raised. Darrel smiled. She was good.

"Here, I'll help with that." Linda took the sack out of his hand and walked towards the kitchen.

"You can't avoid her forever." Jason said. "*That* woman will tie you to a chair if she has to. Face her and get it over with."

"Do I smell croissants?"

"Saved by the bell," Jason whispered.

Darrel laughed. "Yes, and I suggest we join Linda before she eats them all."

"I heard that."

Darrel walked into the kitchen and sat the rest of the food on the counter. Linda was setting out paper plates so he began to pull food out of the boxes.

"So, what culinary delights do you have for us tonight?" Penny asked.

"Penne pasta with spinach alfredo sauce and grilled garlic chicken. Three cheese lasagna with Italian sausage. And..." Darrel pulled the last container out. "...tiramisu."

Penny sighed deeply. "A man after my own heart. Point eight, your favor."

Linda took the tiramisu from Darrel. "I'll put this in the fridge to stay cool while we eat."

"Where are we going to eat?" Penny asked.

Darrel smiled. "I stopped and bought a few things; one of which was a card table and chairs."

"I'll get them," Jason said. "Give me your keys."

"I'll help," Penny said.

"I can get it my..."

Linda held up her hand. "No you don't, Mister. You're going to stay right here and help me."

Jason snatched the keys out of Darrel's hand and he and Penny headed for the front door.

Darrel crossed his arms. "I don't think I've ever been so neatly outmaneuvered."

"That was good, wasn't it?" Linda grinned. "Look, I'm just going to get to the point. I didn't mean to be rude or snobbish this morning. And I certainly didn't mean to imply that you were beneath us because of what you drive or how you dress. It's just that..." Linda paused. How did she say what she needed to say without saying too much?

"What?"

Linda closed her eyes. Father, help me say the right thing. Looking at Darrel, she waved her hand at the room. "It's just that I know this isn't your kind of thing."

"My kind of thing?"

She sighed. Darrel still had his arms crossed and his tone of voice was skeptical at best. She took a deep breath and rushed on. "I just didn't want you to be stuck here because you used all your money to help us."

*****

Darrel felt the band that had been squeezing his heart expand. He took a deep breath and let his arms fall to his side. Linda kept shifting from foot to foot like she was standing on coals. There was no doubt she was sincere. He ducked his head to hide a smile.

"So? Am I forgiven?"

Darrel looked up and bowed slightly. "How could I not forgive such a beautiful lady?"

Linda crossed her arms. "That's not really an answer."

"It's good enough for me." Penny walked into the kitchen with Jason close behind. "Let's eat."

"I agree," Jason said.

The men sat up the table and chairs while the ladies got the paper plates, plastic forks, spoons, knives and cups.

After they sat down, Linda held out her hands. "My turn to pray. Father, thank You," her voice cracked, "for keeping us through last night and being with us today."

Darrel raised his head and looked at Linda.

"I am so glad You were there for us to lean on; to look to. Thank You for a good place to stay. Thank You for good friends who are willing to stand with us during this troubled time. I know You will show us what to do and when to do it. Thank You for the food and friendship we will enjoy around this table. Bless this food in the lovely name of Jesus. Amen."

Darrel leaned back in his chair. How, after everything that had happened, could Linda still mean the things she had just said? And she *had* meant them.

He started to pick up the lasagna when headlights moved across the window. Someone was pulling into the Brown's driveway. Jason got up and eased out the back door.

"Ladies," Darrel stood and pulled his knife out. He heard a gasp. "I need you to get in the pantry now."

"What?"

"Linda, just this once, don't question; just go." Darrel waited until Linda and Penny got into the pantry. He leaned down and quickly kissed Linda. "I'll be back." He stepped back and shut the door.

He stepped out the back door and eased up the side of the house. He was about to round the corner when he heard a thud and then a siren started blaring near his ear. The front door was open so he eased in and almost fell over a body.

Jason slid in from the kitchen. "Anyone we know?"

"Can't tell. Shut that siren off and get the lights." When the lights came on, Darrel rolled the young man over. His eyes jerked open and drifted shut. Darrel sighed. At least the kid was breathing. The fall probably knocked the wind out of him.

Darrel heard a noise behind him and twisted around. Linda was standing behind him with her hand over her heart and Penny was right behind her. Reaching out, he jerked her into the house and hissed at Penny to come in.

"I thought I told you to stay put."

"You did, but I remembered..."

A low moan came from the person on the floor. Linda looked around Darrel. "Teddy!" She knelt down beside him and gently shook him. "Teddy. Are you okay?"

Teddy opened his eyes. "What—just—happened?"

"You ran into one of Jason's booby-traps."

"Booby-traps?"

Jason walked back into the room. "No one else outside." Pointing, he asked, "who's this?"

Darrel grunted. "Little brother."

Jason nodded. "I suggest you get him to the other house. I'll redo our early warning system.

Darrel nodded and held out his hand to Teddy. "Can you stand up?" Teddy took his hand so Darrel pulled him up. The boy swayed as he stood, so Darrel got under his arm and half carrying him, took him over to the other house. He eased Teddy into one of the chairs. The boy took a deep breath and looked up.

"What is going on and why is everybody in the Benson's house?" Teddy looked at Darrel, "And who are you?"

CHAPTER 37

Teddy shook his head. "You're kidding, right?"

"I wish we were." Linda sighed. "I *wish* I had told you to stay with the Steinberg's for a few more days."

"It's better he's here where we can keep an eye on him," Darrel said

There was a knock on the back door. "Coming in."

"Come on."

Jason eased in the back door. "Everything's moved and reset." He moved in front of Teddy. "You okay?"

"Yeah," Teddy answered. "What are we going to do now?"

Jason got a crate and pulled it up to the table. "I'm going to eat."

Penny waved at Darrel. "What is it with you two and food?"

Jason grinned. "When you've done the kind of work we have, you never know when your next meal will be so you don't pass up food." He spooned some lasagna onto his plate. "Besides, it helps to keep things as normal as possible."

Linda put some penne pasta on her plate. "I know I keep asking this but *what* are we going to do about our situation?"

Darrel pulled out his phone and punched in a number.

"It's Sunday afternoon," Karen said.

"I know. Come in early tomorrow and pull all the files for Dr. Garth Brown and..." Darrel looked at Linda. "What is the polymer project called?"

"142POY," Linda said.

"...142POY". If you need higher clearance to get some of the files, call and we'll see what we can do." Darrel heard a big sigh on the line.

"You know I will have to come in *extremely* early to have all that done before you get there."

"Yes and I know I'm going to owe you big time."

Karen laughed. "Don't think I won't collect, either."

Darrel put up the phone. "That's a start."

Linda cocked her head. "Was that an arbitrary decision you just made?"

"I... Uh... Yes."

Linda shook her head. "I thought so."

"Hey, old habits are hard to break"

Linda raised an eyebrow. "Try harder. Who were you talking to?"

"Karen, my secretary."

"Why are you pulling *all* the files on Dad?"

"Because Jason asked a couple of valid questions this morning: Was your father being followed or harassed in any way?" Darrel paused. "And was the plane crash an accident."

Linda gasped. "You don't think the plane crash was an accident?"

"I don't know," Darrel said. "It's worth checking out."

Linda set down her fork, her appetite gone. "So you're saying these things could have been happening for a long time now."

"Yes."

"Why have they suddenly become so..." Linda searched for a word, "...obvious?"

"That is the real question. What has pushed these people to step up their timetable? Those files might answer that. Detective Acres wants to start at the beginning anyway and review everything we know."

"What do we know?" Penny asked.

"Well," Jason held up his fingers, "One; we know the military is interested in the polymer which could mean big bucks on the black market. "Two; your father died while working on the polymer..." He looked at Darrel and raised an eyebrow. "...but we don't know yet it if was an accident or not."

Darrel crossed his arms. "In my defense, I have only been aware of this for four days, now."

Jason continued. "Three; a man that was following Linda is now dead. Four; there is a new player who we suspect killed the first man and trashed the house."

"That's not much," Penny said.

Jason shrugged. "We've worked with less."

"A lot less," Darrel said. "Look, we could sit here and rehash everything but that is counter-productive. Linda and I have a long day ahead of us tomorrow. I vote we make it an early night.

Teddy stretched and yawned. "I could definitely use some sleep. All that fresh sea air..."

"You mean staying up all night every night," Linda said

Teddy grinned. "That, too."

"First," Jason said "Darrel will be with Linda all day so she is covered. Penny and Teddy, what are your plans for tomorrow?"

Penny looked around the room. "I will be cleaning. Probably all day.

"I have to register for classes tomorrow." Teddy shrugged.

"Okay. I have a man coming at 8:00 am. Will that be early enough, Teddy?"

"A man coming?"

Penny raised her hand. "He wasn't here when we discussed the bodyguards."

"Right." Jason said. "Each of you will have a bodyguard 24/7 until this problem is solved."

"Will he have the suit and sunglasses?" Teddy asked. "That would be awesome."

Linda laughed. "Trust you to focus on the important things."

"Hey, if I have to have one, I might as well be styling."

Jason laughed. "Will eight be early enough?"

"Sure. Registration starts at eight but I don't have to be there right then."

Darrel stood. "Now that that's settled, I suggest we get some sleep."

*****

In the shadows, the young man pushed his knife deeper into the ground. The movements inside the house were easily discernable through the sheet curtains. They looked like one big happy family. It was enough to make a guy puke.

He looked at the house next door. Because the kid had set off the alarm, the new guy had repositioned them all. He shrugged. Not that it really mattered. Although trashing the house had been fun, it was time to end this. Tomorrow, Linda dies.

CHAPTER 38

"Everybody settled?" Darrel asked.

"Yes."

"Good. Go to bed. I'll take the first watch."

"Actually," Jason rolled his shoulders, "I thought we could do some catching up. Want a cup of tea?"

"Hot tea?"

"Yeah, I picked up the habit when I was stationed in Japan. Tea can be soothing. And it doesn't leave you jittery and unable to focus."

Darrel grunted. "I could use some of that."

"What?"

"Focus. I seem to be lacking that right now."

"That's understandable. When someone you love is in a situation like this, it's extremely hard to set that aside and focus on the mission."

"That has no bearing on this case."

Jason put his hand on Darrel's shoulder. "Please. Anyone can see how you and Linda feel about one another."

Darrel shrugged Jason's hand off. "Nothing can come of it."

"Man, love like that doesn't come around very often."

"I know that but...," Darrel shook his head, "...I won't do that to any woman, especially not Linda."

"What do you mean?"

"Saddle them with all my baggage."

Jason shook his head. "Don't throw away the life you could have with Linda because you refuse to forgive yourself."

"Forgive myself. You have got to be joking." Darrel balled his hand into a fist.

"Darrel, what happened that day was an accident. Something totally beyond your control. Valdez's family wasn't supposed to be at the compound. You had no way of knowing they were there much less that his son would jump into his arms at the exact moment you took the shot.

Darrel sat down. "With my mind I know that but here...," he hit his chest, "...here that knowledge doesn't make any difference. I KILLED a kid! How," Darrel's voice broke, "can I forgive that?"

"By accepting forgiveness yourself. It's the only way. Believe me, I know. "

Darrel looked up. "What do you mean?"

Jason sat down. "You know what I was like. How I lived. What I did. We both know I was not an angel."

Darrel grunted. "*That's* an understatement."

"I've done my share of things I'm not proud off. Things no one knows but me." Jason sighed. "Not long after you mustered out, I hit rock bottom. Everything in my life was spinning out of control. I spent most of my free time passed out drunk. I lost my fiancé. Pushed away all my friends. I even considered suicide."

Jason stopped and ran his hands across his face. "Sorry, I get sappy when I remember what God delivered me from."

Darrel paused. Jason was one of the toughest men he had ever known. For him to get sappy, God must have done a lot. "I can tell you've changed."

Jason smiled. "Change is a mild word for what happened to me. God will do the same for you. All you have to do is accept the gift of his son, Jesus."

Darrel started shaking his head. "That won't work for me."

"Why?"

"*Because*, I've done too much."

"No, you haven't."

Darrel jumped up. "How do *you* know?"

"Would you like to have the kind of relationship with God that Linda has?"

"What's that got to do with anything?"

"Answer the question."

Darrel rubbed his neck. "Yes."

"That is the Father drawing you to Jesus."

"What?"

"The Bible says that no man can come to Jesus except the Father draws him.2 That longing in your heart for a relationship with God is that drawing. If you are being drawn to God, it's not too late."

"The Bible says we are not supposed to kill."

"It actually says not to murder. If it meant not to kill anyone, then God himself broke that commandment when he ordered his people to go into the promised land and fight for it. In our line of business, we occasionally have to hurt people but we don't kill them unless it becomes absolutely necessary."

Darrel crossed his arms. "Jason, I intentionally murdered people."

"So did the Apostle Paul. And King David."

"What are you talking about?"

"David had sex with Bathsheba while her husband, Uriah, was away fighting and got her pregnant.3"

Darrel shook his head. "I've seen that happen to good men."

"Uriah was one of those good men. First, David tried to cover it up by bringing Uriah home but he refused to sleep with his wife in the safety of their home when his fellow brothers were still fighting. So David had Uriah sent to the front lines with the command that everyone fall back and leave him exposed and without backup. Of course, Uriah died."

"Wasn't David a great warrior himself?"

"Yes."

"You don't do that to a brother."

"You do if you are only thinking about yourself. David took Bathsheba as his wife and thought everything was fine until God called his hand on it.4 Psalms 51 is where David repented for what he had done."

Jason pulled his Bible out of his backpack and turned to Psalms 51. "Verse fourteen says 'deliver me from bloodguiltiness, O God, thou God of my salvation: and my tongue shall sing aloud of thy righteousness'. Jesus did that for me. When He shed His blood, He delivered me from guilt of the blood I had shed. I just had to accept it."

"Didn't God call David 'a man after His heart'?" Darrel asked.

"Yes, but it didn't give him special privileges. If he had not repented of this sin, it is possible that the title would have gone to some else."

"Still, that was one time. I've assassinated a lot of people."

"So did Paul." Darrel started to speak but Jason held up his hand. "Let me finish. Paul's name was Saul before he became a Christian.

He was a young ambitious member of the Pharisees[5], one of the governing bodies of the Jews at that time. He was willing and eager to do whatever it took to rise in their ranks. He took the job of rounding up Christians and throwing them in prison. He thought he was doing God's work.[6]"

"I don't see the relevance."

"These were the same Christians that were skewered on stakes and burnt alive; killed by animals in the coliseum. Saul knew he was sentencing them to death when he arrested them."

"Then one day, Jesus called his hand on it and gave him a choice. At least the choice is implied. He could either join Jesus' side or have Jesus fight against him." Jason smiled. "Saul chose Jesus and millions of lives have been changed by that choice.[7]"

"Still..."

"Darrel, sin is sin. There are no big or little sins with God.[8] There are some that carry harsher consequences[9] but they are all sin and everybody has sinned[10]. All sins were judged, paid for and forgiven when Jesus became sin and died on the cross.[11] Our part is to accept it.[12]" Jason put his hand on Darrel's shoulder. "I accepted it and the heaviness I had been carrying lifted off of me. Through accepting forgiveness from Jesus, I learned how to forgive myself."

Darrel covered his face with his hands. "If only it was that simple."

"It *is* that simple. You want a close relationship with God. He wants one with you and gave you that option through His son, Jesus. You just have to believe it and receive it."

"How do I do that?"

"The Bible says 'if you confess the Lord Jesus and believe in your heart that God raised him from the dead, you will be saved.[13]"

"Are there some special words I need to say, do I kneel or what?"

"Say 'Jesus, I come acknowledging that I am a sinner."

"Jesus, I come acknowledging that I am a sinner," Darrel echoed.

"I accept the price you paid for my sins."

Darrel repeated. "I accept the price you paid for my sins."

"I confess You as Lord."

Darrel's voice broke. "I confess You as Lord."

Jason grabbed Darrel in a bear hug. "Now you really are my brother."

*****

"Amen." Linda whispered. She hadn't meant to eavesdrop on their conversation but she was glad she had. She swiped at the tears running down her face but they just kept coming. Softly, she eased back around the corner to her bedroom. She knelt beside her bed, tears still dripping down her face. "Father, You are so good."

CHAPTER 39

Darrel shook Jason awake. "It's time."

Jason stretched. "That..."

A scream rent the air.

Jason jumped up. "Go."

Darrel sprinted up the stairs and into Linda's room. She was fighting the covers. "Linda." Darrel moved closer to the bed. "Linda!"

She stilled. "I won't let them, Daddy."

Penny came in the door, "Lin?"

Darrel put his finger to his mouth. Moving closer he whispered, "Let them what?"

"Take the formula."

Darrel hissed. Obsession explained. Teddy stumbled in the door and Darrel motioned for him to be quiet.

Linda whimpered. "Don't go. Daddy, don't go-o-o!"

Darrel touched her shoulder. When she didn't swing at him, he gently shook her. "Linda, wake up!"

Sitting down on the edge of the bed, Darrel pulled Linda into his arms. "Wake up."

Linda sighed and snuggled deeper into his arms.

For one second he hugged her closer then he shook her a little harder. "Honey, wake up."

As Linda slowly opened her eyes, the memories returned with a rush. The crash, the rending metal and the sudden silence. She buried her face in Darrel's shoulder. "He was alive."

"What?"

"Daddy was still alive after the plane crashed."

Looking at Penny and Teddy, Darrel asked, "Did you know that?"

"No," Penny wiped at the tears on her face. "Well, not for sure. Daddy was..." She choked up.

Teddy put his arm around Penny. "When the plane crashed, the passenger side was lodged in the tree. It was so crumpled, it took several hours to cut Linda out. Dad's side...," he paused, "...fell taking the fuselage with it. They said it exploded on impact. Dad's body was burned beyond recognition."

Linda started sobbing and Darrel pulled her closer.

"Linda didn't know?"

Teddy sighed. "When she woke up in the hospital, she didn't remember anything. Not even that Dad was dead."

"I remember now."

Darrel sighed and sat her away from him. "I know this will be hard but we need to discuss this. You okay with that?"

Linda nodded.

Darrel stood and held out his hand. Linda took it and he pulled her up.

"I vote we go downstairs and have some tea while we talk."

*****

Linda took the cup of tea and sat it on the table. "Thanks."

"Are you ready?" Jason asked.

Linda reached under the table and took Darrel's hand. "I... Yes," she said and fell silent.

Darrel gently squeezed Linda's hand. "Just start at the beginning and tell us what you remember."

Linda nodded. "I was enjoying the trip because it had been a long time since I had Daddy all to myself. We were talking about...," Linda shrugged, "...stuff. Catching up on our lives. Then that storm came up. Daddy tried to fly below it but the winds were too rough. He tried to get above it..."

Linda paused. "Then out of nowhere, lightning struck almost right in front of my face." She shuddered.

Darrel squeezed her hand.

She took a deep breath. "The engine just...stopped. Then we started falling. Blinded by the lightning, I never saw the trees. Daddy probably didn't see them either..." She shook her head. "He wouldn't have been able to do anything if he had."

With a shaky hand, she took a sip of tea. "When I woke up, the silence was deafening. All I could move was my head and my left arm. There was blood everywhere." She bowed her head.

"Do we need to take a break?" Darrel asked.

Linda looked up. "No. I'm...okay. Daddy was alive, barely. He said Homeland Security approached him about using the polymer to catch a man who has been on their radar for several years. Evidently this guy will steal and sell anything he can. With Cyrus' permission, Daddy agreed to work with them." She sighed. "He told me to talk to Wade, that he would fill me in on everything." She jumped up. "All this time I have been driving myself crazy over this polymer when I could have..."

Darrel reached for her hand and tugged her back into the chair. "That explains a lot."

"It does?" Teddy asked.

"Yes, it does. Now we know why Linda is so obsessed with finishing the polymer."

"Why?" Penny asked.

Darrel smiled. "Linda's scientist subconscious probably figured the best way to protect the polymer was to go public with it. That meant finishing the formula."

Penny nodded. "I can see that."

"Plus," Jason said, "now we know the crash *was* an accident. We also know that Wade is part of the solution and not the problem."

Darrel nodded. "True. We need to talk with him first thing in the morning."

"But why would I not trust him, especially if Daddy said Wade could explain everything."

"Remember when you told me the way he acted didn't fit his persona?"

Linda nodded.

"It's my guess Wade works for Homeland Security and is undercover at the lab. That could explain why he looks one way but acts another. It would also explain why he wasn't offered the Head of Research position." Darrel shrugged. "Of course, this is all just supposition. We won't know for sure until we talk to Wade."

Jason looked at his watch. "I hate to break up the party but it's almost 2:00 am. Everybody finish your tea and go back to bed. I think we are going to get a lot of answers tomorrow."

CHAPTER 40

Wade slammed the receiver down. He didn't care if it cost him his job. It was time to bring this investigation to a screeching halt. He walked up to Linda's office and flung the door open. "Is it true?"

Linda and Darrel both looked up.

Linda had the phone in her hand. "I was just about to call you."

"Was your house broken into?"

"Yes."

Wade turned to Darrel, "Did you find a dead man in your apartment?"

"Yes."

Wade ran his fingers through his hair and it came away sticky. "Uhg! I hate this stuff." He grabbed some tissue and started wiping his hand.

"I wanted to..."

Wade held up his hand. "Let me go first. My name *is* Wade Waters and I work for Homeland Security. Your father was working with us to catch a man called The Broker."

"I know," Linda said.

"You do?"

Linda shrugged. "At least some of it. Daddy told me about it before he died but I only remembered it last night."

Wade crossed his arms. "Do you also know that the polymer was finished before we came on board and we have the data to prove it?"

"No... Daddy didn't say anything about that." Linda's eye narrowed. "Where is the finished formula?"

"You look at it everyday."

"Impossible. That formula won't hold under pressure."

Wade sighed. "Only because I've been sabotaging the tests."

"You what!" Darrel stepped forward. "You're saying that you have been letting this woman work herself to death over a formula that was already finished?"

Wade threw up his hands. "Whoa. I was just following orders."

"That is no excuse!"

Wade looked at Linda. "I agree."

"Why are you telling us this now?" Linda asked.

"Because things have gotten out of hand and we're no closer to catching this guy then we were a year ago. Going public with the polymer should stop anything else from happening to you." Wade laid a CD case on the desk. "This is all the data. If you want further proof, we can run the test again right now. I promise you the polymer will hold."

There was a tentative knock on the door and Casey stuck his head in the door.

Linda smiled. "Good morning, Casey. Do you need something?"

"I couldn't help but overhear. If you are going to test the polymer, I would like to help."

Linda fingered the CD sitting on the desk. "This has everything we need?"

"Everything," Wade said.

"I've done enough testing on this polymer. Let's get this information upstairs." She looked at Casey. "No testing today. Did you need anything else?"

"No, Ma'am." Casey started to turn away. "Wait. I could use some direction on one of Bob Johnson's projects."

Wade smiled. "Casey, that's two sentences without stuttering. Way to go."

Casey's eyes shifted between them. "I-I-I've b-been working on it."

Linda smiled. "Good for you. Give me a few minutes and I'll come over to look at that project with you."

"I can do that," Wade offered.

"No," Linda said. "It's time I started taking care of my department. Besides, after today, you probably won't be here."

Wade laughed. "After today, I might really need this job."

Linda looked at Casey. "Give me thirty minutes?"

Casey nodded and walked off.

Linda slid the disc into her computer. She opened one file after another and looked through them. "This is very thorough."

Wade nodded. "Your father was very meticulous when it came to research. I really enjoyed working with him."

Linda sat back. "And you will confirm that all this data is accurate?"

"I will."

"Let's get this upstairs," Darrel said. "If they do a controlled press release on it today, maybe this Broker will call off his men."

"I'm all for that. Just let me compose a cover letter and I will send it out."

Wade grimaced, "I need to check in with my office in person and let them know what is going on." He paused, "I'd just as soon get it over with if you can spare me."

Linda waved her hand. "Go."

"Thanks. I'll be back."

Darrel chuckled. "There goes a man in deep trouble."

"Why?"

"He has been here all this time without saying anything to you about this investigation. I doubt his superiors gave him the green light to do so today."

"But...," Linda cocked her head. "Oh-h-h."

"Percisely." Darrel's radio squawked. "Go ahead."

"We show a heat source in the men's restroom right outside of the research lab on the seventh floor. Eli is on his way to check it right now."

"A heat source? I haven't heard any alarms."

"It doesn't register as a fire but the heat sensors show the temperature rising in that bathroom."

"Go," Linda said. "I'm going to send this email and then check in with Casey. I'll stay in the lab until you get back."

Darrel rubbed the back of his neck. That feeling was back. "No, my men can take care of it. I'm here until you leave."

Linda clicked the send button. "There, the polymer research is now public." She raised her hand. "I solemnly promise not to leave the research department without you."

"I don't..."

"GO." Linda stood. "I'm going to help Casey."

Darrel sighed as Linda left the office. He clicked the mike on his radio. "Eli, where are you?"

"Passing the sixth floor."

"I'm close. I'll take this."

"Yes, Sir."

*****

Linda rounded the corner but didn't see Casey. "Casey?"

Suddenly a hand clamped over her mouth and a large knife came into view.

"Ms. Brown, don't struggle. Or make a sound. I am going to take my hand away and put a piece of tape over your mouth. If you scream, my hand might jerk and accidently cut your throat. So, don't scream. Okay?"

Linda nodded and Casey put the tape over her mouth.

"Now, you're going to turn around so I can bind your hands. But move very slowly or the knife might slip."

Linda nodded and slowly turned around. He bound her hands and she almost fell when he spun her back around.

"Now, we are going to leave using the service elevator."

Linda stood still until he nicked her cheek with the knife.

"Ms. Brown, we *are* leaving. You can either be all alive or mostly dead. I don't care."

Linda closed her eyes. Father, I need strength. Help me.

"Let's go."

CHAPTER 41

Darrel waited until Linda rounded the corner then he opened the door to the lab. That nagging feeling crawled up the back of his neck again. He turned around and studied the research department. He was missing something.

He clicked the radio, "Eli?"

"Yes, Sir."

"Still on your way up?"

"I'm stepping off the elevator now."

"Good, come ahead and let me know what you find."

"Yes, Sir."

Darrel looked towards the back corner. Wade had said...

"Boss?"

"Go ahead."

"There's a heat lamp pointed at the sensors."

A heat lamp? The only department that used heat lamps was... Darrel started moving. Casey had not even hesitated in his speech until Wade had brought it to his attention. People who stuttered didn't suddenly become better.

Darrel hit his radio mike. "Call the police. Let them know we have a hostage situation."

Rounding the corner, he heard the faint swoosh of elevator doors. He eased past the work station and into a small holding area. The service elevator was going down. He hit the radio mike. "I need to know where the research lab's service elevator stops."

He ran out of the lab to the stairs and started down. God, he thought, I know I'm new at this but please let me get there in time. Keep Linda safe.

The radio squawked. "Parking garage."

"Activate the security measures." Darrel jumped over the railing to the bottom landing. He jerked open the door, ran out into the garage and did a quick 360.

"What took you so long?"

Darrel turned toward the voice and his heart stuttered in his chest. Casey and Linda were standing on the low wall of the garage. There was a knife pressed to Linda's throat and a trickle of blood on her cheek. He took a deep slow breath. If ever he needed focus, it was now.

He started easing toward them. "Casey, don't do this. The polymer is public now and of no use to your boss. It's over."

Casey waved the knife around Linda's face. "The boss quit on this yesterday. This has nothing to do with him or the polymer." He slid the knife up Linda's cheek.

Linda gasped and it was all Darrel could do to keep from lunging toward them.

Casey smiled. "It's all about you."

"Me?" Darrel kept easing forward. "Then let Linda go and we'll settle it like men: face to face."

Casey laughed. "Face to face! You're a top of the ridge, miles away killer." His eyes narrowed. "A coward that dresses up as bushes and hides behind trees to shoot little boys."

"Casey, I don't know what you've heard but..."

"Oh, I haven't heard, Ghostman, I know. *I—am—Ramon—*Val*dez.*"

Darrel suddenly saw the little boy jump into his father's arms. Saw the bullet slice through them both. Saw them drop to the ground. He sighed deep within himself. His past had finally caught up with him and now it threatened Linda. God, he prayed, help me. Show me what to do.

Darrel studied Casey. Anger radiated off the boy in waves. Could he make Casey mad enough to let Linda go and come after him? Risky, very risky but right now it was the only thing he could think of. He took a deep breath and made himself relax. He strolled towards them. "How many men have you killed?"

"What?"

"Men? How many have you killed? One, two," Darrel shrugged, "three?" He sneered. "After all, you *are* just a boy...*Casey.*"

"I told you my name is Ramon."

Darrel stopped in front of them. "Says you. Every record we have says your name is Casey. Casey, the lab *boy.* Labeled discard after use. Your boss thought so." He curled his lip. "*He* dropped you like trash at his feet."

"I am *not* anyone's trash." Casey touched the knife point against Linda's throat and slowly applied pressure. Linda's eyes widened and she tried to pull back but Casey held her tightly. A small drop of blood oozed past the blade tip. "I am the one in control."

Darrel balled his hands into fists. "You think cutting a defenseless woman means you're in control?" Darrel snorted. "It just proves you are a coward."

Casey pointed the knife at Darrel. "*I* am not the one who hides to do my killing."

Darrel rolled his eyes. "Right...who's the one hiding behind a woman?"

Casey roared and brought the knife handle down on the back of Linda's head. She crumpled and he flung her onto the grass below.

Darrel lunged and caught Casey around the thighs. They both went over the wall and hit the ground with a bone jarring thud. Casey brought the knife down but Darrel rolled sideways and it grazed his arm. They stood at the same time.

Casey moved between him and Linda. Darrel desperately wanted to make sure she was okay but it would have to wait. He raised his hands. "Casey, I can not undo what I did but you have to know I never meant to kill the boy."

"The *boy's* name is Phillipe..."

"I never meant to hurt Phillipe. Please, put down the knife. I don't want to fight you."

Casey smiled. "Of course, you don't want to fight me because I'm going to kill you." He pointed at Linda. "But you will see her die first." Casey grabbed a handful of Linda's hair and exposed her neck.

"Wait!"

Casey dropped Linda's head and laughed. "I knew she was the way to get to you. You don't have to worry. I'm not going to kill her...yet. I want the blood spewing from her neck to be the last thing your dying eyes see."

Casey started shifting his knife from hand to hand. "I know you carry a knife. Get it."

Without taking his eyes off Casey, Darrel slid his knife out. He flipped it; blade down, cutting edge out. Casey started moving from side to side and Darrel mimicked his movements. Casey lunged and Darrel easily deflected the blow.

Casey jabbed his knife in quick succession but Darrel deflected each move.

Casey stepped back. "I'm glad."

"Glad?"

"That this won't be over quickly." Casey pointed at his arm. "I am going to enjoy cutting you before I kill you."

Casey moved in with quick, short, slashing motions. A flurry of knife strokes rained down around him but Darrel met them blow for blow. The ring of steel hitting steel was the only sound until a soft moan emanated from behind Casey. Darrel feinted forward then took three quick steps back and moved left.

Casey didn't follow. "Good try." With his foot, he pushed Linda backwards. She rolled the two feet to the street and stopped with a solid thwack. "But not good enough."

Suddenly, Casey pivoted left and lunged. Darrel blocked the blow but Casey's knife slid along his knife's edge and across his arm.

Casey backed off. "Cut two."

Darrel didn't take his eyes off Casey. "Pure luck."

Casey smiled and lunged.

Darrel met him head on deflecting each strike. He felt that old calm rise within him as he zeroed in on the flying blade. The boy *was* good but his rage would be his undoing.

A muffled scream filled the air.

Darrel jerked. Casey lunged. The knife slid into his side before he could dodge it. Pain radiated around his mid section. He eased back.

Casey backed off. "Cut three."

Darrel glanced at Casey's knife. There was blood on two inches of the blade so the wound wasn't deep. Painful but not deadly.

"Darrel?"

Darrel glanced at Linda. She had rolled over. Blood oozed from a cut along her hairline and the spot on her neck. A bloody piece of tape hung from her cheek. She was the most beautiful thing he had ever seen. Darrel breathed under his breath. "Thank You, God."

"Oh good," Casey sneered. "The girlfriend's awake. Now, you can watch one another die." Casey lunged.

Darrel turned into Casey and barely deflected the blow. He rounded with his elbow and drove it into Casey's chest. Then he swung his fist up and smashed it into Casey's nose. There was a satisfying crunch and blood spurted across his hand.

Casey fell back; his nose was obviously broken.

Darrel raised his hands. "We don't have to do this."

Casey looked at him. He gently wiped his sleeve across the bottom part of his face then slowly brought his knife up.

"You won't win."

"Oh, I'll win." Casey eased down the slope until he was in front of Linda. "You're the only loser today."

Darrel moved down the slope and into the street. His mike crackled.

"The police are on the way."

Darrel keyed his mike. "We're in the street."

"Got eyes on you now, Boss."

Darrel nodded. "Put the knife down, Casey. Right now the worst charge against you should be assault with a deadly weapon." Darrel let his hands fall to his side. "Do your time. With good behavior you'll be out before you know it. Don't let this ruin your life."

Casey laughed. "Too late. My old man ruined my life years ago."

"It's never too late. I just learned that myself. God has forgiven me and He will do the same for you."

Sirens filled the air.

Raising his knife, Casey charged.

Darrel dropped his knife. Stepping right, he dropped his left shoulder and rammed into Casey's chest. He grabbed Casey around the hips and using Casey's forward momentum, threw him to the street.

The weight of Casey's body pulled him down and Darrel landed on top of Casey with a thud. Casey's head hit the street with a loud crack.

Darrel sat up and felt Casey's neck. There was a strong steady pulse. Thank you, Lord. At least the boy would live. Darrel grinned. But, he was going to wake up with one massive headache.

"Darrel?"

He stood and pain shot around his middle dropping him to his knees. Blood oozed from the hole in his side and the cuts on his right arm. He slowly stood.

"Darrel?"

He walked over to Linda, eased onto the ground and took her hand. "How are you feeling?"

Linda sighed. "Better now. You?"

"Nothing a few stitches won't fix."

"Casey?"

"Down and out."

The first police car slid to a stop in front of them. The officer got out, gun drawn and walked over. "Darrel Foss?"

Darrel nodded.

"Perp?"

Darrell pointed at Casey.

The officer keyed his mike. "All clear. We have three needing medical assistance."

*****

Linda felt her hand move. Slowly, she opened her eyes. The light sent a stab of pain through her head and she quickly shut them. She was obviously in a hospital bed but she didn't remember getting here. The last thing she remembered was...

Her hand moved again. She opened her eyes and this time the pain wasn't as bad. Looking toward her hand, she saw Darrel. He was asleep in a chair with his head on the bed and he was holding her hand. She closed her eyes. "Thank You, Father, for keeping us both safe."

Darrel shifted and pulled her hand to his cheek. "I love you, too."

She smiled. She wouldn't mind hearing *that* for the rest of her life. She squeezed his hand. "Marry me."

"Okay."

Linda chuckled and another pain shot through her head. She jerked and Darrel came instantly awake.

"Hurt bad? Let me..."

Linda grabbed his arm. "No you don't. You're not leaving until we settle this."

"Settle what?"

Linda smiled. "Our wedding plans."

"Our WHAT?"

Linda closed her eyes. "Please, don't shout."

"Sorry," Darrel leaned closer and whispered. "Our what?"

"Wedding plans. I just asked you to marry me and you said okay."

"I did?" Darrel frowned. "But I just... I was..." He crossed his arms. "I don't remember agreeing to anything."

Linda smiled smugly. "Ah, but you did. And, I happen to know that your word is your bond."

"But..,"

Linda held up her hand. "You said that you loved me."

"I did?"

Linda nodded. "Just now. I know I love you."

"You do?"

"Very much." Linda cocked her head. "So, do you or do you not intend to honor your word and marry me?"

Darrel gently brushed her lips with his and sat. "There are some things you need to know about me. After you know..." Darrel's voice trailed off. He picked up her hand and kissed it. "*If* you still want to marry me, ask me again and I will definitely say yes."

Darrel took a deep breath. "I was a Marine sniper. Went straight into boot camp out of high school. I was your typical jock: cocky and full of myself."

Linda gently laughed. "That I *can* believe."

Darrel shook his head. "I was bad."

After sitting in silence for a few minutes, Linda squeezed Darrel's hand. "Just start."

He sighed deeply. "One of my last assignments was to assassinate an arm's dealer in South America..."

SCRIPTURE REFERENCES:

1) pg 141. John 5:32
2) pg 207. John 6:4
3) pg 208. 2 Samuel 11
4) pg 208. 2 Samuel 12:1-25
5) pg 209. Acts 7:58-Acts 8:3
6) pg 209. Acts 9:1-2
7) pg 209. Acts 9:3-22
8) pg 209. James 2:10-11
9) pg 209. Matthew 18:6
10) pg 209. Romans 3:23
11) pg 209. Romans 5:6-10
12) pg 209. John 3:14-18
13) pg 209. Romans 10:9-10

PRAYED SCRIPTURE:

Genesis12:3a And I will bless them that bless thee...

Psalms 3:5-6   5.Trust in the Lord with all thine heart; and lean not unto thine own understanding.   6.In all thy ways acknowledge him, and he shall direct thy paths..

1 Peter 5:7 Casting all your care upon him; for he careth for you.

2 Corinthians 2:14 Be ye not unequally yoked together with unbelievers: for what fellowship hath righteousness with unrighteousness? and what communion hath light with darkness?

John 5:32 And ye shall know the truth, and the truth shall make you free.

James 1:5 If any of you lack wisdom, let him ask of God, that giveth to all men liberally, and upbraideth not; and it shall be given him.

Psalms 91:1-16 He that dwelleth in the secret place of the most High shall abide under the shadow of the Almighty. I will say of the Lord, He is my refuge and my fortress: my God; in him will I trust. Surely he shall deliver thee from the snare of the fowler, and from the noisome pestilence. He shall cover thee with his feathers, and under his wings shalt thou trust: his truth shall be thy shield and buckler. Thou shalt not be afraid for the terror by night; nor for the arrow that flieth by day; Nor for the pestilence that walketh in darkness; nor for the destruction that wasteth at noonday. A thousand shall fall at thy side, and ten thousand at thy right hand; but it shall not come nigh thee. Only with thine eyes shalt thou behold and see the reward of the wicked. Because thou hast made the Lord, which is my refuge, even the most High, thy habitation; There shall no evil befall thee, neither shall any plague come nigh thy dwelling. For he shall give his angels charge over thee, to keep thee in all thy ways. They shall bear thee up in their hands, lest thou dash thy foot against a stone. Thou shalt tread upon the lion and adder: the young lion and the dragon shalt thou trample under feet. Because he hath set his love upon me, therefore will I deliver him: I will set him on high, because he hath known my name. He shall call upon me, and I will answer him: I will be with him in trouble; I will deliver him, and honour him. With long life will I satisfy him, and shew him my salvation.

Also G Psalms 138:2. I will worship toward thy holy temple, and praise thy name for thy loving kindness and for thy truth: for thou hast magnified thy word above all thy name.

COMING NEXT

WITNESS

Penny Brown's life had been carefully plotted out since she was twelve. Graduate High School with honors, go to law school, graduate with honors, join a prominent law firm, move up to partner and sometime during that journey, get married and have her 2.5 allotment of kids. Now it was doubtful if any of that was going to happen. Accidents, that were increasingly dangerous, kept happening around her. Then she got the note and knew the accidents were meant for her. But why?

Wade Waters was not a field man. He had the FBI training just not the experience. Yet once again his boss had sent him undercover in, of all places, a mission his sister ran on B Street. Then the accidents started and they seemed to all be centered around the newest volunteer, Penny Brown. Did they have anything to do with his assignment? Did she?

They will have to join forces to find out who is behind the accidents before it's too late.

AUTHOR BIO

Barbara Arent lives in the Piney Woods of East Texas with her pets and a large loving family. Two of her favorite pastimes are reading historical markers and wandering through old cemeteries. She is a graduate of Basic Writing from The Institute of Children's Literature.

From chasing Indians or aliens in the woods as a child to writing romance-suspense as an adult, she has been constructing stories for years.

Visit her
On Twitter: @BarbaraArent
On Facebook:
http://www.facebook.com/pages/Barbara-Arent/394674743920464

www.ingramcontent.com/pod-product-compliance
Lightning Source LLC
Chambersburg PA
CBHW061149170626
46809CB00003B/1031